SNR

SNR

SNR - Bob Holt

She's Never

Return

Or would she?

SNR - Bob Holt

For information contact; bobLholtco@yahoo.com

Book and Cover design by Bob Holt

ISBN-13: 978-1977670533

ISBN-10 : 1977670539

SNR - Bob Holt

Dedication:

To my Readers,

Thank You.

"No Way!"

She picked up the invitation and read it again. There was no way she'd ever attend her thirtieth-class reunion, no way! That was only 4 months away. Why hadn't they allowed more time. It didn't matter to her; she wasn't going anyway.

Maybe she should, after all, she still wore the same size 8 dress and only weighed 3 pounds more than she did at graduation and that had to be in her bra cup size. Her breasts grew during her 2 pregnancies and stayed.

At 48, the wrinkles and crow's feet hadn't made their appearances and her emerald eyes still had that sparkle that sent Brian Howard out of his mind 28 years ago. Her auburn hair fell carelessly on and below her shoulders and still had body…plus a little color too but show her a 48-year-old woman that didn't. Her lips were still full and sensuous…That's what Lynn said the last time they dated.

Before she dated Lynn the first time, she stood naked in front of her full-length mirror really taking a critical look at her body. Her breasts were full and firm. There was no ripple or middle age spread. Of course, there was a reason for that. For almost 20 years, she'd gone to the Wellness Center and worked out on the treadmill and exercise equipment. It was like brushing her teeth, it was a habit, a good habit, and she was proud of it even though there were times when she almost talked herself out of going.

Looking again, it was plain that she hadn't had a bikini cut in years and she'd let her tan go too. Maybe it was time to put a little color on her body?

Why was she doing a self-exam, she wasn't going, she'd seen so few of her classmates over the years and for the most part, that was a good thing.
School had been okay, but that's all, just okay.

SNR

The first through the eighth grades were just that, eight grades, eight years but high school, that was different. That's when she started dating.

Born in 1961, Kayla Denice Herring was in the middle of Raymond and Dolly Herring's brood. Ander was the oldest, followed by Donna, then Kayla and after her, Gary and the last was Linda.

They lived on Allen Chambers Road just up Hwy. 11 from Guilford East. Her daddy went to work there when it opened; first as a shift worker but after he was promoted to supervisor, he was on day shift and gave up farming, renting his tobacco acreage and tillable land to Rayford Scott holding back 2 acres for the family garden.
He also had a couple of hogs for slaughtering, a milk cow, Molly Mae, and Beautancus, his old mule that he plowed the garden with until he died and then her daddy got an old used B-Allis Chalmers. At least, it had a 3-point hitch making it easy to switch out the plow and cultivators.

Her mama kept chickens for eggs, pastry, and Sunday dinner. When the young'uns reached 8 years old, they were taught how to wring a chicken's neck and how to clean them. Kayla had the worst time of it throwing up the first three times but she conquered the task knowing it had to be done.
Ander was stuck with milking until he graduated and enlisted in the Marines then it fell on Gary only because there were tons of chores that had to be done in the house and garden.

No body escaped shelling beans and peas when the time came and it seemed like forever once the season started but they all knew that was how their hungry mouths were fed all year long. Their aching thumbs would heal after the end of the season.

Her daddy believed in his young'uns working and learning responsibilities. He allowed them plenty of time to play but their chores always came first. That plus whatever their mama had for them to do; it always came first.

Once they were old enough to work in tobacco, the boys hired out to the neighbors. The girls did too except, Donna. All her time was spent in the house helping her mama cook.

By the time she was 9, she was putting all the biscuits on the table. Kayla cooked meats and vegetables too but preferred making cobblers and pies to biscuits. She did an excellent job with chicken and pastry too. Her mama said that she had a special knack at rolling out pastry dough. That was natural though because of her skills with pie dough.

"Duplin Central High School"

With the invitation still in her hand, she closed her eyes, relaxing, while remembering her school days.

They all went to Duplin Central High School located about 3 miles down Hwy 11 towards Kenansville right before the intersection with Sarecta Road. Woody Grady's store was in the intersection. Some of the kids went there during their lunch period preferring the hot dogs and hamburgers that Mr. Grady served, and especially his signature dish, Cheesy Fries.

It was a favorite hangout after school and in the evenings too.

Kayla entered the first grade in 1967 and really enjoyed school, especially that dark-haired boy, Tommy Murray. He was kind of sweet on her too. He sat at the desk directly behind her and was always pulling her hair and whispering stuff about how pretty she was.

He'd been caught by the teacher a hundred times but it didn't matter. He only wanted Kayla's attention. Mrs. Vestal finally separated them but it didn't stop him. In class, he was constantly passing notes to her and spending every minute of recess and lunch with her.

She ate up all the attention he gave her responding with smiles and laughing at all the crazy stuff he did.

He lived over on Hwy 111 near the Rogers Farm so when school turned out for the summer, it ended them seeing each other until school started again in the fall.

Their infatuation ended in fourth grade. Not because they wanted it to, his family moved to Asheville. His father found work that as a park ranger on the Blue Ridge Parkway. They moved during the Christmas holidays leaving Kayla crying inconsolably almost every hour of the day.

Her tears slowed on Christmas morning when the presents that Santa left were opened. The yellow dress she'd written Santa about was there along with the sweater and skirt she'd hoped for.

When school started back, so did the tears. Tommy's desk was taken by someone else and she knew that he would be lost to her forever. They wrote letters until summer but that link was soon broken too.

That summer, she hired out to Dovelle Turner to work on his harvester His farm was about a quarter mile from theirs and he picked her up every day, along with the other workers.

She worked up top looping tobacco. It was a boring job… it would have been boring if it hadn't been for that red-headed, freckled faced, Red Sutton. He kept something going all the time, especially when they hung the tobacco up at lunch and the end of the day.

Kayla knew he'd took a liking to her. He just wouldn't leave her alone. At lunch, he made sure he was sitting beside her. Mrs. Turner knew what was happening but didn't seem to mind if he didn't become a nuisance. He was okay but to Kayla, he was exactly that, a nuisance.

She guessed he tried every way he knew to get something going between them but she was having none of it.

One weekend, she'd gone with Ander and his date, Jean, to Woody's for hot dogs. The jukebox never stopped playing because the boys kept dropping coins into the slots. Several couples danced to almost every record. When Mickey Gilley's Bring *it on home to* me started playing. Red was all over her to dance. Ander kept saying,

"Go ahead, dance with him."

He didn't want to dance, he wanted to smooch. She was back at the table in less than a minute.

"Ander, you put me up to that. If he tries putting his hands on me again, I'm going to slap that stupid grin right off his face!"

He could tell she was hot, and didn't make any more suggestions.

From then on until the end of the barning season, Red wouldn't shut up but he kept his distance although, at times, it appeared that he wasn't going to.

When the summer ended and school began, she was finally rid of him. He was three years older than her and his classes were in an entirely different wing than hers and their lunch periods were different too.

"She Wasn't Seeing Anyone Now"

Only Lynn and he was still in Paris.

Realizing she'd been napping, she lay the invitation on the coffee table and rode over to Parker's Takeout on Memorial Drive to pick up something for dinner.

Returning to her home on Fairlane Road with a chicken breast, fries, and slaw, she placed the bag on the table in the breakfast nook while she poured a glass of iced tea. The house was empty now; her children were gone.

Her son, Kevin, had been gone five years. After graduating from J.H. Rose High School, he went to Appalachian State and married Kylie Hardison. They were living in Concord and had a son, Ray, 3, her only grandchild.

She'd been living alone for the past year since Amy moved to Chapel Hill to attend UNC. Kayla wanted her to attend ECU but Amy refused saying ECU had a reputation for being a party school and she wanted no part of that. With a 4.0 grade average. She had several scholarships and intended using them to satisfy her dream of becoming a doctor's assistant or maybe even a doctor.

Kayla was more than happy knowing her daughter wasn't a party animal like her ex-husband, Jeff Harris.

SNR

Jeff, how in the world did I ever get tied up with him?

She had to admit that she knew. Yes, she remembered. She'd broken up with Brian Howard during her second year at James Sprunt Community College. They'd been an item since Tommy Murry left and began dating during her junior and senior year in high school and they'd continued dating until that spring. It had not been a pretty separation. She'd been very ugly to him. She didn't pay any attention then but now she knew what she'd done.

She was moving to Greenville, NC to attend ECU and he vehemently disapproved saying they should get married and have a family. She told him that she'd been on a farm all her life and that was enough. Being saddled down with a family at that point in her life wasn't going to happen and... it didn't.

She'd moved into a dorm on campus at ECU fully expecting to finish college unattached but that's not what happened. Jeff Harris did.

Arriving in Greenville in 1981, she was totally unprepared for what was happening downtown on Fifth and Cotanche Streets. There was nothing to compare it with back home. Yes, she'd been to Carolina Beach and seen the wild times everyone seemed to be having. She had never tasted a beer until then and thought it was the most terrible stuff she'd ever put in her mouth. It was God-awful!

Her friends told her to keep sipping on it, she'd like it. She'd gotten to a point of it being tolerable but she wasn't prepared for the kegs and cases of it available in ECU's party town.

The only thing good about drinking beer was that she had no interest in drugs and they were everywhere. She watched coeds from her dorm, and on campus, arrive as innocent freshmen and disintegrate into almost inhuman bodies destroyed by drugs.

Mary Ann, her roommate, was one of them. She'd gotten involved with Lester Wood and he turned out to be a user/dealer. He destroyed Mary Ann with his excessive use of drugs.

Her parents finally came to Greenville during the holidays carrying their precious daughter back home. Word came later that they'd put her in a rehab center near Charleston, South Carolina trying to reclaim what was once their beautiful daughter but after the treatment, she disappeared showing up dead in an alley from an overdose.

SNR

Kayla preferred on-campus activities including Mendenhall Student Center, Wright Auditorium, and the library. The student center was where she met Jeff Trip.

It was late September and it was more like him forcing his way into her life. She was sitting with three coeds from their dorm on College Hill when Jeff walked up introducing himself.

"Ladies, I'm Jeff Harris. I'm a junior here and you look like you need my company."

He was the epitome of good-looking, tall, dark, and handsome. Okay, he was over 6 feet tall, his hair was almost black and his eyes, oh, his eyes, they were pale blue. They just begged to be looked into. He was muscular, but slender and was dressed in jeans and a collared polo top.

By the time Kayla had gotten over the shock of the uninvited intrusion, Jeff was sitting beside her asking her name?

Wondering why she did, she replied,

"Kayla, Kayla Herring."

His magnetism was running full bore now with those pale blue eyes and captivating smile, capturing her full attention.

"Kayla, it's nice to meet you. Would you do me the honor of dining with me tonight? Do you like Chinese? We could do Chang Palace."

Chinese, she'd never been in a Chinese Restaurant. Why was she saying that she would but she did?

"Okay, what time?"

He'd hooked her, she knew he had.

"Six-Thirty, I'll meet you in the lobby of your dorm."

With that, he was gone. Her mind was flying a hundred miles an hour.

What have I just done? I can't believe I did that but I did.

For whatever the reason, she was glad she did. The other girls were laughing. Tina was pointing a finger, saying,

"Kayla, are you the Kayla we know? You can't be; you were just swept off your feet. Is it really you?"

Kayla knew she was blushing but it didn't matter. She was already looking forward to their date.

This is Chinese? It's Delicious!

She had no idea what to wear choosing white slacks and gold blouse. She'd only been in the lobby a couple of minutes when he walked in.

Smiling, he walked over offering his hand, saying,

"Hi Kayla, you look very nice tonight. Are you ready?"

He looks especially nice too dressed in tan slacks and a purple collared polo.

"Thank you, Jeff. Yes, I am, where is the Chang Palace? I've never been."

He replied that it was on Evans Street near the intersection with Arlington.

"It's about five minutes away."

In the parking area, he seated her in his 1982 Chrysler LeBaron maroon convertible.

Minutes later, they parked in front of the restaurant and like a true gentleman, he opened the door and offered his hand when she was getting out. He opened the door again for her as they entered the restaurant.

The hostess asked about reservations and yes, he'd made them. They were seated at a table for two against a wall away from the traffic. The hostess placed menus in front of them and took their beverage orders for iced tea.

"Would you like an appetizer?"

She had no clue what she was looking at. It was time to "fess up."

"Jeff, I've never eaten in a Chinese restaurant. I have no idea what I am looking at. Please help me."

He chose to begin with Wonton soup with dumplings.

"Do you prefer; beef, chicken, or pork?"

She played it on the safe side.

"Chicken, please."

When the waiter returned with their soup, Jeff ordered the Sweet and Sour Chicken over steamed rice with egg rolls on the side.

Getting through the soup course wasn't a problem and yes, she did know what chopsticks were but how to use them, no way.

With their main entrees in front of them, Jeff, very nonchalantly, picked up the chopsticks and begin eating but looking across at her, he stopped.

I apologize, would you like to learn how to use the chopsticks?"

She was treading in unknown waters but, why not, she was there. She replied,

"Yes, please help me."

The next few minutes were interesting but progress was made although, ultimately, after many miscues, she chose the fork.

During all the hilarity with the chop sticks, they managed to become more familiar with each other. After hearing her background, he shared his.

"I grew up in Opelika, Alabama. It's the county seat of Lee County. It's not as large as Greenville. The population is around twenty thousand. We live in a subdivision east of town on Spring Villa Road.

My father owns a chain of grocery stores scattered around Opelika. I think there are eighteen of them now. My brother, Johnny, and I, grew up stocking shelves, sweeping, sorting, cashiering…whatever had to be done.

"Don't get me wrong, the work was hard but there were perks too. My father refused to open on Sundays but you can bet We'd all be in Sunday School and Church.

"Saturday nights and Sunday afternoon were ours and Johnny and I made the best of every opportunity. We belonged to Spring Villa Country Club so Johnny and I played golf every chance we got. It was apparent from the beginning that he had pro potential but me, not a chance.

"I was better with a tennis racket in my hand but nowhere good enough to begin thinking about being a pro.

"In school, physics and chemistry were my thing and I graduated Salutatorian.

"Burroughs Wellcome drew me to Greenville offering an opportunity to be mentored by some of the finest chemists in the world."

"I probably have a reputation of being a party animal in this party town but with that said, I know what I want to do when I graduate next year."

"I can't believe I dumped all of that on you at one setting…Hey, we didn't open our fortune cookies."

He cracked open his retrieving the little slip of paper, reading it to her.

'Be ever vigilant, love may be close by.'

"What does yours say?"

Following his example, she cracked it open removing her fortune.

'If you have something good in your life, don't let it go.'

Smiling, he said,

"I could be that something good in your life. We'll see, if you let me."

Admitting to herself,

I'm willing if you are.

When they arrived back at her dorm, he walked her to the entrance not trying to extract a kiss but asked about Sunday.

"We could spend the day in Oriental if you'd like."

Oriental, she'd never been there but she was willing to go with him. If this was what they called, 'being swept off your feet,' she was.

"I'd like that, what time are we leaving and what's the dress code?"

"Around nine, very casual, September on the Neuse River is still pretty warm. I suggest shorts and a polo top."

" Oriental, NC, With Him "

Saturday seemed to drag on forever. She'd spent most of the morning in the library reading up on Oriental, NC and the surrounding county of Pamlico.

After lunching at Mendenhall, she rode over to Pitt Plaza shopping for just the right top for tomorrow. She walked the mall beginning at J.C. Penny's, then Brody's and all the way to Belk's before returning to Brody's. The yellow and white collared polo was perfect but what about shoes. She'd heard the name "Docker's" but when she located them, she couldn't believe the price. She'd wear what she had.

That evening, she contented herself with a salad at Jones Cafeteria and wiled the next few hours away watching the boob tube until sleep finally came a little before eleven.

SNR

Sunday, she was up before light. The excitement was too much. By six, she was having breakfast in Jones Cafeteria wishing the hours away.

A little after nine, they were on their way taking her to what he called, "The Sailboat Capital of North Carolina."

Arriving about ten-thirty, she'd been down roads and through communities she'd never heard of. Names like Grimesland, Chocowinity, Edward, Blount's Creek, Grantsboro, Alliance, Bayboro, Stonewall, and Merritt. They parked on the waterfront and walked along the docks seeing dozens of sailboats moored or anchored out in the harbor.

It was apparent that he'd been there before, perhaps many times. Had he been sailing?

"Yes, one of my fraternity brother's father has one docked here. It's moored to a private dock a few hundred yards further down the Neuse River. It's confluence with Pamlico Sound is only a mile or so from here."

It was getting close to lunch so they enjoyed three-seafood combos at the Trawl Door Restaurant at the foot of the bridge.
    Out on the deck under an umbrella, the setting couldn't have been more beautiful.
    "How often do you come down here?"

"During summer break, if I'm not back home, every time I can wrangle an invitation out of Jeric. We'll go sailing into Pamlico Sound, nowhere in particular although last year we sailed to Portsmouth Island. That was quite an experience."
    "When I graduate next year, all that will come to an end. I'll be working at Burroughs Wellcome."

16

"How about you? You have one more year too. What are you going to do?"

Thoughtfully, she replied,

"With my BS in business administration, primarily, I'll be looking for a position at Pitt County Memorial Hospital but I'll also be filing resumes at Burroughs Wellcome, Grady-White Boats and probably DuPont. There's so much growth at the hospital, I'd really like to get on there. I'll just have to wait and see what's available."

With lunch behind them, he took her to Minnesott Beach via Janeiro. They walked along the Neuse River shore from Minnesott Beach Café to the country club and back.

After watching the ferry docking, it was time to begin their return trip back to Greenville. Leaving the beach, they drove through Arapahoe before turning left on Hwy 55 at. Grantsboro. They followed it to Bridgeton turning north on Hwy 17. Their return route was more populated with traffic but after exiting on Hwy 43 at Vanceboro, the traffic dwindled to almost nothing as they passed Calico, Hollywood, and Bells Fork where they stopped at Hardee's for burgers, arriving back at her dorm a little after 8 p.m.

They arrived back at her dorm a little before seven. Walking her to the entrance, he wanted a kiss and she wanted him to have one.

After that, they dated steadily, most times, on Wednesday and Saturday nights. Sunday's, they spent most of the day together. As the weeks passed by the intensity of their love for each other escalated finally reaching the point of no return in a motel room during the Thanksgiving break.

Neither had gone home knowing somehow, someway, they were going to make love. It was driving them crazy and they didn't want their special moment to take place in a car. No way, it was going to be special and they wanted a bed.

The holiday break began on Wednesday before Thanksgiving and would resume on the following Monday. That gave them more than ample time to make their special moment, memorable.

That afternoon, Jeff rented a room at the Ramada Inn on Greenville Blvd requesting privacy if possible. He was given a room on the back facing Red Banks Road.

Driving back to College Hill, He picked Kayla up. She had a small suitcase and one clothes bag.

Arriving at the room, once inside, what had been planned as a calm, one step at a time, experience, evaporated immediately as their clothes flew in every direction and they came together like two magnets. It was her first time and she managed to get a towel under them before the explosion that lasted only minutes.

Now, out of breath, still clinging together, they began their second accent up the mountain but this time exploring the scenery along the way. His hands moved across her body caressing her breasts while he nibbled on her ears, nose, lips and then everywhere.

She was on fire urging him to continue their second climb to the top. It was either continue now or like the first time, she would arrive at the top long before he did.

She did but that was okay, they had the room for three nights. They lost count of their climbs in the pre-dawn hours of Thanksgiving Day.

Exhausted, they showered and dressed before walking across Greenville Blvd to the Waffle House. It was almost empty. One lone diner sat at the counter and they took a booth in the front ordering coffee first.

Jeff yielded to Kayla.

"I'll have the waffles with 2 eggs, over easy, hash browns, and bacon."

Jeff wanted the blueberry waffles, 2 eggs, sunny-side-up, hash browns, and country ham.

When their meals arrived, they talked little. Both were starving after their first night's activities. There were giggles, smiles, and knowing glances but few words.

Finished, they ordered coffee refills and had calmed enough to actually carry on a meaningful conversation but it was mostly about how they would spend the day…besides that, there would be more, 'that,' but it wouldn't, it couldn't, last all day.

Most of the remaining morning just sort of went away before driving back to Jones Cafeteria for their Thanksgiving lunch.

During lunch,

"Jeff, you know I love you with all my heart."

He reached over touching her hand, replying,

"I love you too. I want to marry you. Will you marry me?"

There was no ring but he promised there would be before Christmas and he was true to his word and she was wearing one the next weekend.

There was no question about marrying him. That's all she wanted. She loved him and he loved her.

That afternoon, they climbed the mountain once before taking in a movie at the cinema.

Afterwards, they went back to Jones Cafeteria for dinner and sleep came quickly afterwards. Their mountain climbing could wait. They still had another day and night together.

Before the Christmas break, he gave her a diamond solitary. He'd planned to go home for the holidays and wanted her to accompany him. She'd already promised to spend the holidays with her family but yes, with tears in her eyes, she responded to the ring as he slipped it on her finger.

Jeff, asking again.

"Will you marry me?"

"Jeff, you know I will, when?"

"Maybe Valentines, go with me to meet my family and we'll set a date then."

"But Jeff, I promised to spend the holidays with my family. They're expecting me."

He wasn't giving up that easily,

"Let's do both, we'll spend time with your parents Christmas and my folks New Year's."

She knew that would be interesting saying she'd call her parents first.

That evening, back in the dorm,

"Mama, it's me, Kayla… No, nothing's wrong but I've got news… No, I'm getting married… No, Mama, of course I'm not pregnant. How could you think a thing like that?... Christmas, we'll come down and spend a few days with you before we go to visit his family… No, Ma'am, he's from Alabama… Opelika… No, Mama, it's spelled; O-P-E-L-I-K-A. That's close enough… His father owns a bunch of grocery stores… No, Mama, I don't think he's rich but he isn't poor either, you'll like him, I know You and Daddy will. Everybody will… I'll let you know, Mama. Christmas is on Saturday. We'll probably arrive on Thursday or Friday and leave for his home on Tuesday or Wednesday. We'll work it out… Thank you, Mama, I knew you'd be happy for us. Tell Daddy that I love him, bye."

That evening, they rode over to the Three Steers for supper and she shared the results of her call with him.

After ordering hamburger steak with onion gravy over mashed potatoes and a trip to the salad bar, Jeff asked about the call?

"What did your parents say? Were they upset?"

Smiling, she replied,

"Of course not, Mama was surprised and I'm sure Daddy was too but she wasn't upset. I told her that we would probably arrive on Thursday or Friday and leave on Tuesday or Wednesday. Does that sound all right to you?"

He was more at ease now, replying,

"That will work, I called my parents and they're looking forward to meeting you. School starts back on Monday, January third.

After visiting your family, we'll leave on Tuesday and spend the night driving down. We'll have some time alone.

We'll drive back on Saturday. We'll probably get a room somewhere and spend the night driving the rest of the way on Sunday."

She was more than ready for that, they had almost no time to really be alone.

"When we get back, I'm going to rent a townhouse. I want you to move in with me but it that bothers you, we'll move you in after the wedding."

She responded saying,

"Jeff, you know I'm ready now. It might not make our parents happy but I'm ready.

His response made perfect sense to her.

"You're 22 and I'm 23, we're full grown. We'll make that decision ourselves."

Christmas, With Her Family

They arrived at Kayla's home a little after lunch on Friday, Christmas Eve, finding all of Kayla's family there, all of them.

After hugs, she introduced her parents first.

"Mama, Daddy, this is Jeff Harris"

"Jeff, this is my parents, Raymond and Dolly Herring."

"Mr. and Mrs. Herring, it's a pleasure meeting my future in-law's."

"Ander, he's the oldest, this is Jeff."

Ander introduced his wife, Narla, and Ander, Jr. their two-year old son, saying,

"Jeff, welcome to our family. I hear that you will be part of it soon."

"Jeff, this is my older sister, Donna. Donna, this is my fiancé, Jeff."

Donna responded,

"This is my husband, Cliff, and our daughter, Sandy; she's four. This is Jerry, he's two."

"Jeff, this is my younger brother, Gary. As you can see, he's in the air force."

Jeff shook his hand asking where he was stationed?

Gary replied,

"When my leave is up, I'll be stationed at Anderson AFB on Guam. I'm attached to SAC, the Strategic Air Command."

"Thank you for your service to our country."

Kayla was down to the last one.

"Jeff, this is my younger sister, Linda. She a senior in high school."

He took her hand, saying,

"Like, Kayla, you're a very pretty young lady. You both take after your mama."

Her mama was asking about lunch.

"We just finished lunch. You didn't say what time you were coming. There's plenty left over it you'd like some."

"No, Mama, we stopped by Bojangles in Kinston. We're good."

After being shown to their rooms, they spent the afternoon with her family crowded in the living room while they became more familiar with Jeff asking question after question about him, his family, and what he planned to do when he graduated next year and where is Opelika, Alabama and how was it pronounced?

Smiling, Jeff responded,

"OPA- LIKA, it's just north of Eufaula."

That was sure to bring quizzical looks, it did.

Ander was first to ask,

"Eufaula, Jeff, you're putting us on, aren't you?"

Laughing now, Jeff replied,

"No, Ander, both Opelika and Eufaula are located just inside the Alabama/Georgia state line just west of Columbus, Georgia.

"Eufaula is located on a bluff overlooking Lake Eufaula, a 45,000-acre lake. The lake is lined with beautiful homes. It's unbelievably beautiful there in the spring, summer and fall. We have a summer home there but it's rarely used except in the summer and on Sundays because of my family's grocery store chain.

"Mother spends most of the summer there and my father drives down when he can. Last summer, and fall, when I was home, we spent a lot of Sunday's there.

"When we're married, I'm sure after Kayla sees it, she'll want to spend some of our vacation time there too."

Kayla hadn't heard about the lake or summer home but then, she knew so very little about Jeff or his family.

I'm really looking forward to meeting his family next week. There's so much I want to know about them and I'm sure that they have tons of questions about me.

Later that afternoon, leaving the rest of the family to talk, Kayla followed her mother into the kitchen to help prepare supper giving them a chance for some girl talk.

"Honey, he seems so nice and I can tell that he loves you. Are you sure ya'll know enough about each other to get married?"

"Mama, I know it seems like we're moving too fast but, Mama, we love each other and we get along so good together. He's got his whole career mapped out with Burroughs Wellcome. That's the huge pharmaceutical plant just north of Greenville.

"He'd been working there with chemists for the past two years. It's part of his college classes and he has a job offer waiting for him when he graduates. He doesn't drink, smoke, or mess with any of the drugs that are so prevalent around Greenville. He'll make a good husband and father of our children. I just know he will."

Putting her hand on her daughter's shoulder, she replied,

"Your Daddy and I dated almost a year and a half before we got married. That's because we were in school most of that time. I guess I knew he was the one after a couple of dates."

"Where are you getting married? You know we can't afford a big wedding but we've got some saved up for it. You've just got to let us know what you want.

"Mama, I don't know yet. I don't want a big wedding. If it's left up to me, we'll elope or maybe get married at the chapel at school. I guess we'll have a better handle on it after we visit his parents. Save the money for Linda, she might want a big wedding."

That evening, everyone gathered around the big dining room table. All but Gary and Linda, they shared a card table in the kitchen.

The big meal would be tomorrow for dinner (lunch) but you couldn't tell it by the fixings her mama had crammed on the table.

The conversation almost immediately began about Christmas past and some of the memories that would never fade away.

Her daddy's favorite story was about the snow storm of 1971.
"The weather man acted like he was scared of using the "snow" word. He said we might get some frozen precipitation but wouldn't touch the word.

"Luckily, we got all the chores done when it started. It wasn't long before it was coming down in flakes as big and quarters. By nightfall, there was already 4" on the ground and it didn't look like it was about to let up.

"Ander, I think he was 12 or 13, wanted to get out a play in it so bad so we sent him to the smokehouse for some dried sausage. After an hour, I was getting ready to go look for him when he finally came in the kitchen door. He was one of the happiest young'uns I've ever seen. He'd built a big snow man right off the back porch and was dying for everybody to see it. Donna and Kayla wanted to but Gary won't sure. I think he was about 6 or 7. Linda was 4, she was more than ready.

"They all got into a big snow fight; I don't remember seeing such a sight in my life. Dolly drug me out into it and the young'uns ganged up on us.

"We were all about froze to death when we came back in. Dolly had the sausage, eggs, and biscuits ready by 8 and the sent the young'un scurrying to bed by 9 saying there won't any way Santa was going to show it if they weren't in bed. Linda and Gary still believed but the rest went along with it.

"Next morning, it was still coming down but had mostly slacked off. I took the yard stick out and measured it off the back porch. We had 22 inches there. Out by the stables, it measured 26." It won't as big as the snow of 47 but it was, and still is, the biggest Christmas snow I've ever seen."

"Luckily, we didn't lose power but it didn't really matter. The REA strung power out our way in 55 and we didn't have much more than lights hung in the middle of the rooms and a couple of wall plugs in the kitchen, living room, and bath room.

"We were heating the living room with a wood heater and the kitchen with a fireplace and a 3-brick gas heater. Dolly had 6-burner gas stove and a Kelvinator. The ice box was on the back porch. I put a 3-brick gas heater in the bathroom when I added it on in 55.

We had a color TV but we won't glued to it like we are today. The kids had too many chores and homework to watch them afternoon shows and at night, they'd rather be outside chasing lightening bugs or playing hide-and-seek.

"Dolly got hung up on, what was it, 'As the world twirls'? Something like that anyway and I guess she still is."

Her mama interrupted, correcting her daddy.

"Raymond, you know it's 'As the world turns.' You watch it sometimes too."

Kayla, and the rest, knew their daddy wouldn't be getting into that discussion.

Clearing his throat, he continued, totally ignoring his wife.

"Where was I? Oh, Linda and Gary were up by 4 a.m. seeing what Santa brought them. The rest of 'em was up by 6. I don't guess Dolly and I got hardly any sleep but it's always been that way every Christmas.

"Anyway, after I fed Flossie, Beautancus, and the hogs, I went by the smokehouse and cut off a big slab of ham for breakfast. You can't hardly get anything any better than that.

They shared other stories until a little after 9 p.m. Most of the family would be doubling up. Her mama put her in the room with Donna, her two kids, and Linda.

Jeff shared a bedroom with Cliff and Gary leaving the extra bedroom for Ander and his family.

Her mama and daddy kept the same bedroom they'd always had.

Kayla knew they'd be putting out gifts, they always had and she was sure they always would.

Santa would leave gifts for Sandy, Jerry, and Ander Jr.

By 10, the house got quiet except for Cliff. Jeff wondered how in the world Donna managed to get any sleep. Cliff's snoring was long, loud, and continuous.

Christmas morning was just as expected; the little ones barely gave Santa a chance to get the gifts out before they came charging down the hall awakening everyone in the house. Santa had managed to eat the cookies and drink the milk that Sandy had insisted on leaving out for him.

By 6 a.m., all the presents had been opened and mama and her daughters were in the kitchen fixing breakfast.

The aroma of country ham wafted throughout the house arousing the attention of all the males present, save the kids. They were too excited to care about breakfast and were hard put to keep still when everyone was seated around the tables.

After the dishes were all clean and put up. Kayla and Jeff walked outside and walked down to the stables, corn crib, and tobacco barn. Unlike the big snow of 71, it was a balmy 55 degrees and the skies were clear.

Holding hands as they walked, Kayla, squeezing his hand, remarked,

"I know next Christmas, we won't have a little one but the next one, we will. I guess that's when we'll start staying up on Christmas Eve."

Jeff, grinning, replied,

"Yes, our little one won't know what's going on but later, we'll have pictures to share with him or her."

Kayla, laughed, replying,

"We could have twins and have one of each."

That stopped Jeff in his tracks.

"Twins? I hadn't thought of that. Do they run in your family? They don't in mine."

Kayla was laughing now,

"I was just kidding. We don't need but one to start with and I don't care if it's a boy or a girl as long as it's healthy."

When they walked back in, her mama immediately grabbed her telling Jeff to go into the living room with the men. The women had a meal to put on the table.

Her mama had the whip.

"Kayla, the turkey's about ready to come out of the oven. Set it over on the sideboard with the ham. The potatoes for the potato salad are cool enough to work with. You remember how I showed you to make it?"

"Yes, Mama, it's only been 2 years. Yes, I remember."

"Then you know to make your daddy a little bit without celery. He hates it."

Karla wondered if Jeff liked it. She didn't have a clue. She guessed she'd know soon enough.

When everything was ready, the family was called to the tables and her daddy did the blessing. He won't much for praying and blessings but he knew it was his time to step up and he did.

"Heavenly Father, I ain't much on praying out loud but I've got a few things I need to thank Ye for.

"First of all, thank You for Dolly, we've been together fer a long while now. When ye made us one, you meant fer us to stay together and we will, Lord.

"Thank Ye fer the children Ye blessed us with. We couldn't be prouder. They've all been blessings to us and our grandchildren, Lord, I ain't got enough words to thank Ye.

"Thank Ye fer our health, we've surely been blessed.

"Thank Ye fer our land, it's provided for us well. We try to be good stewards.

Thank Ye now for the food sitting before us. Make us truly thankful for every bite of nourishment we are about to receive.

"Most of all, Father, thank Ye for Jesus, without him, we'd all be lost. We don't go to your house much. I hope we can get better at it. We're gonna try, Lord. Amen."

Among the siblings, there wasn't a dry eye. They'd never heard their daddy pray like that.

As the food was passed and enjoyed, more stories were shared, mostly about Christmas but not all of them.

Ander shared the one about his daddy catching him smoking out behind the corn crib.

"Daddy never put one in his mouth and he made sure that I'd never want another one. That's the most I ever heard Daddy say. He was calm but unrelenting. The tongue lashing was enough but he wasn't done. He told me to drop my pants and bend over the Flossie's feed trough. By the third lick, I was crying like a baby. He never said another word, just hung the leather strap up and walked off.

"To this day, when I see somebody smoking, I remember that leather strap. No way will I ever touch one again."

He laughed before saying,

"Maybe after he's been in the ground 10 or 20 years. I want to be real sure he ain't coming back."

That brought laughter from everyone as the stories continued through dessert.

After supper, everyone seemed ready to turn in early. They'd been up since the wee pre-dawn hours. They got no argument from Kayla or Jeff.

Sunday morning, everyone was up by 8 a.m. Kayla, Donna, and Linda were in the kitchen helping their mama with breakfast

Donna wondered,

"Kayla, what if something happened to Jeff's father? Will he give up his career and move back to Alabama?"

Kayla had wondered the same thing herself, she replied,

"No, Jeff says if something happens or when his father retires, either one of his two brothers' will take over or the business will be sold. That's about all I know right now but I'm sure I'll know a whole lot more after meeting the family"

"When does he graduate?

"Spring of 84, the same time I do. It seems like a long time but it isn't. I'm already sending résumé's out."

Linda was asking now,

"What do you want to do. What kind of positions are you applying for?"

"Administrative mostly. I'd really like to get on at the hospital. It's expanding like crazy. The new facilities opened in 1977 and they've been adding on ever since. I'd like to get on in purchasing or accounts receivable or payable. It doesn't matter. If I'm lucky enough to get on; I'll find out then where I want to be."

"Where are you going to live after you get married?"

"A townhouse, probably, they're springing up everywhere. We don't want to live in the area where most of the students live. We'll probably lease something near the hospital. We don't want to be north of the river either. It's too far from everything."

Donna's mind was churning,

How long would Jeff's commute be?"

"Fifteen minutes, tops. Probably more like ten."

He mama broke up the inquisition, girls,

"Girls, get the tables set, Kayla, get the biscuits out of oven, Donna, get the jelly, butter and molasses, Linda, find out what they want to drink. It's time to get it on the table.

"Kayla, put the grits in a bowl and set the ham, sausage, and bacon on the sideboard, we'll let them march through and serve themselves. This is the last of it. The scrambled eggs are ready. Call em' to the table."

When they were all gathered in a circle, Ander said the only blessing he knew.

"Father, bless the food to the nourishment of our bodies and us to thy service. Amen."

Her mama was barking out instructions,

"Ya'll pick up your plate and file past the sideboard. Tell Linda what you want to drink."

Her daddy went first and then Jeff and Kayla since he was the honored guest. After that, it was age before beauty leaving Linda and Gary to bring up the rear but it didn't matter. There was plenty of everyone.

During breakfast, questions abounded, including, school, the air force, the farm and Woody Grady's store.

Kayla wondered if it was still as popular with the teenagers as it was when she graduated in 1979.

Gary said it was when he graduated.

"Mr. Grady still ran a tight ship but he reckoned that was the reason parents didn't mind their children going there.

"He didn't put up with no mess. If he smelled alcohol on you, you were gone and as far as I knew, there wasn't any drugs around either."

"He put Amos Stroud's son, Jamie, in jail when he hit Doug Williams across the head with a Pepsi Bottle giving him a concussion."

She wanted to ask about Brian Howard but wouldn't. She didn't know why he crossed her mind anyway but he did. She guessed she must have loved him but there was no way he was going to trick her into marrying him and being stuck in Duplin Country for the rest of her life. She knew she was right. She was with Mr. Right now, and they had a bright future ahead of them. She'd told Brian when she left that she was going to make something out of herself and she was; he'd see. Everybody would.

After breakfast, at Jeff's request, they drove to Kenansville and she pointed out the Kenan Memorial Auditorium, the hospital, courthouse, Liberty Hall, the Graham House, Grove Presbyterian Church, the Cowan Museum that had only been open a year, and the Village Squire and Inn before retracing their route past Woody Grady's store, Duplin Central School, and Guilford East where her daddy worked.

"We could ride down the Tram Road."

"The what?"

"Tram Road, I don't know why it's called that but it is. Turn here."

Jeff turned left and followed the winding road to Woodland Methodist Church.

"Where does this go?"

She wasn't sure.

"Outlaw's Bridge, I think."

"Outlaw's Bridge, real Outlaws?"

Kayla was laughing now.

"No, silly, it's one of the family names. They, and the Grady's, are   the largest family groups in this section of Duplin County. The Smiths are probably next. They have a huge combined family reunion every year and I think there's a museum too."

It didn't take them to Outlaw's Bridge but connected them to Outlaw's Bridge Road and took them to the crossroads. Turning right on Hwy 903/111, they drove through Albertson joining Hwy 11 a few miles further down.

Her mama had warned them that there'd be no Sunday dinner, after their big breakfast, so they drove back to the Country Squire and enjoyed brunch before returning to Kayla's a little after 2 p.m.

SNR

Later, the family gathered in the living room listening to stories about the early years of their parent's marriage.

Mr. Herring was sharing about their first winter together.

"We lived in the tenant house up yonder by the woods. It was what they called, a 'shotgun house.' It was straight through from the front room through the 2 bedrooms into the kitchen. Out back, a little ways, was the outhouse. You ain't lived until you used one of them in the dead of winter."

"Your mama bout' made me have a heart attack, maybe a month after we moved in. I was in the kitchen trying to fix the flue pipe that connected the stove to the chimney stack when she let out a yell that would have woke up the dead."

Their mama tried to stop him from telling it but there was no way.

"I tore out of the kitchen as fast as I could run seeing her standing by the open-door huffing and puffing like she was going to die. When I reached her, I grabbed her by the shoulders trying to calm her down but I won't getting anywhere with that. When she finally calmed, between breaths, she said there was a spider in there."

"There won't nothing unusual about that, most times, especially in the hot months, you lit a piece of paper and swished it around the opening to kill off the spiders. She hadn't done that but I can guarantee you that she did every time she went out there til we got plumbing back in 55."

"We'd built this house in 53 and knew the lights was coming so we had a room for a bathroom waiting for it."

"A man out of Pink Hill strung the wires when we built the house and did what he called 'stub-ups' for the plumbing at the same time."

"Tri-County hooked us up a month before Ander was born and I bought the Kelvinator from that same man too. He tried to sell us a clothes washer but mama nixed that real fast saying that new-fangled thing couldn't wash nothing as good as she could."

"Daddy died the next fall leaving the farm to me. Sarah got the farm over across Goshen Swamp. She, Seth, and her young'uns that's still home, tend the farm now.

"Mama stayed in the old place and tended the garden until she passed in 1960. The home place is gone now. It won't worth fixing. She didn't have electricity and plumbing. Said she didn't cotton to the them newfangled things.

"She did have a Philco battery radio. It's in the front room. I doubt if it's works but it's something to remember her by. She loved country music, real country music, not that stuff they call country now. I guess she liked what was called, 'Country and Western.' When Patsy Cline or Loretta was singing, you either got in a corner and hushed or you put yourself outside."

Ander broke up the story-telling saying they had to get on the road.

"I got to work tomorrow. Nara does too. We got about a two-and-a-half-hour drive ahead of us so we better get to it."

They were already packed so after all the goodbye hugs were done and the canned stuff mana insisted they take was loaded along with a slab of country ham and several links of their daddy's dried sausage. They wished everybody and 'Happy New Year' and began their drive.

Gary's leave was up at midnight so he was the next to leave wishing everyone a 'Happy New Year.'

"By the time it gets here, I'll be on the other side of the world. I love ya'll. Kayla, you and Jeff, good luck with your wedding."

Donna's family were not leaving until tomorrow around noon but were more than ready to call it a night.

Kayla wanted to sleep with Jeff but she knew that won't going to happen so she bunked in with Linda leaving Jeff by himself.

SNR

Monday morning, the family was stirring early or at least their daddy was. The old rooster had crowed twice and he had the coffee pot on five minutes later.

Kayla was awake listening to the hushed sounds coming from the kitchen. Her mama was up; she knew she would be. Now the only question was whether her daddy would wait for the family or want his breakfast now.

He was off until Wednesday but that didn't matter. He had a morning routine and he rarely broke it.

Donna's family was up. She could hear them down the hall.

All right, Kayla, get yourself up and help your mama fix breakfast.

"Good morning, Mama. What can I do?"

"Morning, Honey, why don't you do the bacon? I've got the sausage and ham going and the grits are on the stove."

Linda walked in saying, good morning, to everyone, Jeff was in the kitchen too sipping on a cup of coffee.

"I'll get the biscuits going. Don't look like anybody else has started on them."

It was poured in concrete. Linda did the biscuits. Everyone knew that.

Mr. Herring came in the kitchen, grumbling.

"That dag-nab rooster, one of these days I'm going to lay him out."

"What's he done now, Hon?"

"He won't leave, Nicey, alone. She's been sitting on them eggs 2 weeks now. Them biddies will be hatching in another week and he keeps trying to get her up off them. I ran him out of the barn and shut the door."

Breakfast was coming together and so was the family. Everyone was seated when Linda took pan of biscuits out of the oven and dumped them into a basket.

"Lord, thank you for taking care of our family and we thank you for this food set before us. Amen."

Wondering, Jeff asked?

"Mr. Herring, how many roosters do you have?"

"I got 3 of em,' Jack's the boss cause he's the oldest. The other 2 whipper-snappers want to be the boss but they ain't nowhere near ready. Jack weighs a third more than either of them and he's been through the wringer a few times. If I don't kill him first, he'll be the boss for 2 or 3 more years before one of other 2 will take him down. When that happens, he's headed for the stew pot."

After spending most of the morning with her parents, Kayla wanted to go to Woody Grady's for lunch. She invited them to go with them and they were more than willing.

Her mama spoke up, saying,

"It's been awhile since we were there for dinner. I guess that's lunch to ya'll now. We stop by there to pick up this and that but we hardly ever eat. I don't know why, he's got the best burgers and hot dogs, I'm ready."

Her daddy agreed saying they needed to get there before noon; they'd have to stand in line if they didn't.

They hadn't been inside 2 minutes when she spotted Brian Howard sitting with a redhead she didn't recognize. She acted as if she hadn't seen him but she had. Mixed emotions surged through her body. No, she didn't still love him but they'd done a lot together when they dated and for the most part, until right at the last, she enjoyed their time together.

She was still upset about the way he acted when she told him she was moving to Greenville, NC for her junior and senior year. She wanted her diploma to come from there.

As soon as they were seated, her mama was asking,

"Isn't that Brian, the boy you dated in high school and when you attended James Sprunt?"

Trying to act very nonchalant, Kayla, asked,

"Where, Mama?"

"Across the room, over there in that booth with that red-haired girl."

She glanced in his direction before replying,

"Yes, I think it is. He doesn't look like he changed much but it's only been a year or so."

Brian had seen her about the same time and taking the red-head by the hand, walked over to the table.

"Hello folks, I haven't seen you in a while. Kayla you're looking nice. Who's that with you?"

She was ready for him, smiling broadly as she replied,

"Brian, this is my fiancé, Jeff Harris. Jeff, this is Brian Howard. We went to school together."

As she had hoped, that totally caught Brian off -guard as he reached over to shake Jeff's hand.

"Congratulations, when are you getting married? Oh, excuse my manners; this is Faye Whaley. Faye, this is Kayla, her fiancé, Jeff, and her parents, Mr. and Mrs. Raymond Herring."
"Faye's from Beulaville. We've been dating a couple of months now."

Jeff, after speaking to Faye, addressed Brian's query.

"We've looking at Easter. Tomorrow, we'll drive down to my home in Opelika, Alabama so my family can meet, Kayla. During our visit, we'll set a firm date. I'd elope with her tomorrow if she'd go but she should be introduced to my family first."

Brian, apparently recovering, asked?

"Jeff, are you in school too?"

"Yes, we both graduate next year. Are you in school?"

"No, Faye's on shifts at DuPont. I work on the far"

Looking at Kayla, Jeff asked,

"Didn't we pass that plant on our way here?"

"Yes, on the other side of Kinston; you remarked about how big it was."

It was obvious that what Brian was hearing was upsetting and after more congratulations, his questions ceased and he took Faye by the hand leading her back to their table.

Woody Grady walked up about the same time their burgers arrived.

"Well, well, look who's back in Duplinville. You're in ECC aren't you?

"Yes, Mr. Grady, I'm a junior. This is my fiancé, Jeff Harris. Jeff this is the one and only, Mr. Woody Grady. When God made him, he broke the mold. There will never be another. He's our local Dick Clark and this is his bandstand."

Shaking hands with Jeff, Woody, replied to her introduction and remark saying.

"Jeff, it's a pleasure meeting you. You've got a gem there but I guess you already know that.
"You're too kind, Kayla, thank you. One thing for sure, since you left, I haven't had to replace G-39. You wore that button out, Kayla."

"Mr. Grady, you know that I love Willie Nelson's songs and *Faded Love* will always be my favorite."

He responded,
"I know, believe me! You know I'm just kidding. It's good to see you, and Jeff. Congratulations. I know you'll be happy."

"Raymond, it's always nice to see you and Dolly. Ya'll come back soon."

That evening, after another fantastic country meal of Salisbury steak with mounds of creamed potatoes, sawmill gravy, butter beans and biscuits followed by more dessert; they called it a night saying leaving early in the morning called for a good night's sleep.

Meeting Jeff's Parents

By 9 a.m., they were packed and ready to go. Her parents were already calling Jeff, son, and he was addressing them as, Raymond and Dolly." One last hug and they were gone.

They were eager to get started knowing they would be spending the night alone. It seemed forever since Thanksgiving and they were more than ready to climb their mountain.

Jeff followed Hwy 11 to Kenansville turning right on Hwy 24 following it through Warsaw, Clinton, and Roseboro to Fayetteville when he picked up I-95 traveling south. They bypassed Lumberton and Rowland before arrived at South of the Border a little before noon. They'd gotten lost in Clinton.

Traffic on I-95 was sparse so getting an early check-in was easy after picking up burgers and fries, they locked themselves in their room gobbling down their food before flinging their clothes everywhere.

Their appetite for each-other had not dwindled since Thanksgiving. If anything, it had become overwhelmingly stronger. Being familiar with each other's bodies only made their climb up their mountain more exciting.

After the third climb, they showered and fell asleep nestled in each other's arms.

They awoke at six p.m. and were starving. Outside, the night air was chilly but comfortable as they made their way to the Sombrero Restaurant.

Ordering coffee, they looked at the menu knowing they didn't want any spicy food.

They ordered the 10-oz. ribeye's with baked potato and salad. She wanted her steak, medium and he wanted his, medium rare.

Their steaks were cooked perfectly and their baked potatoes were loaded with sour cream, butter, chives, and bacon bits. Neither remember what their salad was like barely toughing them.

The only dessert they wanted was each other and by 9 p.m., they were enjoying their dessert.

Next morning, knowing they had a 7-hour drive, they had ham biscuits at Hardee's and were on the road by 9. Driving down I-20, the route was easy and Jeff was very familiar with it. They arrived in Opelika a little after 3 p.m. local time having crossed one time zone.

Pulling into the driveway at his childhood home, he knew everyone would be on the lake and they apparently were. While making a rest stop, he gave Kayla a tour of the spacious tri-level home. She was more than awed having never been in a house that large.

At 4, local time, they drove to Lake Eufaula arriving 20 minutes later. As evidenced by all the vehicles, his whole family appeared to be there and they were. Jim and Elizabeth (Liz) Harris came out first followed by Johnny and a girl, Jeff didn't recognize.

"Merry Christmas, welcome home and this must be Kayla? Welcome to our family, Kayla, we're heard some much about you."

Trying to be proper. Jeff made the introductions,

Mother and Father, this is Kayla Herring, my fiancé. Kayla, this is Jim and Elizabeth, she prefers, Liz, Harris, my parents."

Johnny, this Kayla, my fiancé. Kayla this is my brother, Johnny, he's 2 years my senior and studying to be a doctor at John's Hopkins School of Medicine in Baltimore and this young lady, I haven't had the pleasure."

Johnny reached for Kayla's hand while introducing his lady friend.

Kayla, and Jeff, this is Nelda. She is also studying medicine at Johns Hopkins. Nelda, this is my brother Jeff, and his fiancé, Kayla."

With all the formalities behind them, his mother welcomed them inside. Kayla was in awe a second time. If anything, this 'summer home' was even more spacious than the other and the view was magnificent. It overlooked the huge lake with a commanding view from high above the lake on a bluff.
A roaring fire welcomed them as they found seats around it.

Mr. Harris, asked?

"How was your drive, the traffic wasn't too bad, I'm sure. Come Monday, it will be murderous."

Jeff replied that it wasn't too bad.

"I'm sure, like you say, Monday will be terrible. We're leaving Sunday to get away from that."

He didn't mention that they would break their trip up overnighting somewhere on the way. He was sure that that everyone supposed they would. After all, they were engaged.

Johnny was asking about school. Was he still online for a position with that big pharmaceutical company?

Jeff replied that he was. He was spending the afternoons at Burroughs Wellcome studying under some of the best chemists in the world.

"I'll be assigned to one of them as their assistant as soon as I have my diploma. I've got my fingers crossed that it will be under Dr. Mayank Sahu. He's from the Bihar District of India. It bordered Napal to the north and Bangladesh to the east. He got his PhD studying at Cambridge, England. He has the most inventive mind I've ever known.

Nelda wondered,

"Do you have any problem understanding him?"

Replying, Jeff said,

"In the beginning, I did but once I became familiar with how he structures his sentences, it's no problem."

"There's an epidemic of aids spreading like wildfire in third-world-countries, and here too. That's what he works on. The new building at Burroughs Wellome is dedicated to aids and Dr. Sahu was instrumental in developing the first drug that showed promise in the treatment."

"How about you? Have you chosen a field?"

Johnny replied that he had.

"I'm looking at Neurosurgery."

Jeff was intrigued,

"After medical school, how many years' residency?

"Depending on where I go, 7 or 8 years. I know that's a long time but that's were my interest is."

"I'm impressed, Johnny, how about you, Nelda?"

Responding, she replied,

"Anesthesiology, it required 4 years' residency."

He replied that 4 years was a long but if she was putting him under, he'd want her to have all 4 years and probably then some.

That brought laughter from the group.

His mother joined in the conversation suggesting the Johnny and Jeff take Nelda and Kayla on a tour of Eufaula and the lake district.

"We're having dinner at six, that should give you plenty of time."

Johnny looked over at the girls, asking,

"Are you ladies up to it?"
They were and in minutes, they all piled into Johnny's 1984 Ford van with a custom "Turtle Package" conversion kit that included 4 captain's chairs.

Jeff was impressed,

"You must have just gotten this. It smells brand new."

Johnny replied,

Yes, it is. I got it in October. My mustang had 170,000 miles on it. It didn't owe me a thing."

"What about gas mileage?"

"It has 2 tanks with a total capacity of 37 gallons. We spent the night in Florence, South Carolina. That's about half way. It's about 850 miles. We gassed up the next morning and came on in.

"It is a long drive. If I come back for Easter, I'll fly into Birmingham and rent a car. Summer Break, I'll drive down.

"Nelda will be going home for Easter and she's spending the summer in Spain. Her family owns a seaside villa in Valencia on the Alboran Sea. She's invited me to come over for a visit. I'd really love to but I'm sure Father has other plans. If he didn't, I'd be surprised. Wouldn't you?"

Jeff knew where that came from but when he and Kayla got married, there'd have to be some changes in that routine.

"We'll be married.   Come summer, I'll be working at Burroughs Wellcome. They've already indicated that they want me and after I graduate next fall. I'll be there full time."

Kayla added that she hoped to spend the summer as a 'temp.'

"Hopefully, it will be at the hospital where I can make some contacts. I really want a position there when I graduate. I filed my resume last June."

Eufaula was beautiful, even in the dead of winter with all the leaves on the ground. The evergreens looked as if they were begging from Christmas decorations.

Decorations were prolific everywhere they turned.

Nelda wondered,

"Most all these houses seem to be occupied. I was under the impression that it was a seasonal resort."

Kayla thought that's what she understood too.

Jeff replied that more and more retirees were moving in. There were plenty of summer homes, but like theirs, they also seemed to be occupied more and more.

"Mom, probably spends 60% of her time here. She loves our home back in Opelika, but it' much more relaxed here."

Laughing, he continued,

It's further away from Dad's office too. When she'd got him here; there are no distractions. None that she will allow him to monitor.

"Mr. Allsworth was stolen from Food Lion 2 years ago to take the reins and run the business and he's more than qualified. He's only limited to what he can do by Dad."

"You have to admit, Dad's only 52 and has a lot of good year's left before being put out to pasture and he's determined to use every year he has left. He's proud of what's he's accomplished. We all are but it's grown into a consuming monster and he doesn't know how to turn it loose."

"I'm sure he understands now that we're not coming back to take over the reins. If Mom keeps up her unrelenting nagging, maybe he'll finally take the hint and sell out. He's already had 2 very lucrative offers."

"What am I doing? We're supposed to be Celebrating the beauty of Eufaula and I'm talking business.

"Mr. Jim Harris, look what you've done to your son. When I become a neurosurgeon. Every time I have time off, I'll probably be trying to talk surgery to everyone I meet and Jeff, he'll probably be trying to shove a pill down Santa's throat every Christmas Eve when he's trying to deliver toys to their children."

That brought laughter from everyone and a change in subject.

They finished circumnavigated the entire 45,000 acres' lake shoreline and were almost back home.

"Decisions, Decisions"

Kayla saw the invitation on the counter while cranking "Mr. Coffee" up. It had been a restless night. Memories from her high school and early college days refused to go away. She's rolled, tossed, and tumbled most of the night. Was she going, or wasn't she? One part of her wanted to go and another part wanted no part of it.

After toast and coffee, she left for the hospital and another day on the job. A job that had lasted almost 25 years. No, not the position she had now but she'd been lucky and given a position at the hospital in the accounts payable department.

At first, she'd been excited, especially with Donna Hudson being her supervisor. She was easy going and never seemed to get excited and knew how to handle any situation that arose and being in accounts payable, there were always situations. Mostly, it was vendors wanting or demanding to be paid but Donna would simply tell them that all the paperwork hadn't been signed off on and until it was, no check could be issued.

The one particular situation that made Kayla want to get out was with an arrogant piece of work called Ransom Daniels. He owned a fabrication shop in Nashville, NC and they'd done a lot of counter replacements when the employee pharmacy was renovated. The sum was substantial but 'Building and Grounds' refused to sign off on the work until Mr. Daniel's replaced some of the laminate with the pattern that had been specified. He refused saying that they made the mistake, not him.

On his last demanding visit, he became threating and Donna called security. They escorted him off the property. It ended up in the legal department and a year later, he replaced the laminate and a check was finally issued.

That had been enough excitement for Kayla and she started looking for other positions available in the growing complex.

One position really grabbed her attention, executive secretary to the executive assistant to the VP of Building and Grounds. The qualifications were well within the parameters of her degree and experience. Donna told her that she'd be more than happy to highly recommend her to Mr. Cal Newbold.

"You would enjoy working for Cal. He'd down to earth and apparently not moody at all. He also came up through the ranks. I'll send a recommendation over to him today."

Three days later, she'd been interviewed by Mr. Newbold and immediately liked him. His personality was   tranquil and the atmosphere in his office seemed very peaceful, nothing like accounts payable.

Two weeks later, she was given the position and moved immediately to the 'Building and Grounds' office across campus. From the moment, she arrived she knew that she'd landed a dream job. Working with Mr. Newbold was almost like not working at all. Yes, there were times when situations became hectic but she never once, heard her boss raise his voice. His calming demeanor was infectious and appeared to rub off on whomever he was interacting with.

On her first lunch break, she walked out of the office, on her way to the cafeteria, at the exact same moment as Mary Tyson. After introductions, they walked together to the cafeteria, choosing salads and water.

Sitting together, they talked mostly about family. Mary had been married 5 years. She and David, had 2 sons, Ralph was almost 4 and Billy was 2. They lived in Farmville and Woody worked for Farrior and Sons.

"They're general contractors and do a lot of work for the hospital. David works for James Haislip, one of the jobsite supervisors. David is a rough carpenter now but wants to become a cabinet maker. That's where the big bucks are. James, is a cabinet maker but took the supervisor position when Mr. Farrior offered it to him 4 or 5 years ago. He lives in Farmville too and has a woodworking shop behind his home. David spends a lot of time there learning the trade."

"Lord, look at the time, I guess I've talked your head off. I may let you talk if we do this again."

They did talk, almost daily, becoming the best of friends.

SNR

In late August, they were having lunch and Mary invited Kayla and Jeff to an outdoor barbecue saying it was to celebrate David's upcoming birthday.

"We're only inviting close friends maybe 15 to 20 and I'd love for you to come."

Neither had met the other's spouses and it seemed like the perfect time to make that happen.

"It's going to be Saturday week. It will be very casual and 'No Presents' please. Just bring yourselves and plan to have an enjoyable time. Oh, no alcohol please."

Kayla replied saying,

"We don't do the alcohol thing. Jeff will drink a beer when he goes fishing the some of the guys from work but I don't touch any of it."

"He works shifts so I'll let you know tomorrow if we can go. I hope so. I'd like to meet the man that keeps a smile always on your face."

Jeff was on graveyard so they got a chance to catch up giving Kayla an opportunity to ask if he'd be available for David's birthday.

"Mary says there'll only be about 10 couples. It will be a good opportunity of us to meet new people. We rarely go out and socialize except at church and most times, you're not available and I'm tied down with Kevin."

Their 6-month old could be a handful at times. Jeff looked at his calendar saying he was off, they could go.

"We'll hire a babysitter and let our hair down. It's been awhile."

Kayla was all for it but wanted Jeff to know that there would be 'no booze.'

"Remember, 'no booze,' the party is alcohol free."

"That's not a problem; I only drink beer when I'm with the boys fishing. I'm looking forward to it."

They really hadn't been anywhere except church and visiting her parents since they got married. Kevin arrived 10 months later and they'd allowed him to occupy 99% of their time. When they were not working, they were taking care of him.

Kayla didn't know what she was letting herself in for but Jeff's wondering eyes would become very apparent at the party.

SNR

That Saturday, Jeff came in at 8:20 a.m., showered, had breakfast that consisted of nothing but a bowl of cereal and a cup of coffee.

"I'm going to get some shut-eye. Wake me about 2. If you have errands to run, I'll take care of Kevin. What time's the sitter coming over?"

Kayla replied that she would arrive about 5:30.

"The party starts at 6, that will give us plenty of time to get there. I told her we would be home by 10 p.m. Remember to leave the money on the table in hall."

Kayla didn't really have a lot to do. She already decided to wear Bermuda shorts and a collared top. The weather forecast was for a very warm afternoon with highs reaching into the lower 90s but there was no rain in the forecast.

As lunch approached she fed Kevin and put him down for his nap before having a pimento cheese sandwich with a glass of iced tea. All that was left to do was dust a little here and there and take the garbage out.

At 2, she awakened Jeff and gave him a few minutes to come together before driving to the mall looking for a pair of slip-ons or sandals. Her flip-flops were too be worn to even consider wearing. Finding a pair of white sandals on sale, she was back home a little before 4 p.m.

When she arrived, Jeff was in the living room watching a car race or something. Kevin was lying beside him with a pacifier in his mouth.

"What's Mary's husband's name? I know you told me but I forgot?"

She replied,

"David."

Absorbing that, he asked?

"Did you say he was a carpenter or something?"

"He works for Farrior and Sons on one of their construction crews. They do a lot of commercial work around the hospital complex. He's hoping to become a cabinet maker."

Jeff remembered seeing their signs on numerous constructions sites including Burroughs Wellcome.

"Okay, got that and Mary works where you do?"

"No, she's a secretary in the office building next to the one I'm in."

"Children?"

"Yes, 2: Ralph is 3 and Billy is 1."

SNR

They left their townhouse on Allen Road just after 5:30 taking the new John P East Memorial (264) Bypass to Wesley Church Road. Exiting, they turned right and drove to the intersection with Moye-Turnage Rd. Taking a right, they followed it into the city limits where it became Wilson Street. Just ahead, in front of Farmville Middle School, Wilson and Grimmersburg St merged. They merged onto Grimmersburg and followed it past Sam Bundy School to N. Waverly Street taking a right finding Mary and David's house a few blocks down on the right.

There were several cars in front of their house. Knocking on the door, Janice, a neighbor, led them out back. Mary rushed up to them with a welcoming hug for Kayla.

"Kayla, I'm so glad you could come. This must be Jeff?"

Kayla made the introductions replying,

"Yes, Mary, this is Jeff. Jeff this is my friend, Mary, from work."

David had walked up wanting to be introduced.

"This is my husband, David. David, this is Kayla and Jeff Harris. You've heard me talk about Kayla many times."

Replying, he agreed saying how nice it was to finally meet her.

"And, Jeff, it's nice to meet you too."

Kayla wished him a 'happy birthday' before being introduced to the group.

"Rhonda and Greg, this is Kayla and Jeff Harris. Kayla and I work together at the hospital. Jeff works at Burroughs Wellcome."

Ronda interrupted, asking Jeff?

"Jeff, what section are you in? I'm in the new building."

Jeff's interest was growing by the minute.

"I'm in the new building too. I'm in the lab on the third level. I'm on "B" shift."

Moving just a little closer so he could get a better view, she responded,

"Me too, maybe we'll run into each other in the cafeteria."

Rhonda was dressed in shorts and a sleeveless top revealing an overabundance of cleavage. Mary and Kayla knew it was way too much but she had Jeff's interest and she was bathing in it. She would capture and hold his attention through the entirety of the evening. Kayla spent most of the evening steering him away from her.

Knowing all eyes were on him; he could feel Kayla's, he asked Greg where he worked.

"I'm a deputy with the sheriff's department. I work crazy hours too."

Prying him away from Rhonda's boobs, Mary introduced them to James Haislip and his wife, Ginny.

"James is the 'job super' that David works under. He also has a huge workshop behind their home and he's teaching David cabinet making. He also spends a lot of time at the coast fishing. I think he has a camper at Harker's Island. Is that right, James?"

James replied in the affirmative, saying,

That's right, Mary; David's been down a couple of times. That's where the grey and speckled trout came from last fall.
"Jeff, do you fish?"

Jeff was fishing but it wasn't for trout. He was having problems concentrating with Rhonda smiling back at him from across the yard.

Almost stuttering, he replied,

"I haven't been salt water fishing. I grew up near Lake Eufaula in Alabama. It's a 45,000 acres' reservoir on the Chattahoochee River. I did a lot of fishing there as a youngster. We fished mostly for bass."

"You ought to come go with us one weekend. You might find it interesting. A Puppy Drum will give you as much of a fight as any bass I've ever run across."

Jeff was interested but not in fishing. Every part of his male anatomy was casting bated lines towards Rhonda and she appeared to be more than interested.

"Maybe I can. I'm on shifts at Burroughs Wellcome. Let me know when you're going again."

Duwood broke the conversation up saying it was time to get the burgers and wieners on.

"James, you and Jeff want to help?"

Kayla, uncomfortable with Jeff's continuing interest in Rhonda, suggested that he help David.

"I'm sure Mary has things she needs to do inside. Ginny and I will help her."

Kayla couldn't get over how interested Jeff seemed in Rhonda. Granted, she was showing much more flesh than she should but Jeff seemed overly interested. She'd noticed that the other men in the group were very aware of her exposed cleavage but didn't seem to dwell on her exposure as much as Jeff. Maybe she was overreacting but she didn't think so. She'd let the rest of the evening convict or exonerate him. If he was going to hang himself, he'd have the chance.

When all the food was ready, Mary called for everyone's attention.

"Okay, everyone. Fix your plates, there's enough hot dogs and hamburgers for you to have one of each plus there's plenty of slaw, potato salad, baked beans, mac and cheese, Watergate salad and chips.

"Set wherever you like and yes, there is a birthday cake; a chocolate one, David's favorite and somehow, I managed to get all the candles on it. We can't light them in the house; the flames would probably burn the house down but we'll try lighting them outside."

When the laughter died down, she asked,

"Jesse, would you say the blessing?"

"Heavenly Father, for the food before us, for the friends around us, for the love in this family, we give you thanks, Amen."

After loading their plates, Kayla led Jeff over to a table joining Mary, David, Jesse, and Melva Monk.

David made the introductions.

Jesse and Melva, this is Kayla and Jeff Harris. She works in the same office complex at the hospital that I do. Jeff works at Burroughs Wellcome."

"Kayla and Jeff, this is our chief of police, Jesse Monk and his lovely wife, Melva. She's the lunchroom manager at Farmville Central School."

Kayla noticed that Jeff wanted to sit on the side affording an unobstructed view of Rhonda sitting at the next table. By then, she was sure that he was going to hang himself.

He was aware of her watchful eye and managed to elude getting caught staring although there were several times when he was sure that he had been.

Checking the time, Kayla realized it was 9:30 and they'd promised the baby-sitter that they'd be home by 10.

"Mary, David, this has been so nice but we should leave. Our baby-sitter will be looking for us."

"David, it's so nice meeting you, Happy Birthday and many happy returns."

Jeff chimed in saying how nice the party was and he really enjoyed meeting them.

"I hope we can get together soon. Maybe we can invite you over for dinner. We'll check my schedule. David, Happy Birthday!"

SNR

They said little on the way back home. Kayla really wanted to drill him about Rhonda but refrained knowing the mood she was in would only lead to a confrontation. Something they rarely had, she could only remember the one that involved Jeff not wanting to visit her parents on her mama's birthday. She'd ended up going, taking their 2-month-old, Kevin, with her. She'd told her parents that he was working but sent his regards. That was a lie but she wasn't about to say that he didn't want to go.

This was different and she knew the minute she opened her mouth, there'd be gnashing of teeth. He'd never raised his voice to her but she was pretty sure that accusing him of staring at Rhonda's boobs would. She would wait until she calmed down.

The next year passed without incident; at least none that she knew of but apparently, a lot was going on that she knew nothing about.

The following year, she was pregnant with Amy; in her third trimester, Jeff seemed to be spending more time with the boys and working more overtime and weekends than before. He kept the books so she had no idea how much more money was coming in. She was thankful for every extra dime. They'd need it with Amy on the way.

Amy was 3 months old when she got a call from Becky Matthews. She was in her Sunday School class at church. The call floored her. Becky shared that she was a night clerk at the Holiday Inn on Memorial Drive and she didn't want to be the bearer of bad news but felt that she should know since she had a new baby and everything.

"Your husband has been checking into a room here at least once a week, sometimes more and he's not by himself. He's got a woman with him. Kayla, I'm sure of it. Last night when he checked in, always wanting an outside, lower level room, on the back, I walked through the holidome and watched. Sure enough, there was a woman and they were necking and kissing before they went into the room. I wouldn't have called unless I saw it with my own eyes. I so sorry. Is there anything I can do?"

Kayla was steaming mad. She wanted to kill him but not without proof. There she was with a 3-month old child and a 2-year-old and he was running out on her.

"Becky, thank you so much. Yes, there is something I want you to do. Next time he checks in, please call and tell me what room he is in. I'll take it from there. Don't worry, I won't shoot him or anything like that but I'll have all the proof I need to divorce him. I guess none of us ever know, do we?"

Next day at lunch, she shared her dilemma with Mary.

"Mary, I'm so mad, I could kill him but no, I want him to pay for whoring around, especially while I was carrying Amy. I'm going catch him in the act, I'm pretty sure who the hussy is but when they walk out of that room, I'll have proof positive."

"Kayla, I'm so sorry. You need somebody to be a witness. Have you got anybody you can call at the spur of the moment? I can come but I might not get there in time."

"Thank you, Mary, I don't know a lot of people. Maybe Becky can meet me there. I'll probably have the children with me. I can't get a sitter at the drop of a hat. It doesn't matter, this must stop. He has to go."

Mary, thinking as fast as she could, came up with an idea.

"I'll get David to call Jesse, he'll know what to do. What shift is he on? I'll let you know what I find out tomorrow."

"He's got one more night of graveyard, then he off for 3 days before going on days."

SNR

As promised, Mary made a lot of calls while Kayla did everything in her power not to confront Jeff without any proof. She had Becky's eyewitness proof but she wanted more. When she finished with him, he'd be gone from her and if any way possible, the children's lives too.

The second day he was on days, he told her than morning before leaving for work that he would be working overtime. It would probably be 10 p.m. or later before he got home.

At 5 p.m., Becky called saying he'd just checked into room 155 on the back.
Kayla called Mary and she called Jesse.

Jesse told her that a uniformed deputy would meet her at the front desk. Kayla took her children, Amy was asleep and Kevin was involved with one of his toys.

She walked into the lobby at the Holiday Inn just before 6 p.m. Becky introduced her to Deputy Oaks. He suggested that they drive around back and park close to room 155.

"When we get there, you knock on the door and tell your husband that you know he's in there with another woman. Tell him that you're staying right there if it takes all night. Let him know that the children are in the car. Demand that he come out now."

Trembling, she stood at the door and knocked.

"Jeff, I know you're in there with another woman and I'm pretty sure I know who she is. Come out now. I'm not leaving until you do. The children are here with me. They're in the car."

From inside, she heard excited, muffled, words before he finally agreed to come out.

A few tense moments passed before the silence was broken by the sound of a chain being released on the door. It slowly opened and Jeff appeared, fully dressed although he'd missed a couple of buttons and his pants were unzipped. He was visibly shaken. He looked first at Kayla and then seeing the deputy, was more shaken.

"There no reason for the person in the room to be identified. You've got me. That's all you need."

Kayla spoke very firmly, saying,

"No, I want to see her too."

By now, there were several on-lookers gathering.

She stormed in the room dragging Rhonda Dail out by the arm. It was very apparent to everyone that she'd hastily dressed and her blouse wasn't tucked into her skirt. She hair was a mess. She looked as if her hand had been caught in the cookie jar, only 10 times worse.

When she saw Deputy Oaks, she froze.

Shocked, Deputy Oaks, exclaimed,

"You are Greg Dail's wife. I can't believe it."

He keyed the microphone on his shoulder asking the dispatcher to connect him with Deputy Dail.

"Greg, what's your 20?"

"Allen Road, what's yours?"

"Holiday Inn on the back, you need to come over here."

"What's the problem?"

"I can't discuss it on the air, just get over here."

The rest of the evening was mostly a blur. She'd thanked Deputy Oaks and told Jeff never to set foot in her house again, ever!

"My lawyer will be in touch. You're never to see me or the children again."

She spent the rest of the evening feeding and getting the children to bed. She tried sleeping but it didn't happen. It would be months before she would finally sleep soundly again without reliving the nightmare over and over again.

"Did she want to go or, didn't she?"

She placed the invitation back on the table. She wasn't going to let memories of Jeff's 'woman chasing' ruin her day.

The ringing phone pulled her away from her thoughts. It was Mary.

"Yes, I'd like that, we haven't been to CPW's in a while. What time?... Okay, I'll meet you outside your office. See you then."

Mary had perfect timing. She always had. She'd been there for her during the trying time leading up to the separation and divorce, always supportive, always caring, always knowing when Kayla really needed her.

Seated at CPW's, they didn't need a menu. They always seemed to order the same thing. Iced tea, the Pasta Alfredo with chicken and broccoli.

"So, have you decided? Are you going?"

Mary was the first one she'd told about the invitation and about her indecision.

"Mary, I still don't know. I guess I should but I really don't want to dredge up some of those memories. I just don't know."

Mary had talked with David and they both felt something like the reunion was just what Kayla needed to get out of the rut she'd been in since her daughter, Amy, left for college.

Her son, Kevin came down with his wife, Kylie, and their 3-year-old son, Ray just about every month but for the most part, she was alone. Yes, Amy, came home about once a month but that left the rest of her life empty.

Dating seemed out of the question. Every time, Mary, or some of the other ladies in the office complex, tried hooking her up with someone, Kayla always had an excuse not to be available.

SNR

There's been one exception back in 2007 when they thought Kayla was going to give dating a try. She met Lynn Stocks at First Baptist's Fall Festival. A social hour had followed the crowning of their King and Queen and Mary insisted that they go for coffee and cookies.

Seeing Jesse and Melva at one of the tables, they stopped by and were invited to join them.

"May I join you?"

Kayla and Mary looked up seeing a man dressed in a sports coat and tie talking to Jesse who had stood offering his hand.

"Please do, Lynn. You remember my wife, Melva, and this is Mary Tyson and her friend, Kayla Herring.

"Ladies, this is Lynn Stocks. He's the manager of the Federal Credit Union in Wilson. He lost his wife in a tragic accident about 3 years ago.

"He has a son, Chad. He's in culinary arts school in France. He wants to be a chef in New York."

"Lynn lives in Cotton Ridge Court on West Wilson Street out beyond Farmville United Methodist Church. He commutes every day but from what I hear, he may be leaving us soon relocating to Wilson. Lynn, I understand that your house is on the market. Is that true?"

Speaking first to Melva, Mary, and Kayla, he took as seat across from Kayla and answered Jesse's query.

"Yes, I listed it with Farmville Realty several of weeks ago. Leaving will be hard but since I lost Joann, it doesn't seem, or feel, the same. My neighbors are great but I think I need to move on and find new surroundings."

Lynn's kind eyes had a twinkle in them and the greyish streaks in his wavy hair made him seem so distinguished. Kayla really liked his persona. It seemed so kind and caring.

Those eyes were looking directly into hers when he asked?

"Kayla, it's none of my business but you're not wearing a ring. Are you single, divorced, or a widow?"

Kayla feeling as if she was blushing, replied,

"Lynn, I'm divorced. It's been 22 years. My son was 4 and my daughter was 1."

He was chuckling now.

"How in the world has a beautiful lady like you remained unattached all these years? I can't believe that someone hasn't gobbled you up."

"That's easy, Lynn; I haven't allowed anyone in. My ex apparently had more than one affair in our 4 years of marriage and I don't guess I've ever gotten over it."

She'd probably said too much, but, it was said.

He eased the conversation into another direction saying he'd seen that happen to too many marriages and he didn't have an answer.

"I guess some marriages are destined to failure. Ours certainly wasn't but providence took Joann away. I'll always love her but I don't want to spend the rest of my life alone. I hope you'll find someone that really loves you. You certainly deserve it."

Changing the conversation, he asked?

"Jesse, are you going to the lodge, Tuesday night? We're doing a 3rd degree."

"Planning on it, Lynn. I enjoy degree work with you in the East."

Mary added,

"David's going, he's starting through the chairs. I'm so proud of him."

Kayla didn't have a clue what they were talking about but wouldn't show her ignorance. She'd ask Mary at lunch.

Just as he started to get up, he hesitated and looked across at Kayla.

"I'm going to a play at Wright Auditorium Friday night. It would be a pleasure to have you join me."

At first, Kayla felt caged like a wild animal. Something inside said yes but there were 22 years of, no. She looked first at Mary seeing yes in her eyes then at him.

"Lynn, I think I'd like that. What time?"

"It starts at 7. May I pick you up at 6:30?"

"That's fine, I'm looking forward to it."

She gave him her address and they exchanged cell numbers.

Standing, Lynn wished everyone a nice evening saying,

"Whoever brought Kayla here, thank you."

She couldn't believe what had just happened. It had been 22 years and now, suddenly, she was going on a date.

Mary was all smiles while Jesse and Melva assured her that Lynn was a perfect gentleman and were sure they would have a wonderful evening.

Her First Date in 22 Years

Saturday seemed to take forever to arrive but finally, it had. All week, the only conversation each day at lunch with Mary seemed to be a replication of the preceding day.

"I can't believe I'm doing this after all these years. Mary, am I making a mistake? Please tell me that I'm not."

Each day, Mary would give her the same reply,

Kayla, it's time to break out and Lynn's the perfect man to do it with. We've never known a finer gentleman. He's involved in all the community activities and he's always in church on Sunday. His personality is delightful but then, you already know that. Go, enjoy; it's high time that you did."

"Should I tell my kids? What would I say to them?"

"Kayla, it's only one date. If there are others, there will be plenty of time to tell them. When's the last time they saw their father?"

"It's been years; I think he remarried. That's his business as long as he keeps up the alimony payments. He didn't miss any child support payments and after his father's estate was settled, he set up educational funds and lifetime trusts for Kevin and Amy.

"After he transferred to the Research Triangle Park, I didn't hear from him again until his lawyer sent a copy of the 'paid-off' mortgage on my house."

"If he has remarried, I pity the poor soul that married him. She wouldn't have a clue about him. He'll do the same thing to her that he did to me."

"I know you're right, Mary but I'm more nervous than when I was back in high school. It's like I've finally allowed myself to open a new chapter in my life and I think that I'm finally ready.

"I guess at 48, it's now or never and the more I think about it, the more I'm sure that I don't want to spend the rest of my life alone.

"Years ago, when I changed my name back to Herring, I thought I was ready but I wasn't. Now I think I finally am."

Saturday finally arrived and although she was as nervous as she's ever been, she was ready when the doorbell rang.

"Lynn, you're right on time. Would you like to come in or do we need to leave? It's been so long since I went to a play at the auditorium, I don't remember about parking."

"First, Kayla. You're absolutely beautiful. I'm looking forward to our evening together.

"Yes, we should get started. Parking is always a problem on campus."

Picking up her purse and wrap, she walked with him to his car He opened the door for her before getting in the driver's seat and they were on their way.

She really liked his Lincoln Navigator, it was plush, very plush. She wasn't accustomed to that kind of luxury. Her, paid for, 2002 Camry, was more her style and it was affordable for her too.

He drove down Fairlane to Hooker Road, taking a right and then a left on Greenville Blvd. After several intersections, he made a left on Elm crossing 10th. Street finding parking near the auditorium.

They had excellent seats in the center section, row B, with an aisle seat. She never been that close to the stage and she already felt special knowing that she/they were going to enjoy the performance.

Nunsense, was more than just entertaining. It was fun and the audience, at times, became part of the play.

During intermission and after the final act, Lynn kept running into friends and business acquaintances introducing, Kayla, simply as a friend but it was very evident by their looks that it had been a long while since they'd seen him with a female companion and she bathed in their appreciative remarks.

It was almost 9 p.m. when they got back to his SUV. After opening the door for her again, he got in hooking up his seatbelt.

He looked over at her asking?

"Would you like a cup of coffee before I take you home?"

She wasn't ready for the evening to end so she replied,

"Yes, that would be nice."

He retraced his route back to the intersection with Hooker Road and turned right into Coffee by Darla's parking lot.

"Have you been here?"

She hadn't, she'd never noticed it before.

"No, I don't know why I never noticed it until now."

"Do you like old fashioned coconut cake?"

"Lynn, am I going to have to jog around the block when I get home?"

Laughing, he got out and opened the door for her. Walking through the entrance, she was struck by the atmosphere. It was quiet, the lighting was subdued but not too dark. The hostess seated them in a booth along the wall with windows facing Greenville Blvd.

Looking at the menu, she saw more varieties of coffee than she ever knew existed. Since she wasn't a Starbucks fan, coffee was coffee to her, and only one way, black.

The other entrees, including the coconut cake, butter pecan, chocolate, and strawberry were only part of the offerings. There were a dozen different cupcakes and just as many donuts.

When asked, she chose the house blend coffee and a slice of the coconut cake. His order mirrors hers.

"This is nice, it's so quiet and relaxing. Almost everywhere in Greenville, the music is loud, the TV's are blaring, and the patrons are loud and boisterous. Now that I know it's here, I'll come back often. Thank you."

The waitress placed their entrees in front of them and he took a sip of his coffee before replying.

"Kayla, it is nice. I'll be eternally grateful to Martin Buck for bringing me here a couple of years ago. It was my first year in the East and I'd just done my first 3rd degree. To say that my nerves were jittery would be putting it lightly. I'm sorry, you probably aren't very familiar with the Masonic Lodge.

"This is my second year in the East. That means I'm the Master of the Lodge. Normally, you hold an office for a year and then rotate off so the next in line in the chairs becomes Master. The member scheduled to be Master, became sick and the second in line wasn't ready so I was re-elected."

"That's enough about the Masonic Lodge. Maybe there will be another opportunity to share more about the lodge with you soon."

"How's your cake? Does it taste homemade to you?"

She looked into his kind blue eyes, replying,

"Yes, it reminds me of my Mama. With each bite, it takes me back to the times I would watch her make one. Back then, she had to crack open the coconut, break out chunks of the white meat and grate it on an old tin grater.

"Lynn, she would always scrape at least one knuckle and it would bleed. She never said a word wrapping a cloth around it while she finished the chore always allowing me the clean out the mixing bowl with my fingers. It's been a long time but I'll never forget those days. They were some of the happiest of my life.

"I made coconut cakes for my children but I used cake mix and grated coconut from Food Lion. They loved my cakes and yes, they were allowed to clean out the bowls with their fingers. They didn't know about 'made from scratch' and I never told them. Even on visits to my parents, the cakes were already made not allowing them to experience what I did."

Taking a bite of his cake, he paused for a moment before continuing their conversation.

"My mother made coconut cakes too. She made them just like your mother. I got to lick out the bowl until my sister arrived. From then on, her place was in the kitchen and mine was outside doing chores around the dairy.

"Dad had 60 Holsteins and they had to be milked twice a day. There was never a dull moment. That, I can promise you.

"As soon as I was old enough to push the wheel barrow, hauling manure was my job and those cows never took a day off. I was chief manure hauler 7 days a week until I was old enough to hook up the milking machines and the manure hauling job became my younger brother's job.

"There were other chores and jobs too. One of the easiest ones was herding the cows out to pasture each morning after milking. There was nothing to it. All I had to do was watch Jake, our collie, do all the work. He was amazing. In the afternoons, when he got the command, he'd round them up and bring them in for the second milking.

"He died the year I was a senior in high school and I guess I cried like a baby. He'd been my constant companion for thirteen years. Randy, our other collie, took over Jake's position when he was 11, He still came out to the barn every day and watched Randy take the cows out and bring them in."

Wow, I'm getting melancholy. I didn't mean to; I'm sorry."

Kayla, mesmerized by his way of sharing his life was shocked when she realized that they'd been there well over an hour. It was closing time.

He paid their tab, leaving a tip, and they walked outside to his SUV.

Opening the door for her, he walked around, getting into the driver's seat and buckling up, he looked over at her apologizing for keeping her out so late.

"I'm sorry, I'm really enjoying your company and I completely lost track of time."

"Don't apologize, I've enjoyed our evening too. It's been so many years since I enjoyed the company of a man."

Arriving at her home, he walked her to the door but before he said good night, he asked if she would go out again with him.

"Yes, Lynn, call me. I'd love to go out with you again."

Inside, she was like a teenager dancing around the living room. It had been more fun then she could have ever imagined. She was already looking forward to the next time. All he had to do was call. She'd be ready.

SNR

Monday morning, as soon as she arrived at work, she called Mary about lunch. The morning breezed by and they drove down Arlington to the K&W.

Mary chose the pasta salad, a piece of blueberry pie and iced tea. Kayla was too excited to eat but knowing she should eat something, chose Watergate salad, fried okra and iced tea.

Finding a booth along the wall, they removed their food from the trays and sat down to eat.

"Kayla, you're going to have calm down, you're going to have a heart attack. Tell me about your date."

For the next 20 minutes, Mary barely got a chance to sneak a word in here and there. It was more than obvious that Kayla had escaped from the land of all alone, to the mountaintops of happiness. The kind of happiness that could only be attained when in the company someone of the opposite sex that has your full attention.

"Mary, I can't believe that I wasted 22 years of my life being alone. How could I have been so foolish? Okay, I know how, but for 22 years? I can't believe it. It's as if a veil has been lifted and for the first time in a long, long, time, I can see life as it should be; not like I've seen it."

"Lynn is such a gentleman, a wonderful conversationalist…oh, I guess I could go on naming every superlative I can think of. I guess what I'm trying to say is that he is a very special person."

"We enjoyed the play and afterwards, he introduced me to so many people before taking me to Coffee by Darla for coffee and cake. I've been by there dozens of time but never noticed it. I will go back. Anyway, we lost track of time and closed the place. Time just seems to evaporate when we're talking."

"He asked if he could call again. You know I told him that he could. I'm so excited. I hope I didn't make any mistakes in the office this morning. Cal said that I looked unusually happy this morning. I told him that I was."

"Kayla, David and I are so happy for you. We've hoped and prayed for years that we would see you this happy again. It's a blessing, it truly is."

Bobby's with Lynn

Tuesday evening, Kayla answered her ringing smart phone knowing it was Lynn.

"Good evening, this is Kayla… Lynn, what a pleasant surprise, I feel honored… Of course, I am… Saturday night?... Yes, I'd love to. Where are we going?... Bobby's, really?... No, of course not, they wouldn't let me in the door…No, I'm joking, it wouldn't fit into my budget and besides, I'd only want to go with someone very nice, like you… Thank you, Lynn. 7 p.m., I'll be waiting… Good night to you too."

"Wow, Bobby's!"

All she'd ever heard about Bobby's was that it was very nice but very expensive too.

I'll have to buy a dress; I wouldn't be caught dead wearing anything hanging in my closet. Arlington Village, here I come.

Wednesday, after work, she drove to Arlington Village stopping at Sara's. She was tempted to look at the cocktail dresses but that wasn't her and she knew it. Instead, she settled on an emerald green, ruffle sleeved, sheath dress with a V neck, fitted waist with a tie and flattering seams. It fitted perfectly, it was her. She already had 4" black heels and a string of pearls with matching earrings. She was ready.

The rest of the week evaporated and it was finally Saturday. After coffee and cereal, she drove to the Wellness Center and spent an hour exercising. She understood she should come more than once a week but always seemed to come up with excuses. With her employee discount, being a member was affordable and she'd been a member for 10 years.

Back at home, after showering and washing her hair, she made her hair appointment at 11 and had a 'Cubbie Burger' afterwards, sans the fries. Of course, she wanted them but!

By 3 p.m. she'd done the washing, changed the bed linens, and done her nails. What was wrong with the clock, it just refused to move forward

When the doorbell rang at 7, she'd been ready for almost an hour. She couldn't believe how excited she was.

"Lynn, my, aren't you handsome."

He was dressed in a white dinner jacket, black slacks, and wingtips. She wasn't sure 'handsome' was adequate, there must be other superlatives that at the moment, they escaped her.

"Kayla, I love your outfit. Emerald is your color. It highlights your emerald green eyes. You are beautiful, positively beautiful."
"We should get going, our reservations are for 7:30."

Beautiful, when's the last time anyone told me that I was pretty, never beautiful.

Taking a right on Memorial, then a left on Arlington they followed it to Hwy 43 turning left. A few minutes later, just past Rock Springs, they turned left on VOA C Road making a final right into Bobby's.

When they entered the reception area, the hostess welcomed Lynn saying their table was ready. They followed her to a secluded table for 2 in a quiet corner near the dance floor and stage.

Someone was playing soft background music on a piano. The ambiance was perfect. They were going to have a perfect evening. She was sure they would.

Their waiter approached placing menu's in front of them asking about beverages?

Lynn, looking across at Kayla, asked?

"Would you like a glass of wine or prefer something else?"

She couldn't remember the last time she'd had wine, maybe the time she and Mary had a glass to CPW's.

"That would be nice. Please order for us."

He responded saying,

"Let's pick out our starters and marry the wine to that. Which one would you like?"

She hadn't looked at the menu. Opening it, she studied it for a moment not having a clue what to order but she was going to try.

"I'd like the stuffed mushrooms, please.

He chose the spicy shrimp and ordered 2 glasses of Chardonnais Napa Valley Chardonnay.

"A few years ago, I was attending a conference in Napa Valley and our group toured a vineyard and did a wine tasting. Please don't misunderstand, I don't know a lot about wines but manage to get through a meal.

"Their Chardonnays are different from North Carolina's. I've toured the winery at the Biltmore and a couple others in the western part of the state. Duplin wineries are unique in their own way. Depending on our main entrees, we may try one of theirs with our meal."

She didn't have a clue what he was talking about. She'd tasted some of their neighbor's wine when she was young and a couple from Duplin Winery that Mary brought back from one of their trips to Myrtle Beach.

"You must come here often, the hostess recognized you."

Smiling across the table, he replied,

"Often enough to be recognized. The owner, Bobby Carraway, is from Farmville. I've known him a long time.

"When my board meets, this is where I always bring them. Bobby has an excellent restaurant. I believe, I certainly hope, you'll agree when the evening is over."

"Speaking of Bobby, he's coming our way."

Bobby Carraway approached, addressing Lynn first.

"Lynn, it's nice to have you dine with us again; as always, welcome."

"Bobby, this is my friend, Kayla Herring. Kayla, this is Bobby Carraway, the proprietor, chef, money changer; he does it all."

"Kayla, welcome to my restaurant. I hope you'll enjoy the evening. Lynn, I hope to see the 2 of you dancing."

With that, he moved to his next guests.

"That was nice, he must have a loyal clientele and everything is so plush. This is way out of my league. I knew it existed but I've never been out this way. I see a couple of doctors from the hospital and that's Danny Moore, one of the VP's from Vidant.

"It's the most expensive restaurant in Pitt County but well worth it. It reminds me of Ruth Chris Steakhouse in Cary. Their menus are similar but Bobby offers personally prepared dishes.

"He began his career with Franc White at the old Sportsman Restaurant in Farmville back in the 60s or 70s and learned his trade very well He has a unique touch combining foods, seasonings and textures. You'll see what I mean when our starters arrive."

Their starters arrived confirming what Lynn said about Bobby's way with food. Hers was delicious.

Lynn had suggested the lobster bisque and like her stuffed mushroom, it was delectably delicious. She'd never tasted anything like it.

They were ready for their main entrees.

"May I suggest Bobby's 10-ounce filet. It's cooked to perfection. I highly recommend it"

She chose it with asparagus and the sweet potato casserole.

"Medium rare, please."

His choice mirrored hers excepting the sides.

"I'll have the creamed spinach and baked potato please and bring a bottle of Siduri Pinot Noir too."

While they were waiting, Kayla asked about his move?

"I've leased a townhouse on the western side of Wilson. It's in a nice upscale community and not too far from the credit union. The commute is 5 minutes unlike the 40 minutes I've been doing for years."

"I'll still doing commutes back to Farmville to church and the masonic lodge but that's fine."

Kayla asked,

"When do you plan on moving?"

"Next week, the house will be empty. I've donated the furniture I can't use and yard items to Masonic and Eastern Star Home."

"Doesn't your son want any of it?"

"No, Chad has no interest in anything in Farmville, or North Carolina for that matter. When he graduated from high school, he went to culinary arts school in Atlanta graduating with honors. His grades got him into the school in Paris. Now, he's studying under some of the best chef's in France. I doubt if he'll ever come back to North Carolina.

"He was much closer to Joann than me. I was gone too much of the time. It's my fault but there nothing I can do about it now.

"He was in France when Joann died. Her memorial service was delayed a week so he could attend. We spent 2 days together afterwards. I encouraged him to go through her things but he took little with him when he returned saying I could do whatever I liked with the rest.

"I donated all her clothing, jewelry, and personal items to charity keeping only pictures and a few small mementos.

"I did go to his graduation in Atlanta and if he invites me, I'll attend his graduation in Paris. That's next spring."

She sensed melancholy and remorse. He was so kind and gentle but he was hurting inside.

The waiter was back with their food. It was perfect timing. It broke the mood allowing them to enjoy the rest of the evening.

"Lynn, this is delicious. Enjoying this kind of dining will make returning to the K&W difficult. How is you steak?"

"Delicious, it always is. That's why I come as often as I do. When I move, I'll be torn between Bobby's and Ruth Chris Steak House in Cary.

"One of the pluses of living in west Wilson, is being so close to Raleigh, Durham, and Chapel Hill. There's so much to do; dining, cultural, entertainment... it's all there."

And you'll be an hour away from me with all those things pulling and tugging at you.

What was she thinking? This was only their second date and she was already trying to build a fence around him.

Get real, Kayla, remember the fence you were behind only a month ago. The gate's been left open. If he drops out of the picture, there will be others. Be happy; you're no longer a prisoner behind the barbed wire fence; a fence you built yourself.

"I know you're looking forward to living so close to your work and the Raleigh area. Driving in that traffic is scary to me. I guess it's because I'm never in it."

He agreed,

"Yes, that's all it is. We're products of our environment. Wherever we are, that's where we've most comfortable."

The waiter was back clearing the table and asking about dessert?

"Would you split a dessert with me?"

"That would be nice, yes, thank you."

"Waiter, we want to share Bobby's, Chocolate on Chocolate."

He looked at her, asking?

"Would you like coffee with your dessert?"

"Yes, please."

"Add 2 coffee's, black, please."

She returned attention to the couples dancing.

"Would you like to dance?"

"I'd love to."

It had been over 20 years; she hoped she remembered how. She did; dancing with him was like a dream. His steps were so smooth; it was as if she were floating on a cloud.

The whole evening had been as if she'd been floating on a cloud or maybe in a hot-air balloon with Lynn at the helm.

She knew she'd never be able to go back to her lifestyle of hiding from reality, from love. She was lonely and now she was ready to admit it. Maybe she'd even allow herself to fall in love again.

She wondered if that was what was already happening. If it was, she had no control over it. She would succumb to whatever was happening. It had been so long since the feelings she was experiencing surged through her whole being. It was wonderful.

The dance ended and he led her off the floor. Their Chocolate on Chocolate and coffee were waiting.

Their enchanting evening was drawing to a close. She didn't want it to end but knew it must.

When he walked her to the door, he kissed her tenderly on the lips thanking her for a wonderful evening.

"No, Lynn, thank you. It's been wonderful being with you. You've opened my eyes and heart to a life and feelings that I've locked away for too many years.

"Thank you, I do so much enjoy being with you."

Closing the door behind her, she floated into the living room reliving bits and pieces of her entrancing evening. He'd been captivating, charming, adorable… she could not put her finger on the right word. Romantic, debonair… he was all of them and more. She felt as if she was a teenager again and fallen in love for the first time.

Was she letting her feelings run crazy with wild abandon? Should she slow down? She didn't want to think about it. She really wanted to enjoy it. 22 years of her life had been wasted but no more. If it wasn't destined to be Lynn, someone out there was waiting for her and when she met him, she'd be ready.

S N R

Sunday morning, she was up at the crack of dawn feeling as if she had the best night's sleep in… she couldn't remember. It had been a long, long, time.

After showering, she drove over to 'Coffee by Darla" enjoying a cup of coffee and one of their, freshly baked, cinnamon buns.

After a second cup of coffee, she drove back home and dressed for Sunday School and Church. Following church, she had lunch at "The Three

Steers' on Memorial Drive enjoying their 'one trip to the salad bar.' They had the best salad bar in Greenville. Nobody contested that. She preferred their Steer Burgers over the fast food places too. Their burgers were made fresh every day.

Arriving back home a little after 2, she changed into her comfortable slacks and tee. It was time for a nap and she was more than ready for it.

Would He Call Again?

Other than sharing her Saturday night with Mary, Monday and Tuesday were mostly blurs. Lynn hadn't texted or called and she was so hoping that he would. Maybe she'd read too much into that kiss. Maybe she was just a passing fancy. Maybe he was gone; moving on to greener pastures in Wilson or Raleigh?

There she was again, ever the pessimist. He was in the middle of a move and selling his house. There were probably many things he needed to pay attention and time to. After all, he was involved in so many community clubs including the masons. She'd forgotten to ask him about them. She would on their next date… if there was a next date? Her mind was driving her crazy and she was loading the gun.

That evening, she started to call but resisted thinking it would be too un-lady like to call. Maybe he was just busy. She'd give him until the weekend.

A little after 8 p.m., her smartphone alerted her to a call from him.

"Hello, this is Kayla… Lynn, it nice to hear from you… you're where?... Washington, DC?... What in the world are you doing in Washington?... Oh, okay. I can wait until Saturday night. Where are you taking me?... Yes, I love seafood… Baxter's Seafood out on Hwy 33, no, I haven't… Okay, casual is the word, good. I'm looking forward it…Okay, have a safe flight home. See you Saturday, bye."

What in the world was he doing in Washington, DC? She didn't have a clue but guessed she'd find out Saturday night. Maybe Mary knew; she'd ask her tomorrow.

"Mary, do you know why Lynn's in Washington, DC? He called last night from there. When I asked, he said he'd tell my Saturday night. We're going to Baxter's Seafood for dinner."

Mary looked puzzled.

"No, Kayla, I couldn't begin to guess. He travels a lot though. It's probably just another conference. It it's a federal anything, all they like to do is talk and never get anything done. I don't know why we don't just clean house and start over. Lord, forgive me, here I am talking about politics. I'll be cussing if I don't change the subject."

"Baxter's Seafood? We went there last spring before the "R's" ran out. They're got a great oyster bar."

Oyster Bar? That never crossed my mind. When he said seafood, fried was all that came to my mind.

"Steamed oysters… Mary, it's been years. Jeff took me to the oyster bar in Williamston. I can't remember the name of it. It was my first time and I loved them. Now you've got me salivating. I hope that's what he has in mind."

Mary replied,

"It's the Sunnyside Oyster Bar across the intersection from the Holiday Inn. A group of us still go 2 or 3 times a year. We love it there."

"He said to dress casual, it must be the oysters. Now, I'm hoping it is."

Baxter's, The Shucker's Were Waiting

Lynn arrived a few minutes before 7 dressed in slacks and a collared knit. She opened the door welcoming him.

"Lynn, come in, I've missed you."

He stepped inside saying,

"Good evening, Kayla, I've missed you too. It's been a whirlwind week for me but admittedly, it happens to my schedule very often; probably more often now but I'll explain all that to you after we eat.
"Do you like steamed oysters?"

It was going to be steamed oysters,

"Yes, Lynn, it's been a long time but yes, I do."

"Are you ready? The shucker's are waiting."

They drove down Hooker Road taking a right on Greenville Blvd following it to 10th Street across from Hastings Ford. Turning right, they followed it (Hwy 43) to Baxter's. It was on the left near the Portertown Road exit.

Seated at the oyster bar, Lynn ordered a half bushel of oysters and 2 pounds of steamed shrimp.

The shucker's were extremely fast and very efficient easily keeping up with them. The steamed shrimp too more time. They had to be peeled.

"Are they as good as you remember?"

"Probably more, they're so large. I guess I prefer the cocktail sauce to the drawn butter but they're delicious either way. The shrimp are too. I've never had them steamed."

When the half bushel was gone, he asked if she wanted more?

"No way, Lynn, I'm more than satisfied but you order more if you want them."

"I'm good. Let's go to Darla's for a cup of coffee. It's too noisy to try talking here."

She was getting more apprehensive by the minute. There was something serious in his comment. What was he going to tell her? She didn't know but her nerves were beginning to fray.

"That sounds nice. It is too noisy in here."

Arriving at Coffee by Darla's, they were seated in the same booth as before. They ordered coffee and bacon caramel donuts.

He looked across at her beginning,

"As I told you on the phone, I've been in Washington all week. I've been meeting with our Congressman, Jerry Bowers. Jerry and I were in college together. I guess you could say that we were 'best buddies.' Jerry serves on the House Financial Committee.

He wants me to serve as his liaison. It would require me to move to Washington. He's in his second term and won't come up for re-election for almost 2 years. If he's successful, and I'm sure he will be, I'll probably be asked to serve again and I couldn't refuse. What he's doing is very important to our country and I have a lot of knowledge when it comes to financing."

"I'm going to miss seeing you but I don't think I have a choice. There will be times when I'll be back home and I would hope that I could see you then."

Kayla had been broadsided. She felt as if her heart was in her throat. How could she feel so strongly for him? They'd only dated three times. It didn't matter, she was falling and falling fast. Maybe this was a good thing. It would certainly put the brakes on her runaway romance. She didn't know but right then, at that moment, it hurt.

At 46, she'd finally chosen to come out of her hiding place opening her heart to this man, this wonderful man, and he was being pulled away from her clutches. How was she going to respond? She knew she had to and it had to be now.

"Lynn, I'm almost without words. I guess I'm stunned. I fully understand what you're saying and I know you're doing what's right. We only met a few weeks ago but I feel as if I've known you forever. Being with you has given my life back to me and I will always be eternally grateful. I'm going to miss our time together but I'll look forward to the times when we might be together again.

"I'm sorry, I'm almost speechless. I really don't know what to say except to wish you luck in your endeavor. I know your life will be in a turmoil too.

"When are you leaving?"

"Monday week. Next Thursday is Thanksgiving and I want to spend it with you if you're available.

"I don't have much to do to get ready for the move. Most of my things are still unpacked. I rented an apartment in Arlington, Virginia. It's a 2-

bedroom, 2-bath with 950 sq. ft. That's close to what I just moved into and it's a quick commute to the capital.

"Getting acclimated to the traffic and population density will take time but I'll adjust. I always have.

"Flight time from DC to RDU is only 1 hour and 10 minutes and it's only 4-hour drive to Wilson."

"I guess I've covered all the bases. I haven't but Jerry's staff has."

Spending Thanksgiving with him was fine with her, she hadn't planned on visiting back home or the children and they hadn't contacted her.

"I'd love to spend Thanksgiving with you. I could cook a turkey if you'd like."

"That's putting you to too much trouble. We'll dine at Greenville Golf and Country Club. I have a membership there and they do a grand job for Thanksgiving, Christmas, and New Year's. Maybe we can celebrate New Year's there too. If not there, Bobby's but I'll have to make reservations now."

She was still trying to assimilate what she was hearing,

"I want to spend Thanksgiving and New Year's with you too. I usually go down to my parents on Christmas. Kevin and Amy usually go too.

"Last Thanksgiving, I went to K&W for lunch. The weather was nice so afterwards, I drove over to Washington and spent a couple of hours on the waterfront. It was lonely but I'm used to that. New Year's, I picked up a barbecue plate at Parker's and curled up on the couch intending to watch the new year arrive on TV. About 12:30 a.m., I awoke and went to bed. I don't remember the last time I stayed awake until midnight. Unless I'm with you, I'm sure this year will be no different. New Years, either place is fine, I'll let you make that decision.

He reached across the table taking her hand.

"This year will be different, we'll be together."

Thanksgiving, Yes, It Was Different

It was different, very different. Thanksgiving, they dined at the country club enjoying a lavish buffet that seemed endless with their wide variety of entrees.

All the traditional entrees, including turkey with stuffing, baked ham, oyster dressing, cranberry sauce, potato salad, green bean casserole, macaroni and cheese, collards, cabbage, carrots, stewed corn, rolls, biscuits, cornbread and hushpuppies were offered along with a roast beef carving station, grilled salmon, stuffed flounder, fried shrimp, stuffed pork chops, and fried chicken.

The dessert line seemed just as endless with coconut, sweet potato, pumpkin, cherry, chocolate, pies, banana pudding, coconut, chocolate, German chocolate, and red velvet cakes

By the time they got back to her home, they were stuffed and spent the afternoon watching ballgames on TV.

That evening, they had coffee and a cupcake at Darla's before parting a little before midnight.

When he walked her to the door, she turned into his arms squeezing him tightly as their parting kiss lingered. She didn't want to let go and it was apparent that he didn't either.

Long forgotten feelings were stirring deep within her. Feelings she hadn't allowed to awaken for too many years. They were awake now and she was having a problem subduing them. She wanted to invite him in but managed to stifle the desire. If he asked or tried, she'd welcome him into her home, her bedroom, her bed.

She knew that he was fully aroused but he backed away. One moment longer and there wouldn't be any backing away. She couldn't believe how ready she was. It had been so long but she hadn't forgotten.

SNR

The feelings he left with her were nurtured throughout the night. She was fully aroused and it took hours before calm finally subdued her passion.

Finally, sleep arrived and with it, he was in her arms as they climbed the mountain of love. Not just once, but again, and again.

When she awakened next morning, a smile was still firmly affixed on her face.

She was having coffee when her smart phone alerted her to a call. It was from him.

"Good morning, Lynn. Thank you for yesterday. It was very special… No, not a thing. I'm off until Monday… Let's see, how about Yoder's?... You haven't, Lynn, I can't believe that you've never been… It's on that highway between Grifton and Vanceboro…It's country cooking; as I recall, their lunch menu had: fried chicken, livers, country fried steak, pork chops, fish, mac n cheese, green beans, pinto beans, black eye peas, corn, broccoli casserole, cabbage casserole, beets, mashed potatoes, rice and gravy, biscuits, rolls, fresh baked bread and their desserts are down-right sinful. Lynn, they have sticky buns that are to die for… I knew you would… 11? No, Lynn, we need to be there by 11 or we'll have to stand in line…About 30 minutes from here…I only know one way. That's down Hwy 11 to Grifton and take that road to Vanceboro. There may be a better way, Google it…Okay, 10:30 here; I'll be ready, bye"

Now, she was starving knowing she'd better eat something or she'd go crazy when they got there. She satisfied her hunger with a bowl of corn flakes before going over to the Wellness Center to do her workout.

The whole time she was on the treadmill and doing the exercise machines, her mind was spinning.

Today's going to be the day. I can feel it in my bones. Bones? I can feel it all over. I'm ready, I hope he is…I know he is!

Back at home at 5 of 10, she rushed to get ready coming together about 5 minutes before the doorbell rang.

There was a hug and kiss and they were on their way.

The route he chose took them down Fairland to Hooker, right on Hooker, then left on Greenville Blvd and then right on Red Banks Road and another right on Arlington that became County Home Road on the other side of Fire Tower Road. Driving past the Senior Center, Alice Keene Community Schools Center, the Farmer's Market, Winterville Primary and Elementary, they stopped at the all-way stop intersection with Worthington Road before continuing on. Stopping at Hwy 102, they crossed driving until they encountered the Cox Cross Road intersection. The flashing red light alerted them to how dangerous the intersection was. After stopping, they continued on stopping and making a right turn in Gardnersville onto Stokestown Road passing through Honolulu (yes, Honolulu) finally arriving at Hwy 118. Turning right, they had arrived. It was 10:55 and there was a short line but they were seated 10 minutes later.

They were laughing about Lynn's choice of routes when their waitress placed menus in front of them asking about beverages?

They chose iced tea and would order when she returned.

Minutes later, with their iced tea in front of them, Lynn asked Kayla to order first.

She chose the country fried steak over mashed potatoes with plenty of gravy along with the broccoli casserole.

"I'd like the rolls."

"And you, sir?"

"I'd like the pork chops…they are fried, aren't they?"

"Yes, sir, country style, swimming in gravy."

"Perfect, rice and the cabbage casserole. I'd like the rolls too."

Looking across at her, smiling, he said,

"I can't believe that I've never been here. It appears to be a complete farm and seed supply with all that lawn furniture outside and those buildings across the highway; it's out here in the middle of nowhere. How long has it been here?"

"Lynn, I don't know. I think it was here when I moved to Greenville about 25 years ago.

"I came with a group from Reedy Branch Church about 15 years ago. I think there were 3 couples. I was the only single. We met one Saturday morning at 6:30 a.m. Pastor Willis Wilson said if you didn't want to stand in line, you had to get there by 7 on Saturday mornings. They open at 7:30 during the week.

"I can remember it like it was yesterday. I ordered the French toast with bacon. Lynn, those slices of bread were almost an inch and a half thick and they make their own honey-butter-syrup. It's to die for.

"There was no way I could begin to eat it all so I asked for a takeout tray and had the rest of it Sunday morning before church. I also got a sticky bun. Lynn, it was so big, I quartered it and had it 4 mornings in a row with coffee."

Their waitress placed their entrees in front of them saying she would be back to refresh their tea.

They held hands while Lynn returned thanks. The next few minutes little or no conversation as Lynn sampled each entrée on his plate with an ever-broadening smile covering his face.

"Kayla, I can't begin to thank you enough for sharing this place with me although I'm thankful I didn't find it earlier. I'd probably weight a ton. These pork chops remind me of my mother's cooking and this cabbage casserole is unbelievably delicious and the rolls…melt in your mouth."

A memory raced through her mind. Her daddy used to say that they fattened up the hogs before they slaughtered them. She stifled a laugh. Yes, she was probably fattening Lynn up for the kill. She wasn't going to push him, she didn't think he needed to be but one way or the other, he was going to have her special dessert before the weekend was over.

He'd seen the stifled laugh and asked,

"What did I miss?"

Smiling, she replied,

Nothing, I'll tell you later."

She would, after he tasted her special dessert.

As the minutes passed, they enjoyed their meal and time together prompting him to observe,

"Kayla, I do so wish we could have met after my wife died. Each time we're together, I wonder how it would have been, could have been, if our chance meeting could have taken place 3 years ago?"

Reaching across the table touching his hand, she replied,

"Lynn, although those 3 years have slipped by, I'm glad we didn't. Had we, I wouldn't have opened the door. You, no one could get in. The door had been sealed and I wasn't ready. I am now. I am ready for you."

He squeezed her hand, replying,

And I am so ready for you."

Too full for the beckoning desserts, he paid their tab while picking up 2 sticky buns along with 2 chocolate chip and molasses cookies. They spent the next hour walking through the complex on both levels discovering so many items neither had seen in years.

Outside they tried the different swings, chairs, and rockers, deciding that a swing was needed in her back yard. Somehow, he would make that happen, perhaps during the Christmas holidays. Time would tell.

They'd just turned off Hwy 118 onto Stokestown Road when his phone alerted him to an international call.

Pulling off the road, he looked over at her saying,

"It could be Chad; I'll have to take it."

"Lynn Stocks… Yes, this is Chad Stocks father. Is there anything wrong?… Is he critical?… I understand, I'll fly out on the first possible flight… Yes, I'll call this number when I arrive in Paris, good bye."

"Lynn, what wrong??"

"Chad was in an automobile accident on the outskirts of Paris. He's in the American Hospital of France intensive care unit in critical condition. They've put him into a coma while they access his injuries. I have to get over there as soon as possible.
"I'm sorry, Kayla, but I must go."

She reached over touching his shoulder, saying,

"Lynn, I understand. You need to be with your son."

What she didn't say was she knew he'd lost his wife only 3 years ago in an accident. He couldn't lose it son too. It might destroy him.

On the way back to her home, he made several calls including getting reservations on an international flight out of Reagan in Washington. boarding at 10 p.m. that evening. He was going to have to drive back to his apartment in Arlington to get his passport and official papers. He would be traveling as an official of the Congressional House Services Committee and would be afforded with diplomatic immunity.
She understood. He had to go, it was his son. Whatever she'd hoped would happen would have to wait. She'd been on hold for a very long time. She could wait until they could be together again however long it took.

Arriving at her home, he walked her to the door and there was a longer than expected, lingering, kiss.

"Kayla, this is not how I'd hoped our Thanksgiving weekend would end but I'll be back. Please pray for Chad."

She squeezed him replying,

"I'll pray every day for Chad, and you. I'll be waiting when you return. Be safe."

She watched his car rapidly moving away from her down Fairland Road until it disappeared.

Walking inside, she sat in the recliner in the den, she mind twirling.

To be so close and now so far away. Not only in distance in time too. I can't believe how close we were. I was so sure that I would be complete again.

What Was She Going to Do?

It was time to a decision, was she going or wasn't she. She looked at the contact information.

Travis Sutton? She didn't remember him? Admittedly, there were 227 in her graduating glass but she didn't remember him being one of the officers.

Trying to remember where her high school annual was, she rummaged through several boxes on the shelf in her closet. Finally finding it, she found the pages with the officers. Just as she thought, he wasn't an officer. Paging through the superlatives, she found him. "Most likely to succeed." She still couldn't place him but it didn't matter.

Was she, or wasn't she? She was, she was going. Why not, what else was she involved in? Nothing, her life had turned back into nothing 2 years ago when Lynn got that faithful call.

Yes, they'd been in contact but only on the phone, texting, tweeting, and on Facebook. Chad had been in the hospital for almost a year and Lynn was by his side every day.

Congressman Bowers, had gotten Lynn transferred to American Embassy and he was working under one of the diplomat's liaison's.

When Chad was released from the hospital. He was still unable to walk without a walker and the doctor's wanted him in a convalescent home near the hospital. Chad didn't want to come back to the US and Lynn, readily agreed.

Now, 2 years later, he was walking without any aid but had a noticeable limp. That didn't deter him from returning to culinary school.

In their last conversation, Lynn said that he was coming back to the US during the Christmas holidays and he was coming to see her if she wanted him to. There was no question, she really wanted him to. She had been on hold since the accident but in no way, did it deter her feelings for him.

She filled out the RSVP, along with a brief resume stating the she was divorced and no longer a Harris.

I legally changed my name back to Herring years ago. I have 2 grown children. The oldest, Kevin, is married and has a son. Amy is a sophomore at UNC-Chapel Hill.

She dropped it in the hospital mail next morning.

She was going. That was final. Starting tomorrow, she'd go to the Wellness Center every day. She didn't need to lose weight but if she was going to make an appearance, she was going to be a knockout.

Next morning, she texted Mary saying they should have lunch.

Mary texted back,

Abrams?

Kayla almost said no, but relented knowing she's probably gain a pound eating their county food.

Yes, Abrams, U drive.

Arriving at 5 after 12, there was a line but it wasn't too long. When they got to the servers, Mary chose the hamburger steak in gravy over mashed potatoes, collards, and cornbread. Kayla wanted the hamburger steak and gravy over rice with a side of cabbage and cornbread too.

Seated, Mary observed,

"Okay, give. You look like you're about to explode."

Kayla was. She excitedly shared that she had finally decided.

"I'm going to the reunion. I mailed the RSVP this morning. Now that I've finally decided, I'm excited. I don't know why but I am."

"Will that guy be there? What was his name?"

"Brian Howard, I don't know. The last time I saw him was back in 1983 when I went down for the Christmas holidays. Mary, I don't know what any of my classmates are doing. The invitation indicated that 3 have died but it didn't say which 3.

"I guess that I should have gone to some of the reunions but I chose not to. I was too wrapped up in my self-pity and hatred for Jeff. I can't believe that I was that stupid but I can't go back an erase a day. I can only move forward.

"Mary, I was so sure, 2 years ago, when I met Lynn that my self-exile was over. Life has a way of changing everything, it did for me, it did for us. Lynn says he's coming back to the US for the Christmas holidays and he's coming to see me and I'm so ready to see him."

Mary, wiping her lips, asked?

"The reunion is in October. That's, right, isn't it?"

"Yes, the 27th; I'll probably take a vacation day and drive down Thursday night after work. It will give me some time to spend with my parents and I'm sure I'll visit my old hangout, Woody's, to do a little reconnoitering on Friday.

"Mr. Grady is probably getting up in age now. I haven't seen him in 26 years but I'm sure if anything had happened to him, mama or daddy would have called. All the teenagers I grew up with, loved him. He had a very special way of treating us and…keeping a lot of us out of trouble."

"Anyway, I've got until October to get ready and I promise you that I will be ready when I go."

SNR

That afternoon, after work, rather than go home, she went to the Wellness Center. She'd made up her mind and she was sticking to her plan.

Changing into her exercise outfit, she began her regimen on the treadmill setting it at 8 degrees and 3 mph. As the time drifted by and heartbeat increased, she watched the others on treadmills and the TV monitors mounted above and in front of them.

Some were wearing earpieces so they could listen to the channel they chose but not Kayla, she'd been locked away for too many years. Locking herself away from the activities surrounding her wasn't going to happen. Her self-exile had ended and she wasn't going to allow any part of it to creep back in. She'd broken her horrible mold for good.

30 minutes later, feeling good about herself, she wiped the perspiration off her face, neck, and arms, while walking around the track 3 times to wind down before attacking the exercise machines.

With that done, she showered and dressed stopping by the Three Steers for a salad. One of the ladies in the office complex was there and inviting her over to join her.

Ginger was a secretary for Dennis Strickland. She was in the office complex on the other side of Mary.

"Hi Kayla, please join me; I don't remember seeing you in here before. I usually stop by here right after I get off work but today I had an errand so I'm running about an hour behind my usual schedule."

Thanking her for the invitation, sitting down, she replied,

"Thank you Ginger; I'd love to join you. I eat too many meals alone. I guess that comes with being divorced plus being an empty nester but I guess, by now, I'm used to it."

Ginger replied,

"Me too, I've been divorced a little over a year. Our marriage fell apart when our son left to join the air force. Our lives had been so wrapped around him. He was very active in school sports. Not good enough to get a full scholarship so he chose to spend 4 years in the service and let them pay for his education. When he left, we'd already lost touch with each other. I cried for 6 months until my neighbor practically drug me to her church demanding that I get involved. We've been neighbors for 15 years and she treats me like her sister. Tod, her husband, does the same.
I guess if it hadn't been for them, I'd probably be in a looney bin now."

Kayla, knew exactly what she'd been through. If it hadn't been for Mary, there was no question where she would have been.

Ginger asked, saying that she wasn't trying to be nosey,

"You started dating someone a couple of years ago. Are you still dating?"

"No, Lynn's son was studying in France and was in a terrible accident. He was in a coma for almost a year followed by another year in rehab trying to learn how to walk again without assistance. He has a noticeable limp now but is back in culinary school.
"Lynn is in the US Embassy there as a liaison officer. He was a liaison for Congressman Bowers in Washington before the accident but now it seems that

the embassy has first dibs and trumps over congress. They want him to remain there.

"He's promised to come back to visit during the Christmas holidays and I'm so ready to see him."

Ginger, wondered, asking?

"What do you do after work to keep yourself entertained?"

Kayla replied,

"Not nearly enough but I'm trying to break the mold. My 30th class reunion is coming up in October and I've decided to attend. From now, until then, I'm going to the Wellness Center every day after work. If I'm going, I want to look good."

"30th! Kayla, I can't believe that you're that old. Gosh, I went to my 25th reunion last year and I'd have given a hundred dollars to look as good as you. How in the world do you look so young?"

"Ginger I don't really look that good but thank you. I guess being hidden away for the past 22 years helped. I can still wear the clothes I wore back then and I only weigh 3 pounds more than I did back then. My waist and hips are the same. My bust size changed but that came from the children.

"Whatever it is, if I've got it, I'm going to flaunt it at the reunion."

"That sounds like you left someone after high school."

"Yes, it was after 2 years at a local college. I wanted to graduate from ECC he didn't want any part of it. He wanted to get married and have children. I told him there was no way that was happening to me. I wasn't going to be stuck in rural Duplin Country for the rest of my life."

"Duplin County? Where's that?"

Ginger, it's south of Kinston. Our school, Duplin Central High School, is located on Hwy 11 between Pink Hill and Kenansville, the county seat of Duplin County."

"Oh! We pass by it on our way to Myrtle Beach. I know exactly where it is. We've eaten at the Country Squire too."

"I grew up in Bertie County just outside Colerain. I'm sure you don't know where that is. Since you're not from there, why would you. I went to Colerain Elementary and then Bertie Senior High School. There's only one high school for the whole county. It's located on Hwy 13 a few miles north of Windsor. It's the county seat of Bertie County."

Kayla wasn't lost anymore,

"Windsor? I know where that is. When Lynn took me to visit the Hope Plantation, we had lunch there. It was at the intersection where we turned to go to the plantation. It was beside a huge Ford truck dealership. I remember asking Lynn how there could be such a large dealership there. He said that the county was rural and everyone drove trucks."

"He was right. There are probably 10 trucks to every 1 car. Daddy always drove a truck. Lucky for us, it was one of those 4-door models. It was huge and had big tires on it. We almost needed a ladder to get into it. Mama was always complaining until he put foot rails on it.

Kayla replied that her daddy had an old beat-up Chevy pickup.

"I think it was a 69 model. He works at Guilford East. That's the huge manufacturing plant you pass before the high school. When he went from shifts to days a long time ago, he started renting the farmland out and his need for a good truck ended."

She was laughing now.

"You won't believe it but he plowed the garden with a mule, Beautancus, until he died. Now, he uses an Allis Chalmers tractor."

Ginger replied that her daddy still farmed.

"He has about 100 acres of peanuts. That's the money crop up our way.

"You said that you were going to the Wellness Center tomorrow after work. I'd love to join you if you don't mind. We could come here for supper afterwards."

"I'd like that, Ginger. It would be nice to have someone to talk to. Mary and I usually have lunch together but she spends her evenings with her husband, Harold."

Back at home, she stood before the full-length mirror turning, first this way and then, the other. For a 48-year-old woman, she looked good, very good. No, it wasn't her mind playing tricks on her. She didn't look bad if she did say so herself.

She was going to knock them dead at the reunion. She wasn't chosen the 'Best Looking' in her class but she was sure she was now. She opened the year book finding the superlatives. Andera Grady, Kayla had to admit that Andera was pretty, very pretty, but now 30 years later…

I'll bet she doesn't look that way now. I'm sure that none of us do but I'm close. No, I'm prettier now. I can't believe how I wore my hair. If I'd worn it the way I do now, I'd have easily been the best looking. I'd be in that picture with Perry Outlaw, not Andea. Perry was handsome, I wonder what he looks like now?

SNR

The weeks were slowly slipping by. It was the first week in September and she'd been to the Wellness Center at least 5 times evert week. Meeting Ginger there helped and they were really enjoying their meals after each workout.

Ginger had convinced her to go bowling with her on Wednesday nights. A few of the ladies in her Sunday School Class were meeting at the bowling alley on Red Banks Road.

Kayla had resisted at first but after the first night, she joined right in and all the ladies were more than happy to have her, especially since her score rarely got above 100. Ginger's was mostly in the lower 100s. Janice Whitehurst, was by far the top scorer in their group bowling consistently in the 150s and last week, almost reached 200.

Each night, after they bowled, they met at Darla's for coffee and a pastry or piece of pie.

Kayla, living on cereals and salads, allowed herself that one pleasure, choosing a muffin or piece of pie that she rarely finished.

She was so happy with the way her body was toning up and the pound she'd already lost. Pastries, donuts, and pie wasn't going to ruin her goal. She'd made the decision and one way or the other, she was going to stick to her regimen.

SNR

The second Sunday in September, her smart phone alerted her to a call from Lynn. She was almost too scared to answer. He rarely, almost never called. Their contacts were through texts, tweets, and Facebook.

"Lynn, what's wrong, what happened?... Just to check up on me, I'm honored, thank you... Yes, I'm holding to my regimen; it's working wonders. I can't wait until Christmas to show you. You are still coming aren't you... I'm relieved, please don't let anything happen to cancel your trip. I would be devastated… You know I am, I'm as excited as I've ever been… It's still a little over a month away… Yes, I am excited, not as much as wanting to see you though… Okay, I miss you too… I will, take care, bye."

SNR

By the last week in September, her curiosity got the best of her and she talked Ginger into driving down to spend Friday and Saturday with her parents.

"You'll enjoy meeting them and if Woody Grady's place is still open, there's no telling who we'll run into. We may even drive down to Wallace Saturday night and dine at the "Mad Boar."
"Come on, it beats spending another weekend alone."

They were packed are ready to go when Friday afternoon arrived. After dropping Ginger's car off at Kayla's they were on the way. Kayla told her parents that they'd eat something on the way.

She already knew, after talking to her mama, that Woody's was still the place to meet everyone and for the first time in 20 years, she was ready to do just that.

They stopped off at Skylight Inn in Ayden for barbecue first and then, it was non-stop, except for a few traffic lights, to Duplinville.

It was close to 6:30 when they rolled into the driveway. Minutes later, standing in the front room, Kayla introduced Ginger to her parents.

"Mama, Daddy, this is my friend, Ginger Blount, she works in the hospital complex with me. Ginger, this is my parents, Raymond and Dolly Herring."

They welcomed her into their home saying it was nice to meet one of Kayla's friends. They didn't mention that this was the first time since her divorce that she brought anyone home with her and they welcomed the change.

They led her down the hall to bedroom beside the one Kayla grew up in. It still contained many of the relics from her past.

"Ya'll can unpack later, come and visit with us a little while. We're sure that Kayla wants to ride up to Woody's. I'm sure there's a lot going on. Friday and Saturday nights are his busiest."

"Mama, how's Mr. Grady doing? It's been at least 20 years since I saw him."

"Honey, he's doing fine. He's probably looking at 70 now. His son, Jimmy, pretty much runs the place now but they say that Woody's there every day. He won't ever fully retire, he'll die there. At least that's what everybody says. I'm sure when he passes, they'll do the visitation there. They might even do the funeral there too."

They talked about the upcoming reunion.

Her mama asked?

"Kayla, who have you seen since graduation?"

Kayla had to admit that she'd seen no one but Brian and had seen only him once; the time she took Jeff there.

"No one, Mama, except Brian that one time when ya'll went with Jeff and I, remember?"

Her mama replied,

"I guess you're right. You didn't go to none of their reunions, did you?"

"No Mama, not a one. I wish I had but, no, I didn't. I'm sure nobody will look like I remember them but they won't know me either."

Her daddy replied to her remark.

"No, you won't, honey. We went to my 30th reunion. There won't but 28 in my class and half of them had died.

"When we walked in, Shirley Ann, she's the one that put it together, had nametags with our high school pictures on them. When we walked up to someone, I looked at the picture not the face. I wouldn't have recognized a one of them if it hadn't been for the pictures."

"Lordy, look at the time. If you're going to Woody's, you better get a move on. The night's flying by. We won't wait up for you."

$$\mathcal{SNR}$$

When they arrived, Kayla wasn't surprised by the crowded parking lot.

"It's busy, but I was sure it would be. Come on Ginger. Let's make an appearance."

Inside, it appeared that there wasn't an empty seat anywhere. They walked over to the counter and stood in the end while Kayla surveyed the room hoping to find someone one she knew.

"Kayla Herring, is that you?"

She turned to see Woody Grady holding his arms out. He was older but there was no question, he was still, Woody.

"Yes, Sir, it's me. I'm surprised you recognized me."

Hugging first, she introduced Woody, (he insisted on being called, Woody)

"This is my friend, Ginger. Ginger, this in the one and only, Woody Grady."

"Young lady, you've only gotten prettier, not older like me. It's so good to see you. Your mama said that you were coming to the reunion. I was hoping to see you then but here you are. Let me look at you."

You need a table. Raeford and Sally Jean are getting ready to leave. Follow me.

"Raeford, since you're leaving, please give your table to these young ladies."

"Yes, Sir, Mr. Woody. Ladies, please take our seats."

Woody, seeing them seated, said,

"Ya'll enjoy yourselves. I don't think any of your classmates are here. Johnny Potter, over there by the jukebox, was in the class before or after you. I don't think there's anyone else here.

"Oh! Brian Howard was in here last Saturday night. He said he was going. He never did marry. I don't think he's dating anyone now.

"I don't see a ring on your finger. Maybe you two might want to hook up again?

"Enjoy yourselves. It's really good to see you, Kayla. You too, Ginger. Please come back."

He never married. I can't believe it. He should have been a grandfather by now. I hope our failed relationship didn't sour his outlook on life. What am I thinking? Just look at me!

They ordered Cokes and watched the varied activities that included a large group dancing over by the jukebox.

"Ginger, when I was in high school and at James Sprunt; I was here every free minute I had. Woody told me that I wore out G-39 on his jukebox. That was Willie Nelson's *Faded Love*. That was my song. I loved it. I still do."

SNR

Next morning, she awakened to the aroma of country ham frying in her mama's cast iron skillet. Getting up, she showered and dressed before tapping on Ginger's door.

"I'm up, Kayla. I've already been to the kitchen. I couldn't help it. That aroma was too hypnotizing. It reminds me of being back home.
I'll meet you in the kitchen after I shower and dress."

Kayla found her mother stirring the grits. The biscuits were made and ready to be baked but wouldn't be put in the oven until everybody was in the kitchen. 8 minutes wasn't too long to wait for a hot biscuit. Especially with molasses and homemade butter.

Her daddy was sitting at the table leafing through the Duplin Times. It was a few days old but it didn't matter. Most of the sections he cared about would be news to him.

"Good morning, Mama, that smells so good. My diet is going to be trashed when I leave here but I don't care. I'm so ready for one of your big breakfasts. Ginger is too."

"Good morning, Honey, yes, Ginger's already had a cup of coffee and just a tiny piece of the ham. She says it taste just like her daddy's back home.
"Sit yourself down, I'll pour you a cup of coffee. Still black?"

"Yes, Ma'am. I tried it with cream. Even some of the flavored kind. That's not for me. I guess it will always be black for me."

"Ya'll see any of your old classmates last night? I'm sure Woody was there."

"Woody was but we didn't see anyone else that I knew. He said that Brian Howard was there last week and he said he was going to the reunion. Mr. Woody also said that Brian never married; wonder why?"

"Honey, I don't know. I heard tell that he dated a lot after you left and got pretty serious once or twice but never made it to the alter.
"I guess his business keeps him pretty busy now days."

"What kind of business?"

"I ain't real sure, Raymond, what kind of business is Brian Howard in?"

Her daddy looked up from reading the paper replying,

"He's in the farm equipment business. I hear tell that he's got 4 locations now. The big one, it was the first one, is in Kenansville. It's out on Hwy 24 going towards Beulaville just beyond the bypass on the right. He's got a huge display of International Harvester tractors and equipment. There must be at least 30 home and gardens tractors and mowers too. It's a big operation.
"I think the other 3 locations are in Wallace, Mt. Olive, and Clinton."
He lives in that big old house beside the Graham House in town. He bought it 10 or so years ago and spent a fortune renovating and restoring it. It will have a historic marker out front before long."
"I heard tell that he looked at Joe West's old home first but said that what they were asking was outrageous."

I can't believe that he never married. He was too romantic not to be. He had a temper too but surely by now he must have it under control? It doesn't matter to me, I've got Lynn. I'll see him Christmas. He's the one I want to have a life with.

Who am I kidding? I guess there will always be a soft spot in my heart for Brian. I know that I've forgiven him for how he acted when I left. I should have been more tactful. It was probably as much my fault as his when he blew a gasket.

I could have told him months before I did. What was I thinking? Anyway, it doesn't matter now. There's nothing between us…or is there? Yes, if I were completely truthful with myself; I'd admit that I came looking for him this weekend and I'll be looking for him at the reunion.

Unmarried after all these years? I don't know how I should feel. I'm sure he knows that I divorced Jeff. He probably knows that I'm still unmarried but if he does, why hasn't he tried to contact me?

Brian Howard, I'll be looking for you at the reunion.

When they were all seated around the table, her daddy returned thanks. The country ham wouldn't be denied nor would the eggs, grits, stewed apples, and biscuits.

Ginger slowed long enough to compliment Mama Herring on her spread.

"Mrs. Herring, it's been a long time since I've seen a breakfast like this. Mama made it the same way until daddy's blood pressure shot through the roof.

"One of the toughest things he probably ever did was to quit curing ham, bacon and making sausage but he had to or the doctors told him that he was going to die."

She laughed, before continuing,

"That first 6 months, we all thought we were going to have to move out. You've never seen such a fuss in your life. As far as he was concerned, nothing had any taste. It all tasted like cardboard to him.

"I have to admit that he was right. Nothing tasted like it did when mama seasoned everything with cured meat and cooked with hog lard and plenty of salt.

"I used to slip over to our neighbor's house after school. She knew what was going on and always had biscuits and side meat waiting.

"That's been a long time ago but, thank the Lord, we still have daddy and yes, he's just as cantankerous about his food and how it used to taste but he sticks with it."

She stopped and laughed again.

"He doesn't have much choice since he never learned how to cook. Our neighbor, Mrs. Harrell, the one that fixed biscuits and side meat for me; confided several times that he came over wanting collards and ham hocks but she refused to let him have any."

Kayla's mama replied, saying,

"We've been mighty lucky here. Raymond's in as good a health as he ever was and can eat anything I'm willing to fix.

"We still kill hogs once a year, usually in late January or early February. He cures the hams and bacon and still makes sausage. We like it after its been dried a couple of months.

"He takes the rest of the hog to Raf Miller over yonder on Summerlin's Road. He cuts and packages what we take for the freezer excepting the innards, head, and feet. He keeps all that. They say he makes salse. I don't know. We never bought any of it.

"Daddy used to make something he called 'salse' but after watching him make it, I never wanted any of it. Raymond says it's no different than what they put in potted meat. I don't mess with it either."

Ginger didn't remember anything like that.

"It could have been put in the liver pudding. Seems like daddy used to put everything else in it."

Changing the subject, her mama asked what they were going to do for the rest of the day?

"Weather's supposed to be pretty. You going to ride around or go anywhere special?"

Kayla replied that they might ride down to Wilmington and tour the Battleship North Carolina.

"If it's pretty, we might ride down to Southport and Oak Island. Ginger's never been.

"If it stays cloudy, we'll probably ride down to Carolina Beach and get some Britt's Donuts for lunch and do the Cotton Exchange this afternoon.

"The plan right now is to have supper at the Mad Boar. I think she'll like that. It's expensive but we're good for one trip."

Mr. Herring, listening to his daughter's itinerary, remarked,

"Sounds like a mighty busy day. You're going to be plumb tuckered out when you get back tonight."

"We will be Daddy, but, we'll have a lot to talk about and share with Mary when we get back."

I don't know how much of this I'm going to share with Lynn. If we run into Brian, I know I won't be sharing that with him.

She was beginning to have a guilty conscious. She hadn't expected any of the feelings about Brian. Maybe it was just because she was back home.

That's probably it. When I get back to Greenville, he'll disappear again.

On their way to Wilmington, Kayla turned left at the intersection with Hwy 24. Her curiosity had to be satisfied. She had to see Brian's farm equipment dealership. It was massive. She exited into the lot seeing several salespeople through the huge windows that covered the entire front of the building. Inside, on display, were tractors bigger than any she'd ever seen and the yard had more pieces of equipment that she could count.

Her curiosity satisfied, although she didn't see Brian, she returned to Hwy 11 following it to the intersection with I-40 taking the east-bound lane to Wilmington.

They arrived at the Battleship North Carolina a few minutes after 11. The temps were in the 70s and the clouds had almost disappeared although there was a stiff ocean breeze coming up the Cape Fear River.

When they finished touring a little before noon, the skies had completely cleared and the wind had calmed. They were on their way to Southport. The closer they got to the North Carolina/South Carolina line, the more they wanted seafood platters at Calabash.

15 minutes later, they were seated at Ella's waiting for their 3-seafood combinations to arrive.

"This is as good as I remember. I've eaten a lot of fried seafood but it never tastes like this. It's got to be Calabash style in Calabash."

Kayla agreed as she slathered butter on another hushpuppy. Afterwards, needed a little exercise, they walked along the docks enjoying the surroundings. The fishing fleet was in for the day and they watched as deckhands swabbed the decks and mend the nets. They appeared to be totally oblivious to the gawking tourists.

They finally arrived at Southport a little before 3 spending an hour walking first along East Bay Street and then Yacht Basin Drive. The setting was idyllic and calming.

Ginger remarked that she could spend the rest of her life right there.

"Of Course, I'd have to work somewhere. I could never afford to be here living a life of luxury."

Kayla verbally agreed but secretly thought that being with Brian, they could afford to live there enjoying a life of ease but, if I marry Lynn, I might live in Paris, France.

If I'm going to dream, I might as well dream big.

"You don't know, Ginger, when you find the man of your dreams, he may be the richest man in North Carolina."

Laughing, Ginger replied,

"Of course, Kayla, I'm going to meet him before we leave and he's going to take us out in his 100-foot yacht."

Next, they drove to Oak Island visiting the Light before exiting and turning northward up Hwy 17.
It had been a long, but fun day and they were beginning to tire.

The south-bound traffic on Hwy 17 seemed to increase with each passing mile and the rush-hour traffic caught them when they arrived back in Wilmington. They still had about 45 minutes before reaching Wallace but once on I-40, it was a breeze.

Finally, they were seated in the Mad Boar and yes, Ginger was impressed wondering how in the world a place that expensive was out there in the middle of nowhere?

It took a few minutes to share Senator's Murphy's vision of a gated community and what River Landing had turned into.

"I think it's been added onto several times. They say the occupants come from Wilmington and the surrounding counties. There are a lot of retirees too. Of course, the golf course draws a lot of them too.

"What are we having?"

"We had seafood for lunch, I vote for steak."
Kayla agreed.

They ordered the 12-oz. ribeye's with baked potato and mixed vegetables after trying the tender pork strips for starters.

He was there. Brian Howard was there. She was sure it was him. He'd aged some but not much. He seemed so sophisticated sitting all the way across the room with three other gentlemen.
They seemed very involved in their conversation and he wasn't scanning the room. It was him, she was sure of it. If he had been alone would she have gone over? She wasn't sure…Yes, she was, she would have.

After their steaks, they shared a Whiskey Toffee Brownie that was as scrumptious as it looked.

They finished the evening with cups of hot coffee. It was time to leave and he was still there.
When she stood, wanting his attention, she dropped her purse hoping he would notice. He did, she knew he did. She could feel his eyes on her. She glanced his way once. Their eyes met, she looked away and hurried out the door. She'd gotten his attention, that's all she wanted. It was a preview of coming attractions and he knew when the attraction would be.

Ginger, wasn't blind,

"What was that all about? What am I missing?

Kayla guessed that she'd have to confess. Some of it anyway.

"Remember when we were at Woody's and he said that Brian was going to the reunion and that he'd never married?

Ginger, still puzzled, said she remembered but what did that have to do with you dropping your purse?

"He was there, sitting all the way across the room with 3 other men."

Ginger still didn't get it.

"And?"

When I saw him, I wanted him to know that I was still alive. I guess I wanted him to see what he was missing. Ginger, I don't know. My mind's in a tizzy.

"I want to be with Lynn but hearing what Woody and Daddy said about Brian... I don't know what I want to do now. I guess I want to see Brian, maybe dance with him, maybe talk. I don't know. What do you think?"

"I don't know, Kayla. I've never been in a situation like yours. I guess if Lynn hadn't run off to France, you would probably be married now and this never would have happened but he's been gone, what, 2 years? You say he's coming home Christmas but then he's going back?

"I think you're ready for a man in your life. One that you can put your hands on every day, if you know what I mean. You've been on hold a long time. Somebody had better look out."

She was right, Kayla knew she was right. Lynn had come into her life unlocking hidden chambers of lost love and desire and right at the point of her yielding to him, he was gone and she was left hanging, crying, hurting for his touch, his love, his being one with her.

She'd tried to put a cap on it but, as was so evident tonight, she was coming unraveled. She wanted to be loved, be held, be kissed, be in the arms of someone that wanted and needed her and she was reaching out.

It was all coming to a head. She didn't want to hurt anyone, especially Lynn, but she needed someone to fill the horrible, lonely, gap she'd created so many years ago.

SNR

After tossing and turning all night, not really getting any sleep. Kayla got up when she heard her mama in the kitchen. She showered and dressed before walking down the hall finding her daddy sitting at the kitchen table wading into the News and Observer's Sunday edition. It was huge but more than half its contents were ads.

Her mama was cooking sausage and already had the grits on.

"Good morning, Kayla. Ya'll got in after our bedtime last night. Did you have a good time?"

Kayla replied that they did. No, she didn't share the part about seeing Brian. They didn't have to know about that little episode.

"It was a wonderful day, we toured the battleship first and then drove down to Calabash for lunch and spent a few hours in Southport and on Oak Island.

"We got to Wallace about seven last night and had supper at the Mad Boar. Ginger was surprised to see such a wonderful place in what she described as the middle of nowhere. I filled her in about River Landing. She got the picture then."

"Picture, what picture? Did I hear my name mentioned? Good morning, everyone."

Kayla replied that she was just telling them about yesterday.

"Oh, we did have an enjoyable time. It was great being back in Ella's in Calabash. We spent the rest of the afternoon trying to walk our meal off and as soon as we did, we ate again."

Kayla was holding her breath!

Don't you dare mention Brian, I told you not to, remember??

Luckily, she didn't but her daddy did.

"Kayla, did you ride by Brian's business in Kenansville or Wallace?"

She couldn't deny it, not in front of Ginger.

"Yes, Daddy, we stopped by the one in Kenansville yesterday morning. We didn't stop, just drove through the parking area. It's a huge, impressive place. He must be doing a lot of business."

Her daddy agreed, replying,

"Yes, folks out at the plant and around the courthouse say he's growing fast. Not too fast, they say he has a group of financial advisors out of Charlotte or somewhere like that.

"I heard the other week that he was on the board at one of the banks in Kenansville too. He's really got it together. He's nothing like he was when you were dating him."

Kayla's mind was spinning again.

On the board of a bank, I really want to see him now. I especially want him to see me too. I can't wait until next month.

She had to get off the subject.

"Mama, what can I help you do?"

Her mama replied that other than pouring the juice and getting the jelly and butter out of the refrigerator, it was pretty much done. She was frying the eggs and the biscuits were in the oven.

Kayla busied herself with the condiments and juice hoping the subject would go away. It did but now her daddy was opening another can of worms.
"When have you heard from that man of yours in France? Did you say that he was coming home soon?"

How in the world was she going to answer him, she tried, carefully weighing each word or phrase?

"Daddy, we're in contact almost every day via text, messaging, and Facebook.
"He's coming home Christmas and I'm so looking forward to seeing him."

"Is he going to be home to stay?"

He'd trapped her. Now what was she going to say. The last thing she wanted to say was, no. He was only visiting for a few days before returning to Paris. She couldn't lie to her parents.

"Daddy, he's coming home for about a week. His position with the embassy has turned into a permanent one. He'll probably choose to remain in Paris until his son finishes his studies. He's not sure where his son will want to study after that.
"Becoming a world-renowned chef requires working under chef's all over the world while he develops his own techniques and style. Lynn says he's gifted in marrying foods, spices, and seasonings. Learning about presentation will be his next endeavor.
"We'll talk about all that when Lynn visits over the holidays."

SNR - Bob Holt

"You're not coming home for Christmas?"

"Of course, Daddy, you know I'll be here Christmas Day."

Mama was taking the biscuits out of the oven saying,

"Okay, everyone, the foods on the table, let's eat it while its' hot."

"Lord, make us truly thankful for the bountiful blessings set before us, amen."

That's more like her daddy's blessings. Not one of those long ones when you weren't sure what was coming next. He probably didn't either.

"Ginger, it's so nice to have you visit with us. Are you from up there around Greenville?"

"No, Sir, I grew up in Bertie County. We're below the Virginia state line. Hertford and Gates separates us. I grew near Colerain on a peanut farm."

"Oh, Braxton Bazemore, is in our section at the plant. He's from Askewville, Is that close to where you're from?'

"Yes, Sir, that's about fifteen miles from where I grew up. It's like a lot of little towns up my way. They've about dried up and blown away.
"Colerain's still got a pretty good main street but it's nothing like it was before I left"

Thank goodness, the subject had gotten off Brian; she had to get Ginger out of there before they started up again.

After helping with the dishes, they said their goodbyes and were on the road again. It was a relief getting out from under the inquisition.

Her daddy didn't have a clue what he was putting her through, or, did he? He was smart putting things together. She guessed she'd made a few stupid blunders.

That business of dropping her purse was stupid but she'd gotten Brian's attention and was pretty sure that he recognized her. She's know for sure at the reunion.

"I really enjoyed meeting your parents. They remind me so much of mine. Maybe sometimes you can ride up my way. I think you'd enjoy peanut country, especially during the harvest season. It's all mechanical now, nothing like it used to be when it was done by hand. When I was a little young'un, the plants were turned upside-down and stacked up like hay stacks.

We used to come home from school and run out to the fields eating green peanuts until we about died. They were so good.

"That's when they're best boiled. There's nothing like boiled peanuts; they're so salty. You eat them until you can't hold any more."

The boiled peanuts sounded good, she was going to have to try them. Maybe Ginger would boil some for them. She didn't have a clue how to begin or what was required.

They arrived back in Greenville a little before noon. Neither was hungry after their huge breakfast but agreed to meet at the Wellness Center about 5 and get a salad afterwards.

SNR

After unpacking, Kayla checked for messages on Facebook. Lynn had left two saying he didn't want to bother her during her visit. It appeared that he might be transferred back to Washington in the spring. He would still be attached to the embassy but would finally be back in the states.

She messaged back that they had enjoyed their visit with her parents and had spent Saturday touring the battleship before driving to Calabash, then Southport and Oak Island. She saw no need is sharing the Mad Boar with him.

She was enthusiastic about his possible permanent return to the US and she was still looking forward to his visit over the Christmas holidays.

The noose was tightening; Kayla could feel it tugging and squeezing around her neck. Who was pulling the hardest, Lynn or Brian? She wasn't sure it was either of them. She feared that she was the culprit. She had placed the noose around her neck and was standing on the trap door. Who held the release? Was it her?

She felt as if she'd pushed the time-delayed self-destruct button and there wasn't any reset button. How had she allowed herself to be so overwhelmed by Brian Howard? She'd only seen him for a few minutes. No words were shared, No nothing; just her wild love-starved imagination. She'd taken every word, every remark she'd heard and turned him into her prince charming.

He wasn't her prince charming; he barely knew she existed. She wanted so much to believe that he hadn't married because he was still carrying a torch for her. He must be. Why else had he never married?

Turn it loose, Kayla, before it drives you crazy. You have Lynn although it may take time. Why go looking for a bird in the bush?

She had to go on looking; she was driven by some unknown force; she didn't know why; she only knew that she would.

She desperately wanted to be loved unconditionally, totally, fully, and forever. She was going to be; it was her destiny. She believed that with all her heart. She'd been alone for far too long. The door to her cage had been opened and she was finally free. Free after twenty-two long years.

After their workout, Kayla and Ginger had salads at the Three Steers. While they were eating, Kayla shared Lynn's message with her.

"Lynn says he might be coming back to the states permanently, maybe in a year or 2, he's not sure.

"That sure leaves me hanging and I've been hung up to dry for so long. Ginger, I think impatience is really kicking in. Seeing Brian has really gotten me stirred up and wanting to be unchained.

"Yes, I know that I'm the one that put them on in the first place but they've been on long enough.

"What do you think? Am I moving too fast?

She could tell that Ginger was apprehensive about replying. Why was she trying to put her in a corner? It was her corner. If she wanted out, she'd have crawl out all by herself.

Ginger cautiously replied,

"Kayla, I don't know what to tell you. After seeing your reactions this weekend, I'd have to say that you need to either get Brian out of your life or climb into it with him.

"Lynn showed you love when you desperately needed it but his situation is so iffy, I don't know what to tell you.

"I haven't been divorced nearly as long as you but I can tell you that if there's a next time for me; I'll have to be totally in love before I leap."

"I don't think that you are totally sure and committed to Lynn. I think the reunion will clear that up."

Kayla knew that she was right and she also knew that she had no business trying to drag Ginger into her quagmire of reality and unreality. It was just like being happy. Nobody would make her happy, only her.

Her interactions with other people might steer her into, or away from, happy but only she could make it happen.

SNR

After a very restless night of tossing and turning, Monday finally arrived and with it, her determination to get a handle on her life.

I'm going discuss my weekend with Mary but I'm not going to try to drag her into the middle of my quandary.

The reunion may hold the answer but that would be totally unfair to Lynn. He has a stake in this too.

After showering, and a bowl of cereal, she was ready for another week. Another week as she marched steadily forward to a critical juncture in her life.

She was excited but also, very apprehensive. Two weeks ago, she was so very sure of where her life's path was leading and now there was a Y in her road of life. Either leg appeared to be the direction she should travel but which one was right for her.

Arriving at her desk, she texted Mary asking about lunch.

Mary texted back,

Yes, 11 @ 3 Steers – M

Good, we'll ride 2gether – K

The morning slipped by without any bumps. They arrived at the Three Steers building their salads before spreading Kayla's weekend out. Mary knew about her trip but not about Brian. To say that she was surprised would be an understatement.

She and Harold had brought Lynn into her life and were sure that they were a perfect match.

"Ginger and I had a nice weekend. Mama and Daddy really enjoyed having her visit.

"We spent Saturday morning touring the Battleship North Carolina before driving down to Calabash for lunch. Afterwards, we walked along the waterfront in Southport and visited the Oak Island Light before driving back. We had supper at the Mad Boar in Wallace. It's a very expensive place but I wanted her to see it. While we were there, I saw my old high school boyfriend, Brian. No, I didn't speak to him but I'm sure that he saw me.

"Mama and daddy had already shared that he'd never married. They said it might be because he's so tied up in his business with 4 locations.

"Mama wondered if we might hook up at the reunion. I told her that I doubted it but it would be nice to talk to him and find out why he never married."

She could tell by the look on Mary's face that she'd probably said too much. Her mannerisms were probably dead giveaways too.

Mary, appearing to be uncomfortable, replied,

"Kayla, it's been, what, twenty-eight years since you last saw him? Do you still have feelings for him after all these years?

"What about Lynn, I thought the two of you were so close."

She'd backed Kayla into a corner. She hadn't, Kayla had. She never should have brought Brian's name up. What was she thinking?

"Mary, I think a lot of Lynn and there might have been something for us if his son hadn't been in that accident.

"Lynn's been gone almost two years. He says he may be coming back to the states permanently in another year or two.

"He says he wants to spend some time with me during the Christmas holidays but nothing beyond that. There is no commitment, not even a hint.

"I'll be fifty in two years; my clock keeps right on ticking."

Mary didn't have a retort for Kayla's supposition. Another two years of waiting was a lot to ask of someone when there hadn't been the slightest hint of any permanency.

"Kayla, I have to agree with you. Harold and I hoped that you and Lynn would have gotten married but it didn't happen. It's neither one's fault. No, I take that back. Even though circumstances created the separation, Lynn could and should have been more forthcoming with his feelings and intentions.

"You should go to your reunion with an open mind and if it's meant for you and Brian? to be together, so be it. Love will have conquered all and you know that all I want is for you to be happy."

"Mary, that's all I want and it's nobody's fault but mine that I've waited so long to do anything about it. Now that I'm ready to move on, waiting is like an ever-growing weight pushing down on me. If I don't get out from underneath it, it's going to slowly, but surely, squeeze the life out of me."

She knew that Mary was prejudiced. She couldn't help but be. She knew Lynn, she didn't have a clue about Brian and all she'd ever heard about him was derogatory.

That was Kayla's fault. It the subject ever came up, and it rarely did, she made Brian into a horrible, self-centered, control freak, that only cared about himself.

He was, wasn't he? No, not if I really stop and think about it. I just wanted out. I wasn't ready to get tied down to a bunch of kids in the middle of Duplin County, NC.

Mary pushed the subject aside asking,

"What are you doing tonight? Harold is coaching a 3rd. degree candidate and he'll be tied up at least 3 hours. I'm going over to Belks. I think they are having a sale."

"Ginger and I are exercising right after work. What time are you going?"

"Around seven, that's when Harold will be leaving."

SNR

They arrived at the mall about 7:30 parking at the Belk entrance. In the lady's department, they walked from display to display noting the items on sale.

"Have you decided what you're wearing to the reunion?"

"No, I thought about wearing the dress I bought two years ago when Lynn took me to Bobby's but I think it will be too dressy. I don't know but I've got to start looking. I guess I could start here."

She knew in her mind that it had to be something that would show off her school girl figure and maybe something to draw attention to her fuller bust but not too revealing, maybe a little cleavage.

That will get Brian's attention and probably the rest of the others too.

She turned away from Mary. She didn't need to see that look. She'd read right through it.

Walking over to a rack of what appeared to be evening ware, she looked at each style that was in her size not finding anything that caught her eye. The more she looked, the surer she became of what she was looking for. It wasn't there.

It was almost 8:30 when they left. Mary had picked out two blouses and a pair of slacks. Kayla left empty-handed.

"Let's get coffee and a piece of pie at Darla's."

Mary liked Kayla's suggestion and minutes later, they were seated with cups of coffee and slices of coconut cream pie in front of them.

"This is where Lynn brought you on your first date, isn't it?"

What was Mary trying to do; put her on a guilt trip?

"Yes, we came here after the play. I never knew it existed until then. I come here often now. It's very convenient and a perfect way to end an evening before I go to bed."

If Mary had an ulterior motive in her question, she didn't pursue it.

"This pie's delicious. It would be nice if we had a place like this in Farmville. I guess it's too small to support a place like this."

The pie was good and she was enjoying Mary's company but tensed each time Mary started to speak knowing, almost surely, that it would be about something that included Lynn.

Arriving back at Kayla's, they parted ways saying they would see each other in the morning.

SNR

Inside, after getting ready for bed, Kayla checked in on Facebook seeing two messages from Lynn.

The first one wrote about attending a meeting with a delegation from the French cabinet. He alluded to the boredom of having to listen to the delegates attempt to get the wording right on an official publication.

He didn't have a speaking part and could only pass notes to the ambassador's attaché.

The second one was about a visit to the Louvre. He's posted several times over the past two years and other visits. This one was about the Mona Lisa and how he'd stood, spellbound, for several minutes, enchanted by her mysterious smile.

She replied that seeing the actual painting must have been an exciting experience. Maybe one day, she'd get a chance to do the same. There wasn't anything exciting she could, or would, share with him. She was excited but he wouldn't see her experience the same way she did.

If she was setting herself up for a let-down. So be it. After being out of the game for much too long, it appeared that she'd been dealt two hands and she was going to play both until there was a clear winner, her winner.

SNR

Next afternoon, after exercising with Ginger, they rode over to Arlington Village.

She really wanted to buy something that stood out but knew that would never do. She wanted to be noticed, especially by Brian, but she didn't want to knock him completely off his feet, just stagger him a little.

After trying on several, she chose an orange side ruffle dress with a surplice neckline that was ruched at the side ruffle. It had 3/4 sleeves and was waist length. There was just the right amount of cleavage revealed. Not too much to raise eyebrows but enough to raise interest. Next, she chose 4" heel strappy sandals in a nude color and then an imitation emerald set that included a single stand necklace with a teardrop stone, matching earrings, bangle bracelet and ring.

She was ready, more than ready. The only thing separating her from Brian was time and the clock was ticking.

Ginger couldn't resist, saying,

"He doesn't stand a chance. If you want him; he'll be yours."

Kayla could only remark that she hoped that she knew what she was doing.

"If I'm wrong, Ginger, I could lose both but I've got to do this. Otherwise, I may spend the rest of my life wondering and I've wasted enough time already."

"Ready for a cup of coffee and a piece of pie?"

As they were getting out of the car at Darla's, her smartphone alerted her to a call from her mama.

Seeing it was her mama, anxiety swept through her body. Her mama never called, it had to be unwelcome news.

"Heart Attack!"
Mama, are you sure?

"Mama, are you sure, is he, all right?... Kenansville?... They're air-lifting him here?... When... I'll go over right now, they'll take him to the heart center...No, Mama, it's connected to the main hospital... Who's going to bring you?... Okay, call me when you get here, I'll meet you in the lobby... No, Mama, I'll take tomorrow off...We'll talk about that when you get here... Yes, Mama, I love you too... Yes, Ma'am, I'll pray for Daddy too."

She looked at Ginger who was sitting wide-eyed beside her. She'd heard enough to know that Mr. Herring had suffered a heart attack.

"East Care is air-lifting Daddy here. I'll drop you by the house and drive over there. It's going to be a long night. I'll put in for sick leave in the morning."

"Kayla, I'm so sorry, I have a thousand questions but I'm sure you don't have any answers yet. I'm going to follow you over there. You may need a little support. I'll be there for you."

Wiping tears from her eyes, she responded,

"Ginger, thank you. It will help just knowing that you are there."

This is a horrible way to end September. I hope and pray that October will different. The last week in October may be life changing for me. I'll just have to wait and see.

She arrived at ECHI (East Carolina Heart Institute) with Ginger behind her. They parked in "C" section and hurried to the entrance.

"Has Mr. Raymond Herring been admitted yet? He was air-lifted from Kenansville less than an hour ago."

The receptionist entered the name and waited for the screen to come up

"He's in CICU on the fourth floor. Only family members are allowed in that area."

"We're his daughters. Our mother is in transit and should be here within the hour."

Not questioning Kayla's statement, she pointed to the elevators saying,

"Go to the fourth floor and tell the receptionist who you are."

As the elevator door was closing, Ginger laughed saying,

"That's the quickest adoption I've ever seen. Sis, what are we going to tell our mama?"

"Mama will get over it. Remember, I'm the oldest. What I say goes."

"Yes, Big Sister, I'll follow you."

Their little jest took the edge off the seriousness of the moment and Kayla appreciated Ginger's jest.

When the elevator opened, they walked to the receptionist sitting across the corridor.

"Mr. Raymond Herring, we're his daughters."

The receptionist looked at her computer screen saying,

"I'll walk back with you. You will not be able to go in the cubicle. His team is processing him in."

"Will we be able to see him a little later?"

There was no way the receptionist would answer her and she knew it but had to ask.

"When Dr. Erickson finishes his examination, and confers with the others on his team, he'll post the restrictions if there are any. We will only be able to observe for a few moments. Then, I suggest you and your sister go to the waiting room across from my desk.

"He may ask to speak with any members of Mr. Herring's family. I'll alert you if he does."

They passed through two set of doors before arriving at the five cubicles in that section. Mr. Herring was in the first one on the right.

It was impossible to see her father. He was surrounded by what appeared to be three doctors and two nurses.

Her father appeared to be hooked up to a myriad of tubes and cords connected to monitors above the bed or to bags hanging from two stands.

If he was conscious, she couldn't tell. There was too much going on.

"I'm sorry but we have to go."

Kayla wanted to argue but knew better. The doctors were the ones that needed to be there, not them.

In the waiting room, Kayla texted Mary letting her know what was happening.

Daddy had heart attack – In ECHI – fill U in later- K

Sorry, need me? – M

Tnx – maybe tomorrow – will keep in touch – K

OK – wait 2 hear – praying – M

She didn't know if her siblings had been contacted but she'd wait until her mama arrived. She was strong in situations like this but this time it was different. It was her life's mate.

There was a commotion at the receptionist's desk. Turning to look, Kayla realized that it was her mama.

They rushed up to her. As soon as her mama saw her, she calmed but tears were flowing. She reached out for Kayla hugging her before collapsing into her arms.

Sam Miller, their neighbor, assisted in taking her into the waiting room. Ginger had asked for and gotten a glass of water.

"Mama, everything going to be all right. The doctors are with daddy now. They'll come out and talk to us when their accessment is complete. It may take a little while but he's in good hands."

Her mama looked pleadingly into her eyes but didn't say anything. She wouldn't let Kayla's hand go.

"Mr. Miller, thank you so much for bringing mama. Can I pay you for your trouble?"

"No, Kayla, just being neighborly. Raymond took Harriet to the hospital in Goldsboro a few years ago when I was up there with my gall bladder."
Helping your mama is what neighbors are for."
"I've got her things in the truck, I'll go down and fetch them and then I'll be getting on back. Harriett will be worried."

Ginger interrupted, saying,

"Kayla, I'll go down with Mr. Miller and bring her things back up here unless he thinks I'll need help."

He assured her that she would wouldn't.

"She only brought one suitcase. It's not heavy."

Knowing Mr. Miller didn't have a cell or smart phone, she suggested that he call his wife on hers.

"Thank you, Kayla, I don't know nothing about them phones. Will you call her for me?"

Getting the number, which she saved, she called and handed it to Mr. Miller when his wife answered.

"No, Hun, they don't know nothing yet… Yeah, I'm sure they will… Okay, I'll ask…
He looked at Kayla asking about how long it would take him to drive home?

"About an hour and a half."

"Bout an hour and a half… No, I'm leaving now…I'll tell them."

Thanking her, he handed the phone back to her saying,

"Harriett wants you to be sure and call us when you know something."

She assured him that she would saying,

I saved your number, Mr. Miller. I'll call as soon as I know something. Thank you again, I really appreciate you bring mama up here."

He mama cleared her throat saying,

"Sam, I really appreciate it. You know me and Raymond do."

"Dolly, call if you need us."

30 minutes later, Ginger was back with the bag.

"Did you have any problem finding Mr. Miller's truck?"

Ginger grinned saying,

"A little bit. He couldn't remember where he'd parked but he knew his license number and the make, model and color of his F-150.

"Security finally found it over near the children's hospital entrance. The courtesy patrol offered them a ride when they arrived. All they knew was that your daddy had had a heart attack.

"I stayed with him until he paid his tab at the checkout on Moye Blvd. Walking back from there was easy."

It was a little after seven and so far, not a word from the doctor.

"Mama, I know you didn't have supper, we didn't either. Let's go to the cafeteria and get something to eat."

She didn't want to leave, scared that the doctor would come out to talk to them and wouldn't be able to find them.

"Mama, it's okay, I'll tell the receptionist where we're going. She'll have us paged if we're needed."

Ginger said that she knew it was a little further but she wanted something they couldn't get in the ECHI dining room.

"Let's go over to the main dining room."

Leaving instructions with the receptionist. They took the elevator to the main floor and made their way down the long corridors to the dining room.

Kayla's mama was spry for her age and had no problem walking down the long corridors to the main dining room. She didn't know where she was at but Kayla did and that's all that mattered.

"Kayla, this is a big place. Where do you work?"

"Mama, I'm in is all the way down this long corridor and across the street in an office complex. Ginger's in a separate building but we've close to each other."

Picking up trays, flatware, and napkins, they walked down to the deli line first.

"Mama, what are you hungry for? Fried chicken, pork chops, roast beef?"

Her mama, looking at all the selections, replied.
"Kayla, I don't know, maybe a chicken breast, some potatoes, and green beans. I want a cup of coffee too."

Kayla led her mama through the selections in the middle of the serving area finding everything she wanted. Kayla chose the meat loaf, garden peas, and rice with gravy.

She led her to the beverages getting their coffee.

"Mama, are you sure you don't want dessert?"

"No, honey, this is fine."

Ginger walked up behind them. She'd picked up two pieces of fried chicken and fries. Getting water, she was ready.

Kayla showed the cashier her ID and all three were on her ticket. Ginger tried to protest but lost.

The dining room was practically empty leaving her mama wondering where everyone was?

"Mama, most of the employees eat around six in the afternoon. The line closes at eight but opens briefly around 2 a.m. for those working the graveyard shift. It opens for breakfast at six. That's probably their busiest shift. You can go down the grill line ordering eggs any way you want them."

Her mama was still looking around and still asking questions.

"Honey, this is a big place. How many folks work here?"

Kayla replied,

"Close to ten thousand now, Mama. More come on board every day"

They'd almost finished their meal when there was a message alert.

"Attention please, would the family of Raymond Herring return to the waiting room." It was repeated once.

"I guess we'll meet the doctor now. Mama, give me your tray. Yours's too, Ginger."

She dropped the trays off and they made their way down the long corridors back to the heart hospital and the fourth-floor receptionist.

"Go in the waiting room, I'll let Dr. Erickson know that you're back."

They walked across the corridor taking seats in the waiting room.

Moments later,

"Would the family of Mr. Raymond Herring come with me."

They followed him a few steps away from the room and receptionist.

"I'm Dr. Erickson. Mr. Herring did suffer a heart attack. We have him stabilized but we've also sedated him.

"We will not be able to determine the extent of the damage or what procedures are called for until further assessment is accomplished. We'll do a CT-Scan and MRI first. That will take place very early in the morning. We'll also insert dye in his veins so we can see any blockage. That will determine what actions we'll take.

"After the scans, I'll probably move him to a room if he remains stable through the evening."

Kayla, was the first with a question,

"Dr., how severe was my father's heart attack?"

"Hopefully, it was just a warning. I'll be more able to address your query after the tests tomorrow."

"Since he's sedated, I suggest you not try seeing him until tomorrow. I will be more forthcoming then."

He turned, walking towards the double doors.

"Mama, we'll go down there if you must but we probably should leave him alone since he won't know that we're there."

Her mama knew she was right but she had to see him if it was only for a minute.

"It wouldn't seem right, Honey, we're said good night to each other for over fifty years. It don't matter if he don't hear me. I just want to tell him that I love him."

Kayla knew that arguing with her would be a losing battle. Moments later, they stood at the cubicle. Mr. Herring was totally oblivious of his surroundings. Her mama moved forward touching his foot.

"Ray, Honey, I love you. Sleep good, I'll see you in the morning."

Back in the waiting room, Kayla suggested that they go home.

"Mama, we'll be back very early in the morning."

That fell on deaf ears. Her mama wasn't going anywhere.

"Ginger, why don't you go home and get some rest. You've been an angel. Thank you."

Ginger replied,

"I'll check on you before I punch in tomorrow. Mrs. Herring, your husband will be fine. He's in good hands. I'll pray for him tonight."

One by one, the hours slipped by and finally, a little after 1 a.m., her mama drifted off. She was wrapped in a blanket and rested her head on Kayla's shoulder. Kayla caught fleeting naps but couldn't let go.

A little after 5 a.m., her father was moved to a room on the fifth floor. Kayla awakened her mama and they followed behind.

The nurse said that her father wouldn't awaken before the scheduled scans that begin at five-thirty.

"He'll be awake when we bring him back around eleven."

Thirty minutes later, they watched as her father was prepped and taken away.

"Mama, let's go home, shower and change clothes. We'll have breakfast and come back up here afterwards."

Reluctantly, her mama agreed. Taking her suitcase, she led her mama to the elevator. One the first level, she took her to the entrance telling her to wait.

"I'll get the car and pick you up here."

"I'll go with you, Honey."

"Mama, it's a long walk, wait here."

When they returned, she'd do the valet parking. That would be much better than walking to the far side of "C" section.

Arriving at home, Kayla got her mama's suitcase and led her inside.

"Lordy, Honey, it's been years since me and your daddy were here. I don't remember it looking nothing like this."

It had been a long time. Over 20 years. They'd visited when Kevin and Amy were born but only once after the divorce. She visited home often in the beginning but as the years creeped by and the kids got older, she crawled deeper and deeper into her little corner and her fence got higher and higher, she only went home during the holidays and only then for a couple of days around Christmas so Kevin and Amy could be with the family.

Her siblings visited in the beginning finding an introvert that apparently preferred to be left alone and over the years, she got her wish.

"Yes, Mama, I've done a lot over the years. I'll tell you all about it later."

She led her to Amy's room.

"Mama, this is Amy's room. A bathroom is right across the hall. After you shower and dress, we'll get something to eat before going back to the hospital. There's no hurry, we'll go back around ten."

She showered in her bathroom, dressed and made coffee before texting Mary and Ginger.

Next, she texted Cal Newbold filling him in on her need to be off for a few days.

I'll call later in the morning – Kayla

Her mama walked into the kitchen appearing to be fully refreshed but Kayla knew how close to exhaustion her mama must be.

She poured her a cup of coffee remembering one sugar. She sat it in front of her mama at the table joining her with her cup.

"Mama, let's walk into the den. The chairs are more comfortable there."

Her mama followed her taking a seat in one of the Lazy Boy Recliners. After taking a sip of her coffee, she placed it on the end table and in seconds, was fast asleep.

I'll let her sleep until nine-thirty. That will give us plenty of time for breakfast before we go back to the hospital.

Walking back into the kitchen, she first called Mr. Newbold's office. He was in a meeting but had told the secretary not to expect Kayla saying it may be a few days relating that She had a medical emergency. Her father had suffered a heart attack.

Next, she texted Mary asking if it was all right to call?

Mary called her.

"Mary... yes, it's been a long night... No, I'm home, mama's asleep, daddy won't be back in the room until probably eleven... No, they're doing the scans now... He'd only say that daddy suffered a heart attack. He wouldn't elaborate saying he'd talk to us after the procedures this morning... Okay, I'll see you around noon... Me too, Mary, thank you."

Next, Ginger, it rolled to her voice mail.

"Ginger, we're home, we showered and changed clothes. Mama's asleep in the recliner. We're going to have breakfast at the Three Steers and go back to the hospital around eleven. I'll check with you later today."

She had to call her siblings and children first. She called Donna, then Ander, and lastly, Linda. She had no way of phoning Gary. She'd send him an email. He could be anywhere in the world.

"Kevin, your grandfather had a heart attack... No, he's here in Greenville. They may do a heart bypass operation tomorrow or Friday... No, there's no need to come before Saturday. He'll be in the hospital for at least a week... I don't know, they're running scans now. I should know more by tonight. I'll message you... I'll tell her... I love you too."

Amy's call rolled to voice mail. Kayla shared the same information that she'd shared with Kevin saying she would message her tonight.

Kayla awakened her mama a little before nine-thirty.

"Mama, wake up, we're going to get breakfast first then we'll go back to the hospital."

Her mama was a little disorganized when she awakened but quickly realized where she was.

"Lordy, I musta dropped off to sleep. What time is it?"

"Nine-twenty-five, Mama. Are you ready for some breakfast?"

Her mama was hungry, she could tell.

"I believe I could eat something. We'll get back to the hospital before your daddy wakes up, won't we?"

"Yes, Mama, we have plenty of time."

Arriving at the Three Steers, Janie seated them by the windows. Faye came over placing menus in front of them.

"Is Sandra cooking?"

"Yes, she is."

"Mama, if you want some really good soft-scrambled eggs... like the ones you cook; you'll love these. Sandra fixes them perfect."

Her mama ordered them along with bacon, grits, and white toast. The butter and jelly were on the table.

"I'll have to soft-scrambled eggs too along the home fries and sausage links. I'll have to wheat toast with mine."

When their plates arrived, her mama looked at the eggs, saying,

"Honey, these look just like mine. That cook knows what she's doing. These grits taste like mine too."

"Mama, has daddy ever been sick before? I mean, like now. Has he ever complained about hurting in his chest?"

"Yes, Honey, he had a spell about two years ago. He'd been weed trimming. I saw him grab his chest. He stood there for a few minutes and came to the house. He didn't say anything other than he was going to rest awhile.

"Didn't nothing ever come of it until last summer. He'd come in from work and went out to the stable to knock down some weeds with the bush axe. The weed eater won't strong enough.

"I was watching him from the kitchen window when he dropped the bush axe and grabbed his chest. He dropped down to his knees. I ran screaming out the back door running up to him. His face was as white as a sheet. It scared me to death.

"We walked real slow back to the house. He wouldn't let me call nobody. He sat in the recliner until supper was ready. By then, his color was back and he'd quit shaking.

"Next day, he went off to work but refused to call the doctor."

"Honey, until now he hasn't seen a doctor in fifty years. The first year we were married, his gall bladder gave him a fit and they finally took it out down yonder in Kenansville. It messed his system up for four or five years but the pain was gone."

They finished breakfast and drove over to the hospital using the valet service for parking.

They walked into the room finding Mr. Herring awake but still very groggy.

It only took a few minutes to realize it and after spending a few minutes holding his hand, he dropped back off to sleep.

Just as they were sitting down, Mary walked in hugging Kayla while asking about her daddy?

Kayla introduced Mary first.

"Mama, this is my best friend, Mary Tyson. She works in the same complex that I do. We've known each other for over 20 years."

"Mary, this is my mama, Dolly Herring."

Her mama responded, saying,
"Mary, it's so nice to finally meet you although I would have hoped for better circumstances. Kayla has told us so much about you."

"It's my pleasure, Mrs. Herring. I feel as if I already know you."

Their conversation was interrupted by the arrival of Dr. Erickson.

He greeted them while walking over to the bed.

"Good morning. I see that Mr. Herring is still groggy. He'll be fully awake by noon. One of you might want to call in his lunch. You'll see that he's on a salt-restricted diet.

"There's a lot of blockage in the arteries surrounding his heart. I'm scheduling him for bypass surgery on Friday. We'll do a triple bypass using the minimally invasive robotic technique and Mr. Herring should be just fine.

"However, I must warn you that he must remain on a salt free restricted diet for the foreseeable future. I see that's he's from a rural area in Duplin County and I'm sure his diet has been mostly pork and pork fat. That must end. We want to keep him around for a long, long time."

"Friday morning, he'll be prepped for surgery around four a.m. and taken to the operating theater at five. By then, he'll be very groggy but the family will be allowed to remain with him until he'll rolled into the operating room.

"The procedure usually takes about four hours. Afterwards, he'll remain ICU until Saturday or Sunday. He should be back in his room by noon and we'll have up walking around on Monday or Tuesday.

"He'll remain here, under observation, for another week. I should be able to release him Monday week.

"We'll have time to discuss recovery during his stay here. There will be several teams working with him, and you, on exercise, diet, healthy habits, and stress management."

"Any questions?"

Her mama had one.

"Doctor, when will he be allowed to go back to work?"

"I see that Mr. Herring is 71 years old. being a supervisor, he should be able to go back to work after Thanksgiving. We must remember that the surgery won't be fully effective for six months. He must pay close attention to his, diet, exercise, and stress management.

"You must keep stress to a minimum. I know that's not always possible but you have to try."

When Doctor Erickson left, Kayla called dietary with her daddy's lunch and dinner pics. There wasn't much to choose from but that was all there was.

Stress management, Dr. Erickson, didn't have a clue. She knew when her daddy saw what he was supposed to eat, there's be stress and a lot of it.

Mary and Ginger stayed through their lunch hour saying they'd check on them after work.

By 12:30, her father was fully awake and hungry.

"What does a man have to do to get something to eat around here?"

Dreading it, Kayla was about to answer when the diet specialist came in. She nodded to Kayla and her mama before speaking to Mr. Herring.

"Mr. Herring, I'm Sylvia Hudson. I'm a nutrition specialist nurse. I'm here to help you with your new diet that will hopefully lead to a new healthy lifestyle."

Kayla and her mama could tell by the expression on Mr. Herring's face that he wasn't happy with what he was hearing.

He looked at her with the skin around his nose between his eyebrows all crinkled up, replied,

"New diet, healthy lifestyle, what are you talking about? I'm hungry. When do I eat?"

"Mr. Herring, your lunch is on the way. It's not what you're used to eating but you must make some changes if you want to live.

"The scans performed on you earlier this morning show blockage in the main arteries around your heart. There is almost total blockage in one of them. It's the one that probably caused your heart attack.

"Dr. Erickson will be in later to tell you about the surgery he'll be performing on you. I'm not qualified to do that, sir. It's my job to lead you into a healthier lifestyle and that begins with your diet."

"Your chart indicates that you grew up in a rural environment and your diet included an excessive amount of pork and pork fat. That is where your blockage came from.

"After your operation, it will be up to you as to how successful it is. If you change your diet and begin a new lifestyle, it will be very successful. If you don't, it can't be. As we get older, our bodies are not able to correct our wrongs.

"With the operation, you'll be given a new lease on life. It's up to you, sir, how long you want to live and what quality of life you want."

She'd taken the wind right out of his sails. He calmed right down while she shared dietary charts with him and his wife. She said if it was going to work, it would have to be a joint effort.

When his food arrived, he grumbled but ate the bland food on the tray before dropping off to sleep.

Kayla could tell that her mama's nerves were fraying.

"Honey, what am I going to do? We've lived on pork all our lives. We've had a hog killing every year.

"Raymond's fatting up 2 hogs right now for January. You remember, that's when we usually kill hogs.

"Honey, if I quit using lard, what in the world am I going use? I don't see anything on those charts that we're used to eating. What are we going to do?"

Kayla felt sorry for her remembering when she left home and arrived in Greenville. Jones Cafeteria served pork and beef but most of the greens were new to her. She never saw collards on the line. She adjusted over time and thankfully didn't fall victim to fast food.

She'd raised her children on healthy diets and it became their way of life. Her mama and daddy were in their early seventies. It was going to be a blow to them. It was like they were going to have to start all over again.

"Mama, you'll do just fine. The nurse will give you charts and instructions and if need be, I'm sure there's a nutritional specialist on staff at Vidant Duplin that can help you."

With her daddy asleep, they took the elevator down to the dining area.

"Mama, this is all 'heart healthy' food. See, it doesn't look that bad. Let's try a garden salad with Lite Ranch Dressing."

Seated, she could tell immediately that her mama wasn't into salads but it was a start.

They were back up on the floor when her daddy awakened wanting a Pepsi.

"And don't bring me any of that diet mess. It don't taste good."

"Daddy, what did the nurse just tell you?"

"I know, Honey, I'll start on that stuff when I get home."

She replied,

"No, Daddy, you're already on it."

He acquiesced and she went back down to the food court getting a Diet Pepsi.

About two, her smartphone alerted her to a call from an unknown number with a 910-area code. Thinking it must be a call from Duplin County, she answered.

"This is Kayla... Brian?... He's okay, they've scheduled him for bypass surgery on Friday... Tomorrow afternoon? Yes, that will be fine. There are no restrictions on visitors... Yes, I'll be here... I'll see you tomorrow. Thank you for calling."

She ended the call wondering aloud how he'd gotten her number?

Her mama sheepishly responded saying,

"I gave it to him, Honey. He called about an hour after you left Sunday asking to speak to you. I told him you'd already left and he asked for your number. I hope you don't mind."

She didn't mind, any at all, but why did he want her number? He must have recognized her at the Mad Boar. That had to be it.

Her mind was in a twirl. He called before daddy's heart attack. He wanted to talk to her. She'd be in a tizzy until he came tomorrow. She wasn't sure a tizzy would cover what was happening to her nerves but she was sure that she was more than ready to see him.

"Mama, that's okay; I don't mind him having it."

You don't know how happy I am that you gave it to him. I can't believe he wanted it. My nerves are in overdrive. I must calm down. It may be nothing. It must be something? It just has to be. I'm acting like a teenager but I'm enjoying it.

Later that afternoon, Mary and Ginger stopped by. Mary didn't stay long saying they had something at church but Ginger lingered asking about dinner.

"Let's take your mama somewhere for supper, the Three Steers might be good."

Mrs. Herring declined, saying she'd stay with Raymond.

"When his supper comes, I want to be sure he eats it."

Understanding, Kayla asked if she could bring her something?

"No, Honey, are we going back to your house tonight?

"Yes, Ma'am, whenever you're ready."

"Maybe I can get something then."

Kayla was reading right through that. Her mama wanted something her daddy couldn't have.

"That's fine, Mama; we'll do our exercise first then we'll grab something before I come back."

After exercising that didn't give them much time to talk, they showered and drove to the Three Steers.

Seated, they couldn't refuse the hamburger steak with gravy over rice and fried okra they saw Peggy placing in front of a couple seated at the next table.

Ginger finally got a chance to ask?

"Your daddy just had a heart attack and you're practically bubbling over with something. Come on, give, what's going on?"

Kayla was more than ready to spill the beans. She was about to explode.

"Remember Brian, the guy at the Mad Boar? He called today. He's coming by the hospital tomorrow afternoon."

Ginger was stunned.

"Really, is he coming to see you or your daddy?"

"Both, I guess, he asked if I was going to be there. He also called asking to speak to me about an hour after we left Sunday.
"Ginger, I'm almost shaking like a leaf. I'm reacting like a teenager and enjoying every minute of it. I can't be too excited around Mary. Remember, she introduced me to Lynn."

"Apparently he did recognize you at the restaurant."

"I'm sure he did. He's probably just going to ask about the reunion, I don't know, I don't care. At least he's asking about me.
"I'll try to sort all of this out after I see him, tomorrow."

During their conversation, their meals had arrived but neither had touched theirs.

"Our meal is getting cold, let's eat."

When they finished their meal, they drove down Memorial to Parker's, stopping in front of the takeout, Kayla went in picking up a pound of barbecue, a pint of slaw, a pint of potato salad, 1 fried chicken breast, and a dozen hush puppies.

She dropped the food off at home on the way back to the hospital.

SNR

Back at the hospital, they parted saying they'd see each other tomorrow.

Arriving back at the room, she found her daddy asleep and her mama nodding. It was a little after nine.

She aroused her mama asking if she were ready to go home with her.

Her mama, seeing Raymond asleep, nodded yes and got out of the chair picking up her pocketbook.

They slipped quietly out of the room and down to valet parking. Moments later, they were on their way home.

"Honey, I hope you've got something to eat. I'm about to starve to death.

Kayla grinned knowing the fixings from Parkers would satisfy her mama's hunger.

"Mama, I picked up some barbecue. You want some of it?"
She could see a smile covering her mama's face.

"Yes, Honey, that will be all right."

Her mama was hungry, she ate a huge serving of the barbecue, slaw, the chicken breast and 5 of the hush puppies. There wasn't anything but water in the house but that didn't matter. Her mama didn't complain, she just said,

"Thank you, Honey. This hits the spot. Raymond would kill me if he knew what I was eating."

Kayla really wanted to question her mama about Brian but with her hunger satisfied, all she wanted to do was sleep. It had been a trying day for her.

She had several messages from Lynn. He needed to know what was going on. She'd really been ignoring him for almost a week now.

On Facebook, she messaged that her father had suffered a heart attack and was in Greenville.

He's scheduled for triple bypass surgery on Friday. Mama is here and staying with me. I don't know how long daddy will be in the hospital. I'll take them home when he gets out. It's been a long day. I'll share more later. K

That was probably unfair not sharing more but at that point, it would have to be enough. Her excitement about seeing Brian tomorrow overshadowed Lynn's need to know. He'd been gone 2 long years and her life was filled with nothing but loneliness and emptiness. Even if Lynn came home Christmas, he was going back and truthfully, he didn't seem to know when he might return to the states.

At 48, she was ripe for picking and maybe, just maybe, Brian might be the picker. She fell asleep and was immediately in Brian's arms

Thursday morning, Kayla was up before light. She was much too excited to sleep. Dreaming about Brian all night had been more than therapeutic, it

was too exhilarating to explain or contain. She was best described as, bubbling all over.

After getting Mr. Coffee going, she showered and dressed before driving up Memorial to the McDonald's at the intersection with Arlington. In the drive-thru, she picked up 2 big breakfasts with pancakes and bacon. She knew that would put happy in her mama.

When she returned, her mama was up and enjoying a cup of coffee. The aroma of bacon arrived with Kayla and her mama was more than ready for breakfast.

"Lordy, Honey, your daddy would skin me alive it he knew what I had for supper last night and what I'm about to have for breakfast.

"Don't you ever breathe a word of this to him."

Kayla, sitting the two big breakfasts on the table replied,

"Mama, I wouldn't dare. He'd make me go right out and get him some good food too."

Honestly, Mama, I don't know what you're going to do when you get him home. He'll have to eat what you put in front of him but what are you going to do?"

Her mama, finishing a piece of bacon, laughed, saying,

"I don't have a clue. I'll probably go crazy until he goes back to work and then, I can't do a lot of frying. He'll be on to me as soon as he walks in the house. I guess I'll have to eat what he eats until I go to the drugstore to get his prescriptions filled. Every time I'm over towards Kenansville, I'll stop by Hwy 55 before coming home."

"I'd be scared to stop by Woody's; somebody would see me and tell your daddy."

Finishing their breakfast, they left a little before eight arriving at the hospital fifteen-minutes later.

Walking in the room, they found Mr. Herring fit to be tied. They'd brought his breakfast but there wasn't anything he'd eat but the toast.

"This stuff hasn't got any taste at all. They brought me grits but no butter, no salt, no gravy. How can anybody eat grits, naked?"

Kayla felt sorry for her daddy but there wasn't anything she could, or would, do. He was going to have to adjust or die and she wanted no part of him dying. Too many people loved him

Once her mama was settled, she left saying she was going by her office to check in.

"Mama, I'll be back around noon. You should be just fine but if you need me, just call. I'm no more than 15 minutes away."

"Honey, didn't you say that Brian was coming by?"

"Yes, Mama, he said after lunch. I look for him around two. I'll be back long before then. If he comes before I get back, and wants to see me, I'll come back then."

She wasn't going to say anymore in front of her mama or daddy but she wasn't going to miss seeing Brian.

Mr. Newbold was out front when she walked into the office.

"Kayla, I didn't expect to see you. How is your father?"

She smiled replying,

"Mad at the world. They have him on a bland diet and he's about to go crazy or he's driving us crazy. Seriously, he's stabilized and they have him scheduled for bypass surgery in the morning. The doctor says that with the robotic surgery, he should be up and walking around Monday or Tuesday."

He replied that his uncle had the surgery last year and he was up walking 2 days later.

"That robotic surgery is really amazing. You go back and be with your family. We'll manage without you a few more days but please let us know if you need anything."

There was no way she could have ever had a better boss. No one could.

She'd texted Mary asking about lunch and they met at CPW's enjoying pasta salads.

Hiding her excitement about Brian was almost more than she was capable of but trying hard, she managed to appear subdued and concerned only about her father.

SNR

Knowing the clock was ticking, she was back in the room by one-fifteen. There was no way she was not going to be there when he arrived.

It was extremely evident that lunch hadn't gone well and her daddy was more than upset.

"Daddy, do you remember Ginger telling you about her father's blood pressure shot through the roof and how hard it was for him to adjust to a new lifestyle? With medication, he's stable now but he's still on a restricted diet and will be for the rest of his life."

He remembered but didn't want to talk about it, he was hungry. Hungry for what he wanted to eat. Not that mess they'd sent up to him.

It was almost two when her smart phone alerted her to a call. It was Brian.

"This is Kayla…No, it's fine, come on up… we'll be waiting… Okay, bye."

She knew they were looking right at her.

"It was Brian, he's on his way up. He was in the lobby."

Before the questions could fly, there was a light knock on the door and Kayla responded saying,

"Come in."

Brian walked in wearing a sports coat, tie, and slacks walking first over to the bed greeting Mr. Herring.

"What's this I hear about you being sick or something? Seriously, Sir, how are you doing?"

Her daddy replied, saying,

"Brian, it's good to see you. Me? I'd be better if they'd give me something to eat. That stuff they're trying to give me ain't fit for the hogs."

Laughing, Brian turned addressing her mama.

"Mrs. Herring, how are you, Ma'am?"

"Brian, I've been better but Kayla's doing a good job taking care of me. How are you, son?"

"My health is good, Mrs. Herring. Thank you for asking."

Now he was walking towards Kayla. He reached out placing his hands on her shoulders and leaned forward kissing her tenderly on her cheek.

The sensation was like a bolt of lightning. The shock was there but the pleasure of his touch overwhelmed the shock, the aroma of his aftershave was so masculine but oh so beckoning.

"Kayla, it's so nice to see you again. It's been much too long. You're beautiful, but then, you always were. I hope you're doing well."

Her senses were beginning to stabilize but she was far from being well. He'd blown her away, totally away. She was sure that he was going to but her anticipation wasn't remotely close to the reality, the sensation, the feelings that rushed, rampart, though her whole being.

Regaining her composure, she replied,

"I'm okay under the circumstances I'm doing well. You look as if life has been very good for you. It's been a long time."

Smiling, he replied,

"Yes, Kayla, it's been too long. When I saw you last week, I realized how long it's been."

He had seen her; she knew he had.

"Oh, at the Mad Boar? I thought it was you but I didn't try to speak. You appeared to be in the middle of something."

"I was, the gentlemen with me are all on the same board I am at James Sprunt. We were having our monthly meeting."

He's on the board at James Sprunt too. There sure have been a lot of changes and apparently all for the good. Tell me more; I'm all ears.

"Which board are you serving on?

"The advisory board. I'd like to hear about your life over the past 20 years and share what I've been doing too. Are you possibly free to have dinner with me tonight? I have a meeting at five but it will only last about an hour. I could pick you up at seven."

She looked over at her mama, asking?

"Mama, I could drop you off at the house around six or leave you up here with Daddy until after dinner. Would that be alright with you?"

"Honey, you can just leave me here and pick me up afterwards. I'll be fine, besides, I'm sure ya'll have a lot of catching up to do."

Looking at him, she replied,

"That sounds nice, where are we going so I'll know how to dress?"

"Bobby's"

"Bobby's, you may not be able to get reservations on such a short notice."

"It won't be a problem. Okay, I've got to run. I'll pick you up at seven. I'm looking forward to our catching up."

"Let me give you directions."

Smiling, he replied,

"No need, I already know."

He already knows? Get yourself together, Kayla. This is what you were hoping for.

"Mama, why don't I take you home so you can get a nap. I'll bring you back about six."

She was pretty sure her mama could read right through what she was asking.

She could.

"Ray, if it's alright, I think I will. You can catch and nap and I can too."

Her daddy was more than ready for a nap.

"That's fine, Hon. I'll be right here when you get back."

When they arrived home, her mama beat a path straight to the refrigerator retrieving the barbecue and fixings.

"Kayla, how long's this s'pose to be in the microwave? I don't know nothing about them things."

"Let me do it mama, how much do you want to heat up?"

Her mama dished out about half of what was left and Kayla nuked it for a minute.

Leaving her mama smiling, she walked into the bedroom still unsure of what to wear? It would have to be the dress she wore two years ago or the one she'd picked out for the reunion. The emerald dress won out. If Brian was going to take her to Bobby's, she wanted to look special. She'd wear the same accessories too.

How in the world will he be able to get reservations? Lynn said that under two weeks, it was almost impossible. I'll see. Apparently, he doesn't think that he'll have a problem. I hope not. That's a perfect setting for... Setting for what, Kayla? What do you really want out of this?

She wasn't sure but she was looking forward to it. It was almost seven. She walked back into the kitchen. Nothing was out of place. Her mama had cleaned and put everything away.

She walked down the hall finding her mama fast asleep on Amy's room. There was the doorbell. He was there.

After one last quick check, she opened the door finding Brian in a Camelhair jacket, dark grey slacks, pale blue shirt and striped tie. His shoes appeared to be Black Italian loafers. He looked good enough to eat and his aftershave was all masculine but oh so inviting. She wanted to be held by him so she could be encircled with the aroma. The night was young, maybe she would be.

"Hi, Brian. You look positively handsome."

"Kayla, let me look at you. You're beautiful. Emerald green is your color."

"Would you like to come in?"

"We should get going. Our reservations are waiting."

He'd managed to get them. How in the world did he accomplish that? She was impressed but she had to admit that she'd been impressed from the moment she saw him at the Mad Boar.

A black 750i BMW awaited them. He opened the door for her and helped with the seat belt. Shutting the door, he walked about getting in and fastening his seat belt.

When he touched the start button, the beamer came alive. The surround sound filled every nook and cranny with an instrumental edition of "Faded Love." He remembered. She was more than impressed.

Dining at Bobby's with Brian

Arriving, he parked in a reserved spot near the entrance and walked around to open the door for her. He wasn't missing anything. She couldn't believe this was the same person she walked away from twenty-six years ago. He'd changed so much or it certainly seemed that way to her.

Opening the door to the restaurant, they stepped inside and were greeted by the hostess.

"Mr. Howard, we have your table waiting for you. Please follow me."

What was she hearing? His table waiting for him? Had he been there before?

They were seated in a cozy corner near the piano. The hostess introduced their waiter for the evening.

"Mr. Howard, this is John. He will be waiting on you this evening."

"John, you've waited on me before. This is my lady, Kayla."

"Yes sir, Mr. Howard, it will be a pleasure waiting on you and your lady tonight. Mr. Carraway has chosen a white zinfandel from Napa Valley to begin your evening. Shall I bring it out?"

"Yes, please do."

Kayla was completely confused. All the staff seemed to know him. How was that possible?

"Brian, I have to ask. You've been here before more than once. How did you ever hear about it?"

He waiting to respond until the waiter had poured flukes of the wine. Brian tasted it and asked Kayla to taste it too.

"It's delicious, Brian. It's so smooth, so quieting."

"John, please convey our compliments to Bobby. As usual, he's picked a great one again."

"Did I do something right?"

Bobby had walked up unannounced.

Brian chuckled while replying,

"You always do, Bobby. Good evening. This is my lady, Kayla. Actually, we dated in high school and have just run into each other and I'm so glad we did."

"Kayla, Brian's a lucky man. Any man would be. Welcome to my restaurant."

Kayla, almost to the point of blushing, accepted his compliment replying that it was so nice to see Brian again, it had been years.

Kayla's curiosity had to know.

"You're apparently friends with Mr. Carraway. How do you know him?"

"Yes, we've been friends about nine years. I met him when he operated "Carraway's" in Kinston. I used his facilities on several occasions when I met with my managers. I had two back then and now there are four. I began at the Country Squire but I liked the atmosphere at Carraway's.

"Bobby and I had drinks after one of my meetings and after that, when I needed to get away from Duplin County, I'd go there.

"Bobby had a booming business until Floyd almost ruined him. The water was six-feet deep in the restaurant.

"He opened the Broken Eagle about six months later on Heritage Street and he did okay but that wasn't his dream. He wanted a restaurant in Greenville."

He was interrupted by the waiter asking about starters?

Brian looked over at Kayla saying,

"Let's look at the menu. I hope you'll allow me time to tell you the rest of the story. We may have to see each other several times."

Kayla was ready to give him all the time he needed. She couldn't believe the transformation that had taken place in Brian. It was as if she didn't know him at all, the new him, but she remembered to good part of the old one.

"I'm sure there will be enough time. What do you suggest for starters?"

He responded, saying,

"I like the crab stack. Take a look. How does that sound?"

She agreed: The description looked positively delicious: Colossal blue crab peaks atop a mild melody of avocado and mango, combining a savory flavor in each bite.

"Yes, that would be nice, thank you."

"John, my lady and I will have that and ask Bobby to send out a white wine that will marry well with our starter."

Marry well with our starter, Brian, you don't sound remotely like you're from Duplinville.

"Brian, please tell me the rest of the story."

Brian continued,

"Bobby remained in Kinston for a couple of years but he really wanted to be back in Pitt County.

"He grew up in the Marlboro section of Farmville. His mother operated a Tastee Freez during his teen years and that's when he knew he would one day operate a restaurant.

"In his early years, he learned to cook from one of the best; Franc White. He operated the Sportsman Restaurant in Farmville and had a TV show on UNC-TV and other venues.

"When the restaurant closed, Bobby continued to sharpen his skills working in many restaurants, mostly in eastern North Carolina.

"The restaurant he opened in Kinston was already operating successfully but the operator had his fingers in a much larger enterprise and wanted out of the restaurant.

"After successful negotiations with the property owner, Bobby opened Carraways.

"Now about Bobby's"

He was interrupted again with their starters and a bottle of Tasmanian Chardonnay that was a perfect match.

John was asking about soup or salad?

Brian suggested the lettuce wedge with Bobby's special Ranch dressing.

Kayla agreed looking forward to the special house dressing.

"Where was I, oh, Bobby's. I acquired my third dealership in 2002. It's located in Mt. Olive. My financial advisor was pushing me to invest some of the profits saying if I didn't, Uncle Sam would be the proud recipient of most of it.

"Bobby was looking for financing so I suggested he put together a business plan. He'd already been working with his CPA and shared his plan with me. It included the typical: Logo, Concept, Sample Menu, Service, Design, Target Market, Location, Market Overview, Business Structure, and of course, Financials. It appeared to be well thought out."

Their salads arrived so he suggested they put Bobby aside and enjoy their meal.

While enjoying their salad, Kayla readily admitted that the house dressing was delicious, Brian asked about their main entrée?

"May I suggest the filet. Bobby does something with it. There's just enough sauce, not a jus, that takes it over the top. It's just a suggestion, please choose anything on the menu."

Kayla remembered it from before, she was more than ready to choose it.

When the waiter returned, Brian ordered the steaks,

"My lady will have the filet...

He was looking at her.

"Medium rare?"

She nodded, yes.

"With Bobby's special stuffed potatoes and cheesy asparagus."

I'll have the sixteen-ounce ribeye, medium rare, with the stuffed potato and asparagus too.
"We'd like a bottle of Lambrusco with our steaks."

"All we've done is talk about Bobby, yes, I'll finish my story, but let's talk about you. Tell me about you."

"Brian, there isn't much to tell. You met the father of my children. He turned out to have a roving eye and we divorced when Kevin, my son, was almost three and, Amy was six-months old.
"Kevin is twenty-five now. He's married and has one son, Ray. He's three. They in Concord. Kylie is the perfect wife for him.
"Amy was born in 1986. She went to ECU for two years and is now a junior at UNC-Chapel Hill."
"Me? When I graduated from ECU, I found a job in accounting at Vidant and two years later, landed a dream position as the administrative assistant to Cal Newbold, the assistant to the Vice President in Building and Grounds at the hospital.
"I couldn't have found a nicer person to work for and it's made the years just seem to float by."
There isn't that much more to share. I guess I've been mostly an introvert for the past twenty-two years."

Brian was looking into her eyes now.

"What? No dating, no men? I can't believe that, Kayla. How is that possible? You're a beautiful woman. How could you not have dated?"

How much was she going to share with him? There really wasn't that much to tell.

"Brian, after my divorce twenty-two years ago, I was determined to never let a man do what he did to me again. For the next twenty years, I held steadfast to that determination and dated no one.

"Two years ago, I was introduced to Lynn by my long-time friend, Mary Harrell. He was a perfect gentleman and when he asked me to attend a play at ECU, I accepted. In the beginning, I let my shield down just a tiny bit but allowed it to drop more and more each time we dated until it reached a point of letting him in completely

"At that point, he was on congressman Jerry Bowers' staff as a liaison. He was driving back to Wilson every week but that came to an abrupt halt when his son had an accident in France.

He's studying to be a chef. Lynn flew immediately to Paris. It was very apparent that his son would be incapacitated for a long time so Lynn found a temporary position with our embassy in Paris.

"That temporary position appears to have become more permanent. He plans to come home Christmas but will return after the holidays.

"He says he may be able to return to the US in a year or two but there's nothing poured in concrete."

"I think a lot of him but at forty-eight, I'm not sure how long I'll be willing to wait. Perhaps when I see him Christmas, it will help me to make up my mind. I've wasted over twenty years of my life, which is entirely my fault, but now, I'm ready to move on."

Their meal arrived and they spent the next half hour enjoying the delicious entrees and wine. The filet was as good as she remembered and Brian's choice of wire was perfect. As they were finishing, Brian ordered Bobby's Delight saying they would share it.

"Kayla would you like a cup of coffee?"

"That would be perfect, Brian. Thank you."

177

"Is now an appropriate time to continue your story about Bobby? My curiosity is over flowing."

He really wanted to talk about her, about them, but he continued his story.

"Bobby had put a lot of thought into the business plan and it intrigued me. I took it to my financial advisor asking him to crunch the numbers and I also shared it with three other gentlemen. We formed a financial group and speculate mostly on properties that we think will grow in value.

"A couple of months later, we met at Hilton here in Greenville and discussed Bobby's project. It included driving out here to look at the location.

"The property, ten acres, was listed for sale by a commercial realtor. The location seems a bit remote but its proximity to Rock Springs and Ironwood made it a prime location for Bobby's vision.

"I contacted, Walter LaRoque, in Kinston and he put me in touch with Russ Currie, a realtor here in Greenville. He did the property comps in the adjacent area along Hwy 43 and VOA C road.

"When all the information was gathered, I met again with my financial group and thoroughly went over Bobby's business plan again. We made the determination that it was a solid proposal and would produce excellent returns on our investment."

He was interrupted again with the arrival of their dessert and coffee.

"This is too good to ignore; I'll finish my story later."

After tasting it, Kayla readily agreed, it was delicious and the coffee, she didn't recognize the flavor.

Brian responded to her question saying,

"It's Bobby's special blend. There's some Hazelnut in there but I don't have a clue what else. I must admit, I really like it. In fact, I use it at home."

"Would you like to dance?"

Yes, she really wanted to be held by him. It had been so long, too long.

"Yes, I'd like to."

They took a few steps and were on the dance floor sharing it with two other couples.

The piano player's rendition of *I'll be seeing you*, captured the moment as Brian took her hand and pulled her gently to him. His steps were smooth, his dancing, divine, and his after shave lured her closer.

He'd changed so much; his dancing was nothing like it was so many years ago. It was as if they were dancing on a cloud. She lost all track of time. The tune changed but the tempo didn't and they danced through three more tunes before returning to their table.

She was floating in a cloud. If he was trying to revive their feelings from so long ago, he was succeeding. She was totally captured by his charm and demeanor.

Was she really captured or was her mood self-generated by the desire to be held again. A desire that had been halted two years ago with Lynn was pulled from her arms leaving her unfulfilled with consummation or completion of her feelings for him.

He looked across the table at her saying,

"Kayla, I'm in Greenville often and I'd...

His sentence was interrupted by Kayla's smart phone. It was her mama.

A worried look quickly covered her face.

No Mama, Not Another One!

"It's mama, I have to take this."

"Mama, what wrong?... No! when?... Mama, I'll be there as soon as I can... Yes, Mama, we're on our way."

"Apparently Daddy had another heart attack. We have to go."

As they were standing, Brian got the hostess attention.

"We have an emergency, put the ticket on my tab along with the usual gratuity. Tell Bobby that we had a wonderful evening. I'll talk to him later."

Brian's Beamer whisked them down Hwy 43 to Arlington and Memorial Drive. Turning left on Fairlane and into her driveway. He came to a stop and hurried around to open the door for her. Her mama was standing at the front door.

"She turned towards Brian saying,

"Brian, I had a very special evening with you. Thank you. I'm sorry but I have to get to the hospital."

He wouldn't be denied,

"I'm taking you and your mother. Go change, we'll be waiting."

She couldn't believe he was doing this but there was no time to wonder about it, she was more than happy to have him with her.

Ten minutes later, they pulled into valet parking and rushed up to her father's room. He wasn't there, he'd been taken back to CICU on the fourth floor.

The receptionist relayed that the doctors were with Mr. Herring.

"Please go to the waiting room. I'll let Dr. Erickson know that you're here."

"Kayla, I have to make a couple of calls. I'll only be a few minutes."

He walked over by the windows to make his calls.

In the waiting room, Kayla asked her mama what happened?

"Honey, they called saying it appeared that Ray and had another attack. That's about all they said before I called you. I don't know what happened but I don't have a good feeling about it. I hope the Lord will let him stay here. I don't what I'd do without him."

Tears were streaming down her face. It was the first time Kayla had ever seen her mama scared and it scared her too. They'd been together most of their lives. Going it alone would be catastrophic on either one of them.

My situation was and is entirely different. I'd only been married two years when Jeff's roving eye tore our marriage all to pieces. I was so mad, being alone with my two children didn't matter. My hatred for his actions kept loneliness at bay. Being young helped too. Mama's seventy-one. She tough as leather but if something happens to Daddy, it's going to be hard on her.

Brian was back and sitting beside her.

"It's going to be a long night, lets' take your mama downstairs and get a cup of coffee."

Her mama wasn't arguing. She was afraid of what the night would bring. They took the elevator down to the main floor and the food court.

Getting coffee and a Danish, Brian paid the cashier and they found a table over by the windows.

They allowed her mama to lead the conversation as she reminisced about the years she and Raymond had known each other.

"We got sweet on each other back in the fourth grade. I wore pigtails back then and he wouldn't let them alone. He always sat behind me. It got him in trouble a bunch of time but it never stopped him. He kept right on pulling them and I wanted him to.

"When fifth grade started, mama had cut my hair and done away with the pigtails but it didn't slow Ray up. Not even a little bit. He got to whispering stuff in my ear. I'd almost break out laughing. Mrs. Hill knew what was going on. She put up with his mess but not all of it.

"She sent him to the office a couple of times trying to scare him but it didn't work. He was right back at it when he got back.

"The seventh grade was when we really got sweet on each other. We won't just be poking fun, we were seeing each other as boy and girl. I was taking on some shape and he wasn't missing a thing.

"The eighth grade was a bunch of fun. They were teaching square dancing in the gym and we got pretty good at it. Trouble was, they were teaching other kinds of dancing too. Them slow dances is what kept us in trouble. Ray was always trying to nibble on my ears and he got caught a bunch of times but he never quit.

"At the harvest festival that fall, he kissed me the first time and Lordy, I knew I was in love. Mama told me it was puppy love but I knew better.

"The ninth grade was when…

"Will the family of Mr. Raymond Herring return to the waiting room."

They rushed up to the fourth floor finding Dr. Erickson, dressed in scrubs, waiting.

They huddled with him over by the windows.

Dr. Erickson began,

"Mr. Herring suffered another heart attack. It's not unusual but in most cases, it doesn't happen this quickly. I've assembled the team and Mr. Herring is being prepped for surgery. He's already under. We use this technique to stabilize and calm patients.

"The procedure will take three to four hours using robotic surgery. He'll be in recovery in ICU for two or three hours and remain in ICU for a day. As I told you before, he should be back in his room Saturday.

"You're welcome to stay in the waiting room but I strongly suggest that you go somewhere and get some rest. I'll talk to you after the surgery, either here or by phone."

He turned and walked towards the swinging doors.

At first, her mama wanted to stay but after thirty minutes knowing she wasn't going to see him until probably Friday afternoon, she gave in saying getting some rest would probably be the best thing.

They took the elevator down to the first floor and walked out to Valet Parking. Moments later, Brian took them back to Kayla's home.

He walked them to the door and after thanking him, her mama walked in.

"Put this number in your phone. It's my room at the Hilton. Call me if you need to go back tonight or in the morning. I'll pick you up and take you and your mother to breakfast before we go back to the hospital."

She was so appreciative of what he was doing but it wasn't his place. She started to protest but he placed his finger on her lips. Then he gently removed his finger and placed his lips on hers.

"Get some sleep; I'll see you in the morning."

"Brian, thank you. I'll see you in the morning."

Her mind was spinning when she shut the door behind her. It was almost too difficult to assimilate all that had taken place that evening.

She still didn't completely understand what Brian's connection was with Bobby's but apparently it was financial. That, plus he and Bobby seemed like close friends too.

What he did for her and her mama after the call was a thousand times more than he should have but there was no denying that she appreciated it more than he would ever know.

Yes, she would have gotten through it without him but, admittedly, going through it with him was so much better.

She knew that Lynn would walk away. He was so different from Brianl

Dressed in her pajamas, she pulled the covers up and fell asleep into his arms. Her dream would last until next morning. Exhaustion had seen to that.

SNR

She smelled coffee brewing, her mama was up. Showering and dressing quickly, she joined her mama in the kitchen. It was a little after six.

"Mama, you're up at your usual time. Did you manage to get any sleep?"

"Not much, Honey, a little here and there. I kept thinking the phone would ring but I don't guess that it ever did."

"No, Mama. That's probably good news. Brian's going to take us to breakfast and back to the hospital. What time do you want to go?"

"Right now, Honey, but I don't recon it makes any difference. We can't see Ray until they call."

"I'm going to call Brian and tell him to pick us up at seven-thirty."

"Brian, good morning, this is Kayla… Oh, okay, is seven-thirty too early for you?... That early? You're an early riser too. We'll see you at seven-thirty. I really appreciate you doing this, see you in a few."

He's been up since four and was already on the third cup of coffee waiting for my call.

Her mind was still trying to accept what was apparently happening. Was she falling back in love with Brian. If her mind didn't seem to get the message, her heart did but then, there was Lynn. What about him. He had a stake in this too even though he was four-thousand miles away. Maybe that was the problem, four-thousand miles and two-years.

The bond that existed between Lynn and her was rapidly disintegrating. It had lasted two years but was turning into dust now. Maybe she wasn't being fair to Lynn but was he being totally fair to her? He'd left her hanging. He could have come home to visit if he really loved her. She waited but he never did until now and seeing him was still three-months away.

The wait might not happen. If Brian wanted her back, she would probably be his. She longed to be loved, to be kissed, to be made love to. At forty-eight, she still was just as much woman as she ever was, probably more.

He arrived right on time. Kayla met him at the door. He was dressed in a collared polo, slacks, and some type of casual walking shoes, he looked as handsome as he did the night before.

"Good morning, Brian, we're ready, thank you so much for taking us. I feel like it's really putting you out. You must have tons of other things that you need to do."

"Good morning, Kayla. You look especially nice this morning. Other things? That's what I'm paying my managers and legal staff to do. I much prefer being with you and your mother. I want to be here to lean on if you need someone."

Her mama stepped through the door, ready to go.

"Good morning, Mrs. Herring. Are you ready for breakfast?"

Her mama replied.

"Good morning, Brian, yes, I'm more than ready. I sure don't want to eat that stuff they're serving in the hospital."

Helping them into his car, he asked?

"Kayla, you're much more familiar with Greenville than me. Where would you like to have breakfast?"

That was a given, if it were her choice, it would always be the Three Steers.

When they arrived, Brian commented,

"I've never been here although I've driven by it dozens of times."

Kayla replied,

"You'll come back. Just wait and see."

When they were seated, Kayla told Brian to order eggs any way he wanted them saying they would be perfect.

He replied,

"That will be different, most times, the eggs are never right but I make do."

Kayla and her mama ordered, soft-scrambled eggs, bacon, grits, and wheat toast to go with their coffee that was already in front of them.

Brian looked at Kayla, remarking,

"Soft-scrambled, really? I want to see that. Waitress, I'll have two eggs over easy with link sausage, are your hash brown purchased or made here?"

Surly replied,

"They're made every morning using left-over baked potatoes from the night before and they're seasoned just right."

"With onions?"

Yes, sir, with caramelized onions."

He responded,

"That's perfect and I'll have dry wheat toast too."

When their orders arrived, Brian's eyes darted back and forth from his perfectly fried eggs to their soft-scrambled ones that appeared to be perfectly prepared.

Each time Surly stopped by to freshen their coffee, Brian told her to tell the cook that his eggs were perfect. His whole meal was.

With breakfast behind them, Brian drove them to the hospital using Valet Parking.

Up on the fourth floor, the receptionist told them that Mr. Herring was still unconscious.

"That's expected. Some patients awaken a couple of hours after surgery while others take three, four, even five hours. Dr. Erickson is in surgery now. He'll talk with you when he comes out. That's probably about an hour from now. Please make yourselves comfortable in the waiting room."

They hadn't been seated thirty minutes when Kayla's smart phone alerted her to a call. It was from Lynn. She excused herself and walked out into the corridor by the windows.

"Lynn, you rarely call. To what do I owe the pleasure?... The Rivera, that sounds nice, when's he leaving?... Oh, you're going with him. How long will he be there?... Two years? That sounds like pleasant experience to me.

The background interrupted their conversation.

"Dr. Hardy, dial 1-9 please. Dr. Hardy, 1-9 please."

"I'm in the hospital... No, daddy had a heart attack Tuesday, he was flown here from Kenansville... No, that's a few miles from home... No, he was scheduled for surgery this morning but he suffered another heart attack yesterday and they moved the surgery up to three this morning... Yes, he's in recovery and will remain in ICU probably until tomorrow... Mama's here, my siblings should begin arriving sometime today... No, we're fine, Brian Howard is here with us... He was one of my classmates; the one I dated in high school and the first two years of college before I moved to Greenville... He heard about Daddy's heart attack and was concerned. Mama gave it to him last week. She was sure it had something to do with the reunion... Yes, I finally made up my mind, I'm going, I mailed my RSVP last week... We haven't had a chance to talk about that but I'm sure he's going... We'll be fine, Lynn. Hopefully he'll be able to go home next week... He's seventy-one, Lynn, after the second heart attack, I doubt that they'll let him go back... Okay, I understand, are you still coming home Christmas... Let me know, I have some planning to do, bye."

He didn't mention love and neither did she. In fact, as best as she could recall, the word had never been mentioned.

He was upset, it was easy to tell that he was but he had nothing to be upset about. He'd flown the coop two years ago and now he was chasing his son all over Europe. From the reluctant sound in his voice, she was already writing his Christmas visit off to.

Just as she was getting ready to tell her mama and Brian about the call, Dr. Erickson walked in asking them to join him in the corridor.

"Mr. Herring is still in recovery. There's nothing to be concerned about. It's perfectly normal. We did a triple-bypass procedure with the minimally invasive robotic technique pioneered here. With only three small incisions, your father should be up walking around by Monday. We'd really like to get him up on Sunday.

"As we discussed before, he will have to change his lifestyle, mainly his diet. The dietitian specialist will go over all that again with you. We'll discuss him being able to go back to work later. Meanwhile, let's get him up and moving around. You should be able to visit him later today. The receptionist will let you know."

"Any questions? Good."

He turned and walked back towards the double doors.

Kayla and her mama had plenty of questions but there would be time for that later.

Back in the waiting room, Kayla shared her call from Lynn with them. There was no reason she was aware of to keep the call from Brian.

"Mama, Lynn says his son has the opportunity to study under a world-renowned chef for two years on the Rivera. He's going to accompany him there. I won't tell you that it doesn't concern me that he'll traipse all over the globe after his son but can't fly back to the US to see me. I'm not sure he's coming for Christmas. He sounded iffy to me."

Brian listed intently but made no effort to play a part in the conversation.

About eleven-thirty, he suggested that they get some lunch asking where they would like to go?

Knowing they wouldn't be able to see her father until probably mid-afternoon, she was ready for a break.

"Brian, there's a restaurant across Farmville Boulevard called the Seahorse. They have a country buffet."

Her mama's ears perked right up hearing "Country Buffet." She was more than ready to go.

Walking across Farmville Boulevard was a No-No! Anyone that did, took their lives in their hands.

They rode the elevator down to the main level and walked out to Valet Parking. Five minutes later, they parked near the Seahorse and walked to the entrance. Brian held the door for them and the hostess led them to a booth at the opposite end of the dining room.

Taking their beverage orders, their waitress asked if they were doing the buffet? They were.

"I'll bring the plates and bowls out, enjoy."

Her mama led the way right past the salad bar to the hot food section loading her plate up with country-style steak and gravy over rice, collards, macaroni and cheese, fried chicken and a piece of fish.

Kayla followed, choosing the collards, sweet potato casserole, fried chicken and a piece of the country-style steak.

Brian chose the country-style steak with gravy over rice, sweet potato casserole, cabbage and a piece of the fried chicken.

Back at the booth, her mama eagerly began working her way through the bountiful feast she'd plated paying little attention to the conversation between Kayla and Brian.

"Kayla, I'm probably going to be here through the weekend. If all goes well with your father, I'd like to take you out again tomorrow night or Sunday night but only if your father is getting along, okay."

She was more than ready to go out with him again and accepted if her daddy was improving.

"Brian, I'd like that. We'll see how daddy does. Donna, Linda, and Ander will be coming in sometime over the weekend and my children will be coming in too. He'll have all the company he can possibly deal with."

Her mama, still apparently oblivious to their conversation made her way back to the buffet for her second assault. This time, she began with more collards, the cabbage, a drumstick, and more country-style steak. This time of mashed potatoes.

Karla and Brian were content with their first trip. She'd been before and knew about the cake.

As her mama was finishing up her second plate, their waitress asked about cake.

Her mama stopped in midstream.

"Cake, what cake?"

"Today, we have Strawberry, Lemon, Hershey Bar, Pineapple, Coconut, Old-Fashioned Chocolate and our favorite, Butter Pecan."

Her mama wanted to taste all of it but settled on the Coconut.

Brian looked at Kayla, asking,

"You've been here before, what are you going to choose?"

There was no question for her.

"Butter Pecan, it's to die for. One slice is enough for us."

He looked at the waitress saying,

"1 slice of Butter Pecan more coffee please."

When their cake arrived, her mama eagerly tasted the Coconut cake.

"This taste like Mama's. Lordy, she made a fine Coconut Cake."

From the look on Brian's face, Kayla knew the Coconut Cake would have to work very hard to be as good as their Butter Pecan."

"Kayla, this is delicious. I wish we could take a slice to your father. I know that he'd enjoy it."

She agreed but said that it would probably be a long-long while before he'd get to taste any kind of dessert. The doctor was very emphatic about that.

When they finished, he dropped them off at the entrance saying he had a couple of errands to run but should be back before five.

"Kayla, if you need me, call. I'll come right back. I won't be that far away."
Back in the waiting room, her mama wanted to know what was going on between them.

"He seems very interested in you and you've got that twinkle in your eyes that I haven't seen in years. There was just a hint of it last weekend but there's a whole bunch more now. Tell your mama what's going on, Honey."

Just as she started to tell her, Donna and Cliff walked in saying Sandy was in Texas and Jerry was in Tennessee.

The next hour was spent telling the whole story to them. Kayla knew it would be to do repeatedly until everyone had heard it.

The part about the diet worried Donna.

"Mama, how in the world are you going to get Daddy to eat anything without salt and no hog lard, Mama, what in the world are you going to do?"

"Donna, it's going to be a challenge, but if that's what I have to do to keep your daddy alive, that's what I'm going to do. I ain't nowhere near ready to get along without him. We've been together way too long."

A little before four, Ander and Nara walked in. When asked about Ander, Jr, they replied that he was in Big Surf, California.

"He's engaged to be married Valentines. He's promised to bring Mariana to meet us over the Christmas holidays."

Kayla shared the whole story with them knowing she'd have to do it again when Linda came and then again when Amy and Kevin arrived.

About four-thirty, the receptionist came in saying that Mr. Herring was awake. They could go down and see him but only three at the time.

Donna and Cliff accompanied their mama first.

When they came back, Kayla went with Ander and Nara.

Their daddy was awake and acknowledged them but he was still groggy and understood little that they said. Knowing it was taxing for him, they left after only a few minutes saying they would check on him later.

When they walked back into the waiting room. Brian had just walked in creating puzzling stares from everyone except Kayla and her mama.

Kayla made no attempt at explaining his presence. There would be plenty of time for that later.

Addressing Donna and Ander, she asked if they were staying overnight? They were and already had rooms at the Holiday Inn Express on Moye Boulevard, their spouses were there. Plans were to drive back Sunday night if their father was doing okay.

Kayla's smartphone alerted her to a call from Kevin, they'd just arrived and were checking in at the Holiday Inn Express. They'd already been in contact with Donna and Ander.

"Kevin, you know you're welcome at home. There's plenty of room… Okay, I understand, we'll all up here on the fourth floor in the ICU waiting room in the heart center… Yes, we'll look for you about five-thirty… I love you too, bye."

She got her mama's attention telling her that Kevin and Kylie had arrived.

"They're coming up about five-thirty."

She looked at Brian, saying,

"I told you about Kevin, he'll be here with Kylie about five-thirty."

Brian responded, saying,

"You look tired. Are you sure you're, all right?"

He seems to really care. Finally, there was someone that cares about me, about how I feel, I'm so ready for some of that.

She responded saying,

"I'm tired, but I'm okay. Maybe we can break away and get something to eat after Kevin gets here."

"We'll do that. You need some time away from this. Let me take you somewhere that you can relax and turn loose for a little while."

She had no idea where that could be but she was more than ready to go.

Kevin and Kylie arrived about five-fifteen saying they'd left Ray with a sitter, and after greeting everyone in the ever-growing group, they listened intently as Kayla told the story another time. When she finished she wasn't sure how closely they listened? They appeared more interested in the man sitting beside Kevin's mother.

She'd introduced Brian as a friend but to them, he appeared to be more than just a friend.

"Are you ready to go grab a bite to eat?"

She was more than ready, telling the others that they would be back a little later in the evening. Without giving her family a chance to ask questions, they slipped out the door, down the elevator and out to Valet Parking.

Brian drove west on Farmville Boulevard rapidly reaching seventy miles per hour. She had no clue where he was taking her but knew that she was ready to be with him.

He exited on Wesley Church Road and made a right on Moye-Turnage Road. It became Wilson Street at Farmville's city limits. He continued until he reached Main Street. Turning left, he found parking near the Plank Road Restaurant.

Inside, his reservations were waiting and they were seated at a table for two by one of the walls. It was busy but not loud. The ambiance was warm and inviting.

He ordered the twenty-ounce porterhouse saying it was big enough for both. She chose the whipped cream potatoes and steamed broccoli. He chose the garlic mashed potatoes and seasoned vegetables along with a bottle of Duplin Winery's Carolina Red.

She was amazed, how in the world did he find this place? She'd heard Mary talk about it but had never been. She hoped that Mary and Woody didn't come in.

She really didn't want to have to explain Brian to them. She'd do it later if it became necessary. Right then, all she wanted to do was enjoy Brian's company and a nice quiet meal but it wasn't to be.

Chief of Police, Jesse Monk and his wife, Melva came in and he immediately spotted Kayla.

Walking over, he spoke saying it had been a long time since he seen her and was asking about how she'd been.

There was nothing to do but make introductions that she knew would go straight to Mary.

"Chief Monk, this is a family friend, Brian Howard. My father had a heart attack on Tuesday and he's here to give my family his support."

"Brian, this is Chief of Police, Jesse Monk and his wife, Melva."

They offered their condolences and moved to their table. It didn't matter, the harm was already done. Mary would know about Brian before the night was over.

Moments later, Randy Walters from Farmville Furniture came in and seeing, Brian, walked over to greet him.

Brian stood, introducing him to Kayla.
"Randy, this is Kayla Herring from Greenville. She and I went to school together. Her father suffered a heart attack earlier in the week and I'm up here to offer them my support."

"Kayla, this is Randy Walters from Farmville Furniture. He's looking for some pieces for my home."

Randy offered his condolences and excused himself, moving away to his reserved table.

"How did you find this restaurant and Farmville Furniture?"

She'd been in the store once but realized that their prices were way above her pocketbook.

"I was looking for some pieces for my home and the administrator at Vidant Duplin suggested I come over and talk with Randy.

"We had lunch here and I enjoyed it enough to bring you."

Kayla's mind was spinning. Her world was getting smaller. Brian was all around her and she didn't know it.

She responded saying,

"It's really a wonderful place. I'm looking forward to our meal."

Just as she said it, their meal arrived. The steak was huge. Brian halved the steak giving her all the tenderloin. It didn't go unnoticed.

The wine he'd chosen was perfect. The meal was perfect. The place was perfect. He was perfect.

She looked across the table asking?

"Are you going to tell me the rest of the story?"

"Bobby's?"

She laughed, replying,

"Yes, that story."

"After meeting with my investment group, I made the determination to handle the property purchase through one of my corporations and then I would lease the land to our investment group and we'd finance the building of the restaurant and other costs required to get it open and operating.

I made a personal loan to Bobby to cover the operating expenses for the first six-months. The loan was set up in an account for Bobby to draw from as needed. As it turned out, he only drew from the account for three-months. From the beginning, the restaurant was successful and required no further financing.

"Now you know my involvement in Bobby's. We've become friends and when I need to get away from my corporations, I go to Bobby's. Sometimes, he can break away and we get to spend some time together over drinks. Most times, I don't order, he sends out whatever he's testing and it's always delicious

"Now that I know you enjoy it too. You'll always be with me when you're available."

When I'm available, Brian, I'm always available. All you have to do is call. I'll be waiting.

That's what she wanted to say but wouldn't. She didn't want to seem to be jumping into his arms but she felt as if she were already.

"Please call me, Brian, I've love to go back to Bobby's with you."

They finished their meal sharing a slice of the Chocolate Confusion Cake and cups of steaming hot coffee.

Leaving, they drove back to the heart center finding her mother more than ready to get some rest. They took the elevator down to the entrance retrieving Brian's Beamer at Valet Parking.

Arriving at her home, she was surprised to find a large FedEx box on the steps. Opening the door, she let her mother in and turned to say goodbye to Brian.

He replied,

"Don't say goodbye, I'll be here at least through Sunday night and longer if you want me to. What time do I pick you up in the morning?"

"Brian, you don't have to do this but I really appreciate what you're doing. Eight 0'clock?"

"I'll be here at eight."

He leaned forward kissing her gently on the lips. Backing away, he looked into her eyes, turned and walked away.

Inside, she locked the door and took the box into the kitchen sitting it on the counter. The return address offered no clue. Opening it, she was totally surprised to find a dozen red roses and a note from Lynn saying he should have been more explicit.

I will be home for Christmas and I'm looking forward to spending it with you. Lynn

She placed the roses in a vase thinking,

The flowers are beautiful but Lynn, but you may have let me slip through your fingers.

Lying in bed, sleep refused to come. How had her, ever-so-dull life suddenly become so complicated? For the past twenty-years, she'd closed the door to every man that tried to get in and now, she'd cracked it open just a little and two men were vying for her attention, her love.

Brian was here and doing everything right. Lynn was four-thousand miles away and seemingly doing almost nothing right. The roses were nice but that's the first time since he left that he's done anything like that. He's telling me that he can't come back to the states but has no problem following his son anywhere he goes. Something's wrong with that scenario. Lynn, what are you not telling me?

When sleep finally did overtake her. It was Brian, not Lynn, walking through fields of Lavender with her by his side. Lynn tried to stop them but the gatekeeper wouldn't allow him to pass through.

A little before six, she got up, plugged in Mr. Coffee and took her shower and dressed while waiting for the coffee to make.

When she was ready, she knew the coffee was from the aroma wafting down the hall.

The door to Amy's room was open. She knew her mama was already in the kitchen and probably hungry too. She was.

"Good morning, Mama. How did you sleep?"

"Like a log, Honey and Lordy, I'm hungry enough to eat a barrel of biscuits."

"Mama, Brian will be by at eight to take us to breakfast and then to the hospital. We'll have to wait until then for breakfast."

Her mama was hearing but she wasn't listening.

"Honey, where's the bread and peanut butter. I've got to have something to tide me over."

Kayla retrieved the peanut butter and bread for her mama and it only took a couple of minutes for her to throw together a sandwich.

"Them's pretty roses. Brian give them to you last night?"

This was going to be interesting,

"No Mama, Lynn sent them to me."

"Lynn, you mean that fellow that's been gone for two years?"

"Yes, Ma'am, one in the same."

"He's way out yonder across the big pond. When did you say that he was coming to see you?"

"Christmas, Mama."

"What are you going to do about Brian? He's wants to hook back up with you too. He's here and doing real good. Ya'll always did make a handsome couple."

Kayla could feel the walls closing in around her. How was she going to answer her mama when she didn't know the answer herself?

She had to tell her something. Her mama wouldn't let it go until she did.

"Mama, it's complicated, Lynn came into my life when I needed someone. Now he's four-thousand miles away.
"Brian's here now and would have been here earlier if he'd known that I would see him.
"Mama, like I said, it's complicated."

"Honey, Brian's loved you all his life. You know that's true. Otherwise, he'd been grabbed up a long time ago. Honey, I ain't trying to get into your business but, Honey, you left him, he didn't leave you."

She knew her mama was right. She probably was ugly to Brian when she left, no, she was ugly. She had to agree with her mama.

"Mama, I don't know what I'm going to do. Right now, I'm worried about Daddy. Brian' here and I really appreciate what he's doing but my love life will have to remain on hold until Daddy's back home."

Her mama turned her attention back to her peanut butter sandwich. Apparently, she thought she'd said enough.

Kayla busied herself dusting until the doorbell rung about five-of- eight.

She opened the door knowing Brian would be standing there, he was.

"Good morning, are you and your mother ready for breakfast?"

"Good morning, Brian. Yes, we are."

She turned to call her mama but she was standing right behind her. Apparently, she was still hungry and ready for breakfast.

Turning back to him, she replied,

"Yes, we're ready."

They arrived at the Three Steers a few minutes later. Seated, he allowed them to order first.

Her mama wanted soft-scrambled eggs again with bacon, grits, and a biscuit.

Kayla ordered a bacon omelet, OJ, and wheat toast.

Brian chose the sausage omelet with OJ, and wheat toast.

As before, their breakfast was delicious eliciting a comment from Brian, "When I'm in Greenville, this is where I'll always have breakfast."

Kayla's phone alerted her to a call from Donna wanting to know what time she was going to the hospital?

"We're having breakfast; we'll be there in half an hour... Room 507?... Okay, we'll see you in a little while, bye."

She shared that they'd moved her daddy to a room earlier that morning.

"That's a good sign. He'll be awake when we get there. Donna said that Ander and Amy were there too."

Not rushing, they finished their breakfast and Brian took them to the heart center leaving his Beamer with Valet Parking.

Walking onto Room 507, they found Mr. Herring, wide awake and talking up a storm but a storm was really brewing. He was hungry and wanted country ham.

Kayla walked over to the bed looking sternly into her daddy's eyes.

"Daddy, do you have any idea what you've just gone through?"

He replied,

"Yes, Honey, I had surgery, now I'm hungry and don't want any of that slop they're putting out here."

"You don't realize that you had another heart attack here, do you?"

That let most of the air out of his sail.

"Another heart attack, what are you talking about?"

"Daddy, you had another one night before last and they rushed you into surgery in the middle of the night. The surgeon said that if you hadn't been here... Daddy, you would have been gone."

Now, he was quiet as a mouse. Tears formed in his eyes.

"Honey, I'm sorry, I didn't know. I can't help it if I'm hungry. I reckon I can eat that slop but I don't want to."

"Daddy, I know it's not what you want but do. Do You want to live? Do you want to stay here with us? If you do, you're got to do exactly what they say. Now, tell me what you're going to do. If you want to be stubborn, I'm going home and get ready for your funeral."

Tears were flowing down his cheeks.

"I ain't ready to leave ya'll yet. I'll do what them doctors say. I promise I will."

She leaned over wiping the tears from her daddy's eyes.

"That's better, Daddy, we're not ready for you to leave either."

She stepped back giving her mama a chance to get her hug knowing she wasn't about to tell her husband what she had for breakfast but he asked.

Kayla grinned wondering what her mama was going to tell him but she did good.

"Ray, I had a peanut butter sandwich and coffee."

She didn't lie to him but she didn't tell him the whole story.

Kayla knew that sooner or later, probably the minute they got back home, that her mama was going to have to face up to what was in front of her. She was going to have to learn to eat a totally new heart-healthy diet.

She wasn't going to say anything to her until she was ready to take daddy home. A few more days of eating what she wanted to wouldn't hurt.

The morning slipped by and her daddy's lunch arrived. He didn't say a word but ate everything on his plate.

Donna said that she was going to Logan's for lunch, did anyone want to join her? Ander said he'd like to go and her mama was all for it.

Amy volunteered to stay with her grandfather saying she'd get something later.

Kayla said that she and Brian would probably walk down to the cafeteria which they did.

After their big breakfast, they chose salads and water. Kayla showed the cashier her ID but Brian refused to let her pay.

Finding seats in the middle of the dining room, Brian commented how empty it was.

She replied that on weekends, they operated with a skeleton crew.

"During the week, it's packed."

She wondered when he was going to ask, now he was.

"When are you coming down for the reunion?"

She'd planned to go down Saturday morning and return home Sunday morning. Now she was sure she'd go down on Friday after work."

"I'll drive down Friday after work and probably drive home Sunday morning."

"Will you go with me?"

"Yes, I'd like that."

"Will you have dinner with me Friday night?"

Of course, she would.

"Yes, what time?"

"What time will you get to your parents?"

"Between six-thirty and seven."

"Seven-thirty?"

"That's fine, where are we going?"

"The Mad Boar or the Country Squire. Do you have a preference?"

She hadn't been to the Country Squire in years but really enjoyed the one time she'd been to the Mad Boar. That's where they saw each other.

"The Mad Boar."

"Done, I'll make reservations. I'd really like for you to attend church with me Sunday before you come back. We could have brunch at the County Squire afterwards."

Church, what other surprises are you hiding from me?

"That sounds nice, yes, I'd like that. Where do you attend church?"

"Grove Presbyterian Church in Kenansville."

'That's a beautiful old church, I visited there once, years ago."

It was time for them to get back. Her children would be wondering where they were. She was sure they were waiting for an opportunity to question her about this man that seemed more than casually interested in their mother.

Walking back into the room, they found her mama, Donna, and Ander, back but Amy gone.

Donna shared that Amy had gone to Bojangles for lunch. She'll be back in an hour or two.

Kevin and Kylie walked in greeting everyone. Kayla could see that Kevin was still curious about Brian. She'd have to find the right opportunity to tell him about Brian. After all, he was just trying to look after his mother.

Dr. Erickson came by a little after three. After studying the chart, he asked her daddy about lunch?

Her daddy could only respond.

"It ain't what I wanted but it will do."

The doctor responded,

"That's what I want to hear. You're showing remarkable improvement. Keep it up and I'll have you out of here by Tuesday, Wednesday at the latest. Any questions?"

Her daddy had questions but already knew the answers.

"No, Doctor, I guess I'm good."

Doctor Erickson looked first at her mother and then at her. They greeted him but neither questioned him.

Within a few minutes, her daddy was asleep and her mama wanted to be.

"Kayla, can you take me to the house so I can get a nap. I would appreciate it."

She looked at Brian who had gotten up.

"Yes, Mama, we'll take you. Donna are you and Ander going to stay around for a while?"

She responded saying that Linda had called and would be there any minute.

"Take your time, Mama. Some of us will be here."

When they arrived at her home, Brian suggested that she take a nap too.

"You've had a lot on you. You need to rest. I'll come by to pick you up at five-thirty."

She knew he was right but wanted to protest. He would have none of it. Again, he kissed her tenderly on the lips and was gone.

Inside, she closed and locked the door knowing that her mama was already in Amy's room. Checking, she found her lying across the bed and appeared to be already asleep.

She walked to the den and stretched out in her favorite Lazy-Boy recliner.

In minutes, she was in dreamland, walking hand-hand with Brian. She wasn't sure where she was but it didn't matter, she was with him.

A few minutes after five, she awakened and refreshed. She was all smiles; her dreams of being with Brian were too wonderful to describe. Nothing like the ones she'd suffered through for so many long years. He's put a smile back on her face and awakened the love and desires, smoldering deep in her heart. If she hadn't fallen in love, she was teetering on the threshold.

She hurriedly checked her makeup before awakening her mama.

"Mama, it's almost five-thirty. Brian will be here any minute to take us back to the hospital."

Moments later, her mama was up and ready to go. Kayla was amazed at her resiliency.

I hope that I'm just half that spry when I'm seventy-one.

The doorbell rung, it would be Brian.

"Mama, Brian's here."

"Brian, come in."

He stepped into the entranceway looking directly into her eyes. He didn't have to say a word. She knew what was in his heart.

Her mama interrupted the moment.

"Hey, Brian, thank you for coming to get us, son."

When they arrived at the heart center, they found Mr. Herring eating his supper. It looked horribly bland was he wasn't complaining.

Kayla asked if Linda remembered Brian.

"Vaguely, Mama; Brian, I'm Linda, Kayla's younger sister. It's been a long time."

He responded, saying,

I remember but you were a tomboy back then. You've turned into a pretty lady. Almost as pretty as Kayla."

His compliment didn't slip past anyone there. Especially Kevin and Amy. This man really liked their mother and she liked him too.

Amy asked,

"Mother, didn't you say that you and Brian went to school together?"

"Yes, Amy, all the way from the fourth grade."

Kayla knew her mama was going to but she couldn't stop her.

"And they were sweet on each other the whole time. Fact is, they were sweet on each other until Kayla moved up here to go to school."

Keven wondered and asked,

"What happened. You just stop seeing each other?"

"Distance, Kevin, back then, it seemed like a long way from our little corner of Duplin County to Greenville."

She hoped that would satisfy their curiosity but was sure that she'd hear more questions later.

Her phone alerted her to a call from Mary.
She stepped out into the corridor answering it.

"Hi Mary… Yes, I'm in his room with my family… Yes, Mama, Kevin, Amy, my older sister, Donna, younger sister, Linda, older brother, Ander and Brian, a friend from back home… It's kind of crowded but you're welcome to… No, they'll be here until tomorrow afternoon… He's doing much better, the doctor said he hoped to release him Tuesday…I'm sorry I'm going to miss you but thank you for calling, bye."

She was sure that Chief Monk or Melva had called her. That had to be why they were on their way to the hospital. She wanted Mary to meet her family but wasn't ready for her to meet Brian. She'd see right through them and would know what was happening.

Just as she started back into the room, Ginger stepped off the elevator hailing her.

"Ginger, thanks for stopping by. You'll get to meet most of my family."

Inside the room, introductions were made but the one of most interest to Ginger was the man she'd seen in the Mad Boar a week ago.

"Ginger, this is Brian. We went to school together and he's a friend of the family."

She could tell that Ginger detected the chemistry between them but left it alone. Instead, she hugged Kayla's mama first and then walked over to the bed speaking to her daddy.

"Mr. Herring, you've gone to a lot of trouble just to check out Greenville. Kayla and I would have driven you up here if you'd asked."

Laugher filled the room. Her father appreciated Ginger's humor too, replying,

"Ginger, I'll keep that in mind next time I get a hankering to come to Greenville. It's nice to see you again. Thank you for coming by."

A little after six, Donna and Cliff took her mother out to dinner. Ander and Nora left shortly after going to the Long Horn. Kevin and Kylie said they were going to the Olive Garden. There were no takers leaving Kayla, Brian, and Amy with Mr. Herring and he'd dropped off to sleep.

"Mama, why don't you and Brian get something to eat. I'll stay here with granddaddy."

"Are you sure, Amy. I don't feel right leaving you here alone."

Amy laughed, saying,

"Mother, I'm a junior in college, I'll be fine."

She looked at Brian, asking?

"Are you ready?"

He held out his hand and they walked out the door.

"What would you like to eat?"

She looked at him saying,

"Hamburger steak, rice and gravy."

"And where do we find that?"

"Three Steers."

"Say no more, we're on our way."

Arriving, they found it busy but Lucille seated them in the front dining room by a window.

"Patsy will be your waitress; enjoy your meal."

"What may I get you to drink?"

They looked at Patsy replying,

"Coffee please."

In moments, she was back with their coffee asking if they were ready to order.

Brian replied,

"Yes, we are. Kayla, you go first."

"I'll have the country-style steak over rice with gravy. I'd like the string beans too."

Brian said to duplicate hers.

He looked across at her, asking,

"Do you come here often at night?"

"No, most times, I cook and if I want to get out, I go to Darla's for a cup of coffee and a pastry or cupcake."

"Darla's?"

"Yes, it's across Greenville Boulevard from the Hilton and Convention Center. It faces Hooker Road."

Brian looked puzzled, replying,

As many times, as I've stayed at the Hilton, I've never noticed it. I'll check it out tonight after I take you home. If it's not too late, maybe we can try one of their pastries or cupcakes."

"If it's not too late, we will."

Their food arrived and Brian found the country-style steak just like his mother's.

"I wonder if I could talk the owner's into opening a second one in Kenansville? They'd make a fortune."

Kayla laughed saying,

"I doubt it but you can always ask. It's probably a Mom and Pop place that requires one of them on the property at all times."

Finishing their dinner, they returned to the heart center finding Donna, Amy, and her sleeping father.

"Where's Mama?"

"Ander took her to your house. She was tired and said she could get in using the key you'd shown her. She looked very tired. I'm sure she is. At her age, I don't see how she goes, day after day, after day."

"You're right, Donna. Did the doctor come by?"

"About half an hour ago. Seemed all he was interested in was whether daddy ate his supper? Amy assured him that her grandfather had eaten everything on the tray and didn't grip once. He replied that since Mr. Herring was eating the new diet, he'd probably release him on Tuesday, Wednesday at the latest.
"They've going to get him up in the morning and start him walking."

They stayed until Amy got back. She'd been to the K&W.

Kayla asked, Amy?

"How long are you going to be here?"

Amy replied,

"Probably to ten or eleven. I'm good, why don't you go home and get some rest? I've got a key. I'll let myself in."

"Okay, but you'll probably find mama in your room, just use Kevin's."

"That's fine, Mother, I can crash anywhere."

Kayla looked at Donna, asking?

"When do you have to go back?"

"We'll probably leave around six tomorrow evening. It's about a three-hour drive back to Greensboro and I'm sure Ralph and Gina will be more than ready to give Jerry back to us by then."
"Brian, let's go get that cup of coffee we talked about. We'll see you in the morning. Call me if you need me."

Ten minutes later, they were sitting in Darla's enjoying steaming hot cups of coffee and a Danish but more than that, they were enjoying each other.

"Brian looking across, said,

"I can't believe I didn't know this existed. How in the world did you find it?"

No way was she going to tell him. He didn't have to know.

"A friend brought me here a couple of years ago and I've been coming back often. It's quiet, the coffee's delicious and the pastries and cakes are too. That's the hardest part. When I come in, I automatically want something to go with my coffee and most times, not all the time, back away knowing if I get on the scales, they'll scream."

"Kayla, you're joking. Just look at you. You're the same size you were in high school and college. Yes, there's a little more of you in the right places but, weight problem; no way."

He noticed my breasts, I knew he would. If he only knew how hard I work to remain the same size. I sure haven't worked at it lately. Not since I went back home and now with daddy in the hospital but I've got to get back into my routine, soon.

"I exercise several times a week at the wellness center. It's one of the perks working at the hospital. I work hard at maintaining my figure and so far, I done it."

Brian, still unable to take his eyes off her, replied,

"I belong to three fitness centers but rarely get a chance to use them. My regimen is much too crowded but I must hang in there. I have goals and the only way to reach them is to pay the fiddler.

"The way I look at it, I'll attain all my goals by fifty-five and I'll be able to slow down and really enjoy life."

"Don't get me wrong, I enjoy life now but it hectic, too hectic, but I've only got seven years to go." I can easily handle that."

"It's none of my business but since we're talking about goals, how many businesses do you own?"

If he evades my question, I'll drop the subject. It's really none of my business but one day, it might be.

"Kayla, night now, there are four tractor and equipment dealerships. I'm in negotiations to buy out two more.

"Beyond that, there's the investment group, the property I own including Bobby's, and the property I own between Carolina Beach and Kure Beach.

"I'm also looking at property in Kinston. There's a huge revitalization effort taking place there offering an enormous potential return of property. It may take ten years to realize profits there but that works out perfectly for me. Profit is the last thing I need to show Uncle Sam right now."

"Brian, I'm more than impressed, it's unbelievable what you've accomplished since high school and with no college either. I cannot phantom how you've done it."

He was smiling now. Replying, he said,

"I have a four-year degree in business administration. I did most of it online but finished up the last semester at UNC-Wilmington. That was in 1997. I'm working on my masters now but it's totally online at this point."

She couldn't believe what she was hearing. He'd accomplished so much since high school. She couldn't remember who the "Most-Likely-To-Succeed" was in their class but it should have been Brian.

"You make my life seen mundane compared to yours but I still don't understand why you never married."

He laughed softly before replying,

"Kayla, I thought I'd already told you. When you left, I was devastated, hurt, angry. You were my whole life and I thought that we'd spend the rest of our lives together.

"I guess I pouted for a year before I took bearings on my life or the lack of it.

"I talked with several people seeking their advice and guidance. Mr. Wells, you remember him, our homeroom teacher. He probably gave me the best advice anyone ever did. He told me that life was made up in many levels and stages. No two people were alike and what was waiting for them and what they did with their life would be unique to them and only them. He said that for most, life would include a helpmate but not everyone would have one and others would find them later in life.

"The hardest thing he said was that what I did with my life was up to me. There would be many that would contribute and be helpful and others would be stumbling blocks and hinder, slow down, ever stop my forward momentum

"It would be up to me to separate the helpful ones for the others. After talking with him the third time, I took positive steps to see what I could make out of my life.

"I missed you more than you'll ever know and yes, I dated a little in the beginning and more after seven or eight years but nothing was ever serious. I know I was looking for another you and Kayla, there isn't another you.

"Discouraged, I turned my attention to business and discovered that I had a knack for finding profitable investments.

"Mother and Father were killed in an accident in nineteen-eighty-nine and I sold the farm giving me assets to invest.

"I took a business course at James Sprunt and met Harland Edwards, my instructor. During the course, I found out that he was also a financial advisor. I liked what I saw and heard and retained him. He still is my main financial advisor today.

"In nineteen-ninety, I was made aware that the tractor dealership in Kenansville was going on the auction block. I asked Harland for the business opinion. A couple of weeks later, we met and he presented his findings.

"As I suspected, the business had enormous potential but had been grossly mismanaged causing it to fail.

"I went to see the manager of Southern Bank in Kenansville telling her that I wanted to purchase the business. After she saw my collateral, she told me to come back the following week. She would present my package to her board. The following week, she offered to finance 60% of what I thought the business could be bought for. I could easily handle the balance.

"Two-weeks later, Harland and I went to the auction. After a few minutes, it seemed very apparent that there didn't seem to be anyone there really interested in bidding on it. I low-balled my bid at 25% of what I thought it was worth. Another bidder raised my bid by 5%. I raised it another 5%, and the other bidder raised it another 5%. I countered with another 5% and the other bidder dropped out. It was mine of for 45% of what I thought it was worth. Kayla you'll never imagine how happy I was.

"I spent the next year restructuring the business and replacing most of the sales force and office personal. I retained the service manager and four of the five mechanics.

"The beginning of the planting season the following spring, I added the lawn and garden section which proved to be very profitable.

"During that period, there was no time for dating and it remained that way with each succeeding acquisition.

"Yes, there was time but I wasn't interested. I'd set my goals too high and I hadn't met anyone that came even close."

"When I saw you at the Mad Boar, I knew you were the only one in my life. Now, I'm here to see where I fit, or if I have a place in yours."

She was almost speechless. He'd poured his heart out. What was she going to do? She cared for Lynn and he was at a distinct disadvantage. She owed him an opportunity to claim her too. She would have to wait until he came home Christmas, she just had too.

She reached across placing her hand on his.

"Brian, I don't know what to say. Our history goes back a long way. When I left, I thought that I loved you but I didn't want to be tied down to a marriage and family before even seeing what else was out there.

"I know that I was ugly to you when I left but it was the only way I knew to get you to get me go. There was no reasoning with you. All you wanted to do was get married, have children and farm. I didn't want that then and I don't want it now.

"I made a horrible choice in husbands but my children made it worth the hurt and sorrow I went through. For the next twenty years, I raised my children determined not to ever let a man hurt me again.

"That was a huge mistake. I know that now but I can't go back a single day. Lynn came into my life when I needed him most. Had he not been pulled away to Washington, DC. I'm confident that we would be married now.

"Now you're back in my life and I cannot begin to tell you how strong my feelings are for you but, I must give Lynn a chance. I have do that. I hope you'll understand."

She couldn't detect any hurt of anger in his face, only understanding. He'd changed so much. It would be so easy to let go and love him unconditionally but she couldn't, she wouldn't until Lynn has his chance.

"Kayla, I completely understand. I really do. All I'm asking of you is to let me be part of your life until he comes back Christmas. If it's your decision to marry him, I'll back off and you'll never see or hear from me again. That's a promise and I will keep it."

Standing at her door, she wanted his arms around her, his lips on hers, but as before, he kissed her tenderly on the lips and backed away.

"Eight O'clock?"

She smiled and nodded,

"Yes, eight o'clock, sweet dreams."

"You too."

Inside, still captivated by his kiss, she started undressing hearing an alert from her phone. It was Lynn.

"Lynn, how unusual, you never call on Saturdays… He's better, thank you for asking, they may even let him go home Tuesday or Wednesday… No, they'll all leave tomorrow evening…

She knew he wanted to ask and he was going to have to; she wasn't volunteering anything about Brian. If he wanted to know, he'd have to ask.

"Yes, he's on a bland diet and hates it but I think his team has finally put the fear of God in him. I told him if he didn't go on the diet, I was going home and get ready to go to his funeral… It's hard on her, Lynn… She's slipping behind his back eating everything she can. She knows when she gets home, she'll have to be on the same diet as him. She's like a little child, grabbing anything that has sugar and salt in it… No, I have plenty of sick days accrued. I'll go back after he's home… Probably, I'm sure I'll be taking them home when it gets out… As long as I have to, Lynn. He's the only father I have…

He's scared I'll hook up with Brian if I go back. What he doesn't know is how close I am to hooking up with him here.

"Brian's picking us up at eight. He's taking us to breakfast before we go to the hospital… Why not, Lynn, He's a friend, I've known him all my life and mama thinks the world of him too…

She knew his blood was boiling but she'd asked him once to go meet them but he was too busy and then, he was gone.

"Okay, it must be in the middle of the night there. You sleep well too, bye."

He walks all around the "Love" word but he won't say it. Brian already has.

Lynn Stocks, you're walking on a tightrope and there's no net. If you fall, you are history.

Sleep came quickly but unlike last night, it was a bumpy ride. Brian arrived first taking her on a long walk through a meadow filled with wild flowers but Lynn pushed his way in insisting that she join him for a stroll along the banks of the Seine or a tour of the Louvre. That went on all night and by morning, she felt as if she hadn't slept at all.

SNR

Brian arrived at eight suggesting the Cracker Barrel.

Her mama looked at her asking,

"Honey, have you eaten there? Is the food fittin'?"

Almost laughing, she replied,

"Yes, Mama, the food's good."

It was busy when they arrived but they were easily seated in the middle of the floor in the main dining room. It was still too warm for a fire but there was a small one flickering away.

They all wanted coffee while they studied the menus.

Her mama made up her mind fast. She wanted the "Uncle Herschel's Favorite with scrambled eggs and biscuits.

She chose the pecan pancakes with a rasher of bacon.

Brian chose the 'Country Boy Breakfast with scrambled eggs and biscuits

When they brought it out, you could easily see the gleam in her mama's eyes. Kayla knew that her mama was counting the meals before she'd have to bite the bullet.

Brian commented on how good it was but it couldn't beat the Three Steers. They were the best, hands down.

Between bites, her mama asked,

"Honey, when have you heard from that man?"

Why did she insist on asking about Lynn when Brian was around?

"Mama, his name is Lynn, he called last night to check on daddy."

Her mama wasn't expecting that and immediately changed the subject but Brian was hoping to hear more. If there was more, it would be later when they were alone. Not here, not anywhere with her mama around.

SNR

When they arrived at the heart center, Donna, Cliff, Ander, Nara, Linda, Kevin, Kylie, and Amy were there. They were standing around the bed and Mr. Herring seemed to be entertaining them. He was in high spirits despite the very bland breakfast he'd been served. Amy said that he ate all of it without one word of commentary.

Kayla could easily see the vast improvement from yesterday and she was sure that he was playing a game of "Get me out of here!"

Donna said the he was doing so well and they would be leaving after lunch. Ander was echoing the same sentiments.

Kevin suggested that they all have lunch together.

It's so rare than we're all together. I think it would be fun.

Amy offered to stay with her grandfather.

"I'll get to see all of you, Christmas."

Kayla could easily detect a broad grin on her mama's face. She knew what was going to happen when they got home and she wasn't going to miss a single meal before she started serving her sentence.

Brian, standing beside Kayla, suggested,

Let's call the Three Steers and make reservations. I'll call if you're in agreement."

The vote was unanimous although they were hesitant about leaving Amy alone.

She retorted that it gave her time with her grandfather, one on one.

"Do it, you'll enjoy it."

Kayla was going to offer to bring something back but knew it wasn't a clever idea. Her daddy was doing too good to tempt him.

Brian stepped out into the corridor and made the reservations saying it would all be on one ticket, his. He made the reservations for eleven-thirty.

SNR

Driving two cars, they arrived at the Three Steers and were seated, by the hostess, in the front dining room. Tables had been pulled together and covered with while tablecloths. They were seated three facing three and one on each end.

Their waitress placed the menus in front of each person and took their beverage orders. Donna and Nara took the opportunity to check the salad bar out. The thirty entrees looked more than inviting to them

When their waitress returned, each placed their order, either from the three lunch specials, multi-trip salad bar, or the lunch menu.

Kayla's mama wanted to know about the collards.

"Are they cooked with ham hocks?"

The waitress replied that they were.

"Maybelle only knows one way to cook and that's country. She says she doesn't trust anyone that doesn't put cayenne pepper vinegar on their collards and cabbage."

She had Mrs. Herring's attention.

"Does she fry her cornbread?"

"Yes, Ma'am, she fries it in thin patties in the oven. It's almost like there isn't anything in the middle, just the top and bottom crusts."

Her mama was salivating. She was ready for some country cooking and she wasn't disappointed. She'd never had cabbage collards but remarked more than once that they were better than hers and from the looks of her plate, they must have been.

Everyone, but her, declined dessert. She had a slice on chocolate on chocolate cake capping off with what she termed as;

"A mighty fine meal!'
"Waitress, tell that cook…What did you say her name was?"

The waitress replied,

"Maybelle."

"You tell Maybelle that was some mighty fine eating."

Kevin offered to pick up the tab but Brian said that it was already taken care of.

They all thanked him saying it was very kind of him.

Kayla, sitting beside him, turned towards him and softly said.

"Thank you."

SNR

Back at the hospital, trying every way she could, her mama finally had to admit that's she'd had collards, cabbage and cornbread.

"Ray, what was I supposed to do? They didn't have nothing that was on your diet."

He didn't hear about the pork chop and gravy and the cake wasn't mentioned either.

Kayla had fretted over how her daddy would deal with the bland diet but now, she feared that her mama would be the most trouble.

A little after two, Donna and Cliff said their goodbyes followed by Ander and Nara. Kevin and Kylie left a little before three and Linda left a few minutes later.

Hugging her granddaddy and grandmamma once more, Amy left about five.

Her daddy's dinner was served at five-thirty and Kayla could see the look in her mama's eyes. Her mama was a strong woman but Kayla wondered if she was strong enough to make the transition with her daddy.

Up to that point, she'd shown no willingness to make the transition and time was running out. Somebody was going to have to ride herd on her. She was going to have to call Harriett Miller and ask her to keep a check on her.

She knew Brian would be more than willing to check on them but she couldn't, she wouldn't ask until she cleared the indecision and indecisiveness out of her mind. Really, it was her heart, not her mind.

She was afraid that if she didn't, there was no telling what her mama would do. If she didn't stick to the diet, it was a surety that her daddy wouldn't either.

"Mama, we're going down to the food court and get a cup of coffee. Do you want us to bring you one?"

She knew her mama was trying to remember what was left in the refrigerator. She'd wiped out the barbecue, slaw, and potato salad. All that was left was bread, peanut butter, and jelly.

Her mama replied,

"No honey, I'll wait until we get home. What time are we going?"

"Probably about nine, Mama. Daddy will be ready for sleep by then. He's had a very long and active day."
"We'll be back in a few minutes."

They picked up coffee and a pastry finding a table close to the windows. It was close to eight and very quiet.

"Your mother is going to have a problem when she gets back home. How are you going to handle it?"
His voice showed concern, not just curiosity. He really cared about them.

"Brian, I'm not sure yet. I'm going to call Sam Miller and his wife. They're close by and good friends. I don't want to interfere but mama's showing no inclination towards excepting the change.
When they get home, I'm afraid she might lose it. When I take them, I'm going with her to the grocery store and stock up with what they need.
The stickler is what to do with all the cured meat in the smokehouse. If it's left there, I'm sure she'll be in it before a week's out. I guess I could ask

Sam to take it all to his place and not tell mama a thing. When she discovers it gone, she'll feel too guilty to ask about it.

The lard's got to go too. I know there's one twenty-five-pound stand in the kitchen and I think I remember two more in the smokehouse."

"I'll remove all of it if you want me to. I'll give it away or sell it. It's up to you. I'll get rid of the two hogs he's planning to slaughter too. They can't stay there.

"Who's been feeding the cow and mule?"

'Sam, maybe I ought to give the hogs to him. That's what I'll do, I'll give him everything in the smokehouse too on the condition that he'll never tell mama and daddy what happened to it."

"What about all the pork in the freezer?"

"Mama can cook it without salt if she will. That' going to be the trick. Somehow, she's going to have to learn how to cook without salt and lard."

They took the elevator back up to the room a few minutes before nine.

Her daddy was asleep and her mama was pacing the floor. Kayla knew she was hungry but she was going to be fed a little tough love for a change.

Arriving at home, her mama disappeared into the kitchen leaving them standing in the hall.

"You're going back in the morning, aren't you?"

"Unless you need me. I do need to get back and check on my managers. They're good but as they say, when the cat's away, the mice will play."

"You've already done so much more than you should have. I really can't thank you enough."

"Kayla, you don't have to thank me. I'll always be here for you if you'll let me."

She reached for him and they locked into an embrace, kissing with more than just a tender kiss. The sensations she experienced, sent shockwaves throughout her body, her whole being reawakening desires she'd buried when Lynn slipped away from her.

She eased from him arms finding no resistance from him. He'd changed so much. When they parted twenty-four years ago, he would have fought to hold on to her.

"Thank you, Brian."

One more tender kiss, and he was gone leaving her trembling with desire for him. She was on fire; she had to calm down or she would be a nervous wreck.

Deep down inside something urged her to call him back. If they came together, all her pent-up needs and desires would be answered and she would be whole again. All she had to do was call but she couldn't. Lynn, even though he left her hanging, deserved a chance.

If she made it through the reunion weekend, he would have that chance but first, she had to survive it and she was afraid it might prove too difficult. She was already looking forward to being Brian's date. They would turn heads. She had no doubt about that.

S.NR

Monday morning, she awakened her mama saying they would have a bowl of cereal before going to the hospital eliciting a very troubled look from her.

"Honey, aren't we going to go to that restaurant for breakfast? I really like it there."

Now as a good a time as any, her mama was in for a shock.

Mama, Daddy's going home tomorrow or Wednesday. You're going to have to start eating what's on his diet. You're going to have to start now or when you get home, you won't and when he finds out. There's going to be trouble. He's going to have a tough time as it is without you slipping behind his back cooking and eating food he can't have."

Her mama was almost in tears,

"Kayla, I know there's got to be a change but we've got all that cured meat in the smokehouse and tons of lard. When it runs out, we'll change."

"No, Mama; it you do that, you'll change, daddy will be dead."

"I can't just cut him off, he'll be madder than a snake."

"Mama, he's already cut off and it looks like you want to add confusion and deception to that."

"When I take you home, we'll go buy groceries and we'll use the suggested list they've furnished."

"Now, let's eat our cereal then I'll drop you off and I'll go punch in."

"Punch in? You ain't going to check on your daddy first?"

"No, Mama, I'll check on him at lunch."

She knew her mama was mad but it appeared to be the only way to get her attention. She hadn't been honest with her daddy since his operation. She felt sorry for her but what she was doing had to be done.

SNR

At lunch, she and Mary drove around to the heart center leaving the car with Valet Parking.

Walking through the food court, Kayla picked up a garden salad and a diet Pepsi saying it would be her mama's lunch.

"Our lunch hour will be over before we get back."

"Mary laughed, replying,

After all that food at church yesterday, I need a break. I'm definitely exercising after work too."

"Me too, I haven't been in a week and my reunion is creeping up fast."

Up on the floor, she arrived at the same time her daddy's lunch did. It couldn't have been any less appetizing. There was a serving of roasted turkey, mashed potatoes, no gravy, no butter, garden peas without the slightest hint of seasoning, maybe a dash of pepper, 1 roll and a serving of what appeared to be instant pudding with no topping. She tasted his iced tea. It hadn't been sweetened but there were 2 packets of sweetener.

It made her mama's salad look like steak; not really, but much more appetizing than his.

She had it open as if she were starving.

Her daddy didn't grumble about his, instead, he methodically wiped the plate and containers clean and drank the iced tea without adding the sweetener.

Saying she was proud of him, Kayla rolled the tray away and returned taking her daddy's hand.

"You look so much better now. What did the doctor say this morning?"

Her daddy was smiling now, he replied,

"Wednesday morning, they're going to unhook me from all the stuff in the morning and start me to walking. I feel almost good enough to run…maybe not far but a few steps anyway.

"I haven't had any heartburn or nothing from the stuff they're feeding me. I guess it's doing me good to eat it and that's what I'm going to do. I ain't ready to leave ya'll yet."

"Daddy, that's great news, I've got to get back to work. I'll check on you after I do my exercise.

Mary stood, saying goodbye, and they took the elevator down to the entrance and Valet Parking.

"He does look good, Kayla and I know he's ready to go home."

Kayla frowned, replying,

"He does, Mary. I just wish mama was as ready. I'm afraid I'm going to have a problem with her. She's going to have to eat the same meals as daddy and she's made no effort to try to acclimate to the change. I know it's drastic but daddy has accepted it. Now, she must. If not, she'll pull him right back into eating what they were before and he'll be gone before Christmas."

Concerned, Mary commented,

"Kayla, you can't stay with them. How are you going to keep a check on them?"

"I'm not totally sure. Their neighbors, Sam and Harriett Miller will help and I'm sure Woody Grady will check on them if I ask.
It's going to be interesting. I'll do what I have to."

No way was she going to share Brian's involvement. That would probably be like throwing fat in the fire. Lynn would know it before the sun went down.

After work, she met Mary and Ginger at the wellness center spending an hour trying to get back into the groove.

Afterwards, she and Ginger drove to the Three Steers enjoying chef salads. She'd ordered a 'to-go' for her mama and dropped it off at the house before going back to the heart center.

Brian called as she was leaving the house, she walked back in answering his call.

"Hi Brian, I know you're glad to be back home... Oh, thank you, that's a very nice compliment... Really? I didn't realize there was that much. What should I do... Brian, that's asking too much of you. You've already done too much... Are you sure?... Tomorrow, Mr. Miller didn't think it would be a problem, did he?... Good, that will work out perfectly. I'm taking them home on Wednesday... Not yet, I may know by tomorrow afternoon... Yes, I'll let you know... I doubt it. I'm going to take mama grocery shopping and depending on the time, I'll probably come back... If I do, yes, that would be nice... Okay, I'll call, bye."

He could get five-hundred dollars for the cured meat and lard. She couldn't believe that there was that much. Telling her daddy what she'd done wasn't going to be easy but she wanted him alive, not dead. Mr. Miller was moving the two hogs tomorrow too.

She had another call. It was Lynn. There was nothing to do but take it.

"Lynn, good evening... I'm walking out the door now... He's much better. I think Dr. Erickson is going to release him Wednesday... I don't know. I hope to find out tomorrow... No, I'm taking them. They don't have a vehicle up here; besides, there's no way Mama could possibly drive back home. She's never driven ten miles from the farm... Lynn, I must get them settled in and I have to take mama to the grocery store... Remember, daddy will be on a bland diet and there's nothing in the house that's bland… It doesn't make any difference; if he wants to live, he'll be on a bland diet for the rest of his life… He'll do fine if mama gets with the program. Bland food is not what she wants to eat… Lynn, you haven't been here. You don't have clue… I'm sorry but I've got my hands full with her, I need to get over to the heart center. I'm running late…you too, bye."

It he thinks he can tell me what to do or how to feel and he's four-thousand miles away, he's got another thought coming.

She was upset but she felt she had a right to be. She'd had it up to here with her mama and now Lynn was trying to tell her what to do.

I've been taking care of myself and my children for over twenty years without advice from anyone and no one's going to start dictating to me now.

By the time she reached the heart center, she'd calmed down. She hoped her mama would stay off her case. She'd probably blow up in her face if she said anything.

Walking into the room, she found her mama standing beside the bed. Apparently, they were discussing something but it abruptly stopped when she entered.

She spoke first to her daddy asking what he'd had for supper.

"Honey, I had a piece of grilled chicken breast, rice, broccoli, a roll, coffee, and chocolate pudding. It wasn't bad, I ate all of it."

"Good, Mama, I have your dinner at home."
"Has the doctor been in?"

Her mama replied that he'd been in about four and the dietitian specialist stopped by after he left.

"She gave me a shopping list for things he supposed to have. There ain't hardly nothing on that list at home."

"That's fine, mama, when we get daddy settled in, we're going to Food Lion. Afterwards, all you'll have to do is pick out a breakfast, lunch, and supper menu and fix it. Daddy's got the hang of it, now it's up to you."

I wonder if she really heard what I said? She doesn't look like she understood anything I just said.

She started to tell them what she'd done about the meat and hogs but decided against it. She'd tell them when they got home. Her mama would miss the lard stand as soon as she walked into the kitchen.

It was almost nine. She knew her mama were tired and hungry too.

"Mama, let's go home and let daddy get some sleep. I know that you're tired and probably hungry too."

SNR

Arriving at home, her mama made a bee line for the kitchen retrieving her dinner from the refrigerator. Opening the takeout box, Kayla could see the disappointment in her face.
She looked at Kayla, saying,

"Honey, I'd much rather had some fried chicken and collards. This don't hardly look good enough to eat."

"Mama, I had a garden salad, I could have gotten one for you but the lettuce would have been wilted by now. You need to eat what I brought you. You're going to have to change your diet and you need to start now."

She left her in the kitchen looking as if she'd been whipped.

Mama, I feel sorry for you but this has got to happen. I want both of you around for a long, long time.

Putting on her pajamas, she got into bed and opened her laptop finding messages from Brian and Lynn.

She opened Lynn's first.

Kayla, I'm sorry, I didn't mean to chastise you. I was just trying to understand what you're doing. I know that I have no right to judge. I'm sorry, please forgive me. Lynn.

Lynn, you can't know what I'm going through but at forty-eight, I'm old enough to make decisions for myself. If I feel that I need your advice I'll ask. You've never met my parents and know nothing about what makes them tick. I do, I'm their daughter. Have a nice evening, K

Opening Brian's, she read it.

Kayla, I have five-hundred, fifty dollars for the cured meat. I'll give it to you when you bring them home. Message or text me when you know what time Wednesday. Miss, you, Brian.

What was she going to do? Lynn seemed to be falling further and further away while Brian kept getting closer and closer.

She was up before day, Tuesday morning. Her mama was too. She could hear her in the kitchen. For once, Kayla was glad that she didn't keep eggs or bacon in the refrigerator. Her mama was going to have to make do with cereal or a peanut butter sandwich. She wasn't going to take her out for breakfast.

She knew that her mama was upset but she also knew that her mama didn't have a clue what was waiting for her when she got home

After coffee and cereal, she dropped her mama off saying that she would check on her at lunch.

"Do you want me to bring you a salad for lunch?"

Her mama didn't want a salad, she wanted "grits and grease."

"I'm sorry Mama, they don't serve anything fried in the food court. I told you that you were going to have to adjust. It has to start now."

Her mama was miffed,

"I'll fix me something descent with I get home."

"That's fine, Mama."

SNR

At lunch, she picked up a chef salad with Ranch Free dressing and a bottle of water.

Her father was finishing up his chicken, rice, and peas when she walked in.

"You're doing good Daddy, I'm real proud of you."

He gave her a big smile replying,

"It ain't country ham, Honey, but I'm getting used to it."

Her mama picked through the salad not saying anything. She apparently was still upset.

"Has the doctor been in?"

Her daddy replied,

"Yes, he's checking me out in the morning. I walked to the elevator and back three times this morning. See? I don't have anything attached to me now."

Her daddy was proud of himself and he was ready to go home. Her mama was too but she was afraid for a different reason. Her mama was upset this morning but she didn't have a clue.

Should I tell her tonight? Maybe I should take her back to the Three Steers and tell her then. She'll be too busy shoveling it in to make much of a fuss. I'll get Ginger to join us.

"Daddy, I'm so proud of you. I know you're ready to go home."
"Mama, when I get off work, I'm going to the wellness center and do my exercises. Afterwards, I'll take you to the Three Steers for supper."

She could see a smile erupting across her mama's face.

"That' fine, Honey I'll be waiting."

Back at work, she texted Ginger about exercise and dinner.

Exercise & 3 Steers? K

Yes, C U later – G

After exercising, Ginger went ahead and Kayla picked her mama up telling her daddy that they'd see him come morning.

"I'll be ready to take you home. I love you, Daddy."

She leaned over kissing him on the cheek before walking out with her mama.

Arriving at the restaurant, her mama was already saying that she wanted hamburger steak, gravy, rice, butter beans, and a slice of pie for dessert.

"Order what you like, Mama. Tomorrow will be a new day."

While they were enjoying their meal, her mama was really enjoying hers, Kayla decided that it was time to tell her mama what she'd done. Ginger already knew.

"Mama, I've made a few changes back home."

Her mama was too busy enjoying her meal to be paying much attention to what Kayla was saying until she heard, lard.

"You did what with my lard?"

"Mama, I sold all the cured meat and lard. You can't have it anymore."

Now her mama was paying close attention.

"I can't cook without lard, you know that."

"Mama, daddy can't have fried food and no cured meat, no salt. You won't be able to season with it either."

"That's the only way I know how to cook. You know that."

"Mama, you haven't paid any attention to what the dietitian specialist has been telling you. She gave you recipes and instructions. Remember, we're going grocery shopping when I get you home tomorrow. Mama, you can't go back to the old way of cooking. Daddy will be dead before Thanksgiving."

The slice of pecan pie with ice cream was taking some of the edge off what her mama was being told but her facial expression told the real story. For the first time, the full impact of what was going to take place tomorrow was pouring in around her mama and she knew that there wasn't any escape.

SNR

Next morning, she found her mama sitting at the kitchen table eating corn flakes. She couldn't believe what she was seeing.

"Good morning, Mama. Are you ready to go home?"

"Good morning, Kayla, yes, I'm ready to take Ray home."

By nine-thirty, they were out of the hospital and driving down Hwy 11 towards home.

Arriving a little before eleven. They got her daddy all settled in. It was time to go grocery shopping. Yes, her mama had checked, the lard stand was gone. She didn't go out to the smokehouse; she knew that it would be empty.

While they were shopping for groceries, she got a text from Brian.

R U home? - B
Food Lion now, home 1 hour – K
Lunch? – B
Yes - K
C U then – B

The hardest part of shopping was the meat isle. She'd only allow her mama to pick up boneless, skinless chicken breasts, two turkey breasts, and pork cutlets with as little fat as possible. The ones in the freezer would be too fat and she couldn't trust her mama to trim it off, not yet anyway.

"How about these trout, Kayla? Ray likes trout."

"How are you going to cook them, Mama?"

"Oh, forget it. Ray won't eat them anyway but fried."

When they got home, Brian was already there and helped unload over two-hundred dollars' worth of heart-healthy food.

Finishing, he went back into the living room with her father. After getting everything put up. She helped put together turkey salad plates for her parents.

"Ain't you going to eat something, Kayla?"

No, Brian's taking me to lunch."

That put a smile on her face. She was in Brian's corner. She had been from the beginning.

In the living room, she told her daddy about selling all the cured meat and why.

"Daddy, it can't stay here. It's too much of a temptation. I hope you understand."

"I do, Honey, I'd love to have a big piece of country ham right now but I know I can't. I appreciate you looking after us, up yonder and here too."

"Daddy, I asked Brian to sell it for me. He's got your money."

Brian walked over handing him five one-hundreds and one fifty.

"Mr. Herring, that was some pretty meat, especially the hams. It brought a go

od price. I asked my friends over at the ham place in Warsaw what it was worth and it brought more than that."

Her daddy thanked him saying he didn't realize that there was that much out there.
"Now, I've got to get rid of them two hogs I was fattening up."

Kayla, interrupted, saying,

"Daddy, Mr. Miller came and got them. He'll settle up when they come over to visit."

He was smiling now but visibly tired.

"I think I need to rest a bit, ya'll please excuse me."

"Daddy, I'll probably be gone when you wake up. I'll come back down this weekend to check on you. I love you, Daddy."

She was standing now. Walking over she kissed him and turned to Brian.

"I'm ready if you are."

SNR

Walking into the Country Squire, they were seated in the butler's pantry.

"Would you like glass of wine? You're already had a full day."

"Yes, that would be nice, thank you."

"Waiter, please bring a bottle of Duplin Winery's White Zinfandel."

"Very good, Mr. Howard."

"How did it go with your mother? She seemed okay to me."

With a hint of a smile, she replied,

"She got her dander up last night but by this morning, she seemed to be reconciled to the changes she has to make. When we got here, she went straight to the kitchen. Seeing the lard stand gone, she was pretty sure the meat was too. Thank you so much for doing that for me."

"You don't have to thank me. I want to do for you."

The waiter arrived and poured their wine.

"Taste it; what do you think?"

"It's delicious. Thank you."

Their waiter asked,

"Are you ready to order?"

"Yes, waiter, I'll have the chicken salad sandwich and a cup of the soup-of-the-day.

Liking her choice, he chose the same excepting he wanted the French-onion-soup.

Enjoying their wine, he asked,

"You're coming back this weekend, is there time for us?"

She wanted there to be but didn't know how her daddy would be doing...or her mama either.

"I won't know until I come down. I don't want to tie you up and then not be able to make it."

He reached over touching her hand, saying,

"Tie me up, I want to be tied up by you."

He was doing everything right and saying everything right.

"Are you sure?"

"Yes, very sure."

'Then, yes, I hope there will be time for us."

Their sandwiches and soup arrived and were as delicious as she knew they would be.

Arriving back at her parents, he took his leave but only after kissing her tenderly saying,

"I look forward to being with you this weekend. Drive safely back to Greenville."

"I will. I'm looking forward to seeing you too."

Walking inside, she found her mother studying the diet menus. She looked up at Kayla saying that she'd planned their supper and breakfast in the morning.

"Sam and Harriett are coming over a little later. They want to check on your daddy."

Seeing her mama's positive attitude, she was ready to return to Greenville.

"Mama, you're doing good. I'm going home and do my exercise. I'll be down after work on Friday to check on you."

"I'll fix you supper. What time are you getting here?"

"Brian's taking me out but thank you, Mama. I love you."

SNR

Back in Greenville, she washed clothes first, then texted Mary and Ginger.

Exercise at 5? - K

Ginger texted that she would be there.

Mary said she had bible study. Maybe tomorrow night.

It was a little after four. She checked her messages finding several from her family, and two from Lynn.

She spent the next few minutes answering each one giving them glowing reports.

They're back home now and seem to be settling into their new routines

Now for Lynn,

They're back home and settling in. I'll go down Friday and check on them. May see Mary tomorrow at exercise. Meeting Ginger there at 5. Probably have dinner with her afterwards. I'm tired.

As she was answering Lynn, a message from Brian popped up.

Thank you for having lunch with me. I really enjoy our time together. Hope you'll have time for me this weekend. Always, Brian.

Thank you, Brian. Lunch was very nice. I hope there is time this weekend too. Always, Kayla.

Should I have signed, Always? It doesn't matter now; I did.

By the time she got to the wellness center, Ginger would be there. Opening a bottle of water, she drove over.

There were bits and pieces of conversation on the tread mill and exercise equipment, more on their three cool-down laps. They'd really catch up during their evening meal.

"Let's go to CPW's. I'd like a glass of wine."

"Kayla, I was thinking the same thing. I'll meet you there."

Arriving, they were seating near the wall on the right.

"Have you tried the Duplin Winery Hatteras Red?"

"No, I haven't, Kayla. Is it sweet?"
"Yes, it's dark, sweet and just a teeny bit tart."

They ordered a bottle along with a meatball starter.

"So, your father's doing great and your mother is coming along?"

"That's a clever way of putting it. As you know, she was not a happy camper but somehow managed to pull it together. Once she realized that her lard and cured meat were gone, she had little choice.

"She'll slip and fall. I know she will but sooner or later, she'll toe the line like daddy. I'm so proud of him. He's doing great."

"And what's with you and Lynn?'

Their wine and starters arrived. Their conversation paused while they tasted wine and tried the meatballs.

"This is good, now, tell me about Lynn."

"I told you that he tried to tell me what to do and I put him in his place. He's apologized since and tiptoeing through each word he posts. I think he's beginning to realize that running off and staying gone so long wasn't a clever idea. Between what he'd heard from Mary and my conversations, he knows that I'd not sitting on the couch any longer pining my life away for him. He made a thoughtless mistake and may have to pay for it."

Ginger grinned, replying,

"It sounds like Brian's hanging in there."

"He is, he took me to lunch today and wants to take me to dinner when I go down Friday."

"Bravo, I'm so happy for you. It's taken long enough but now, I think you're ready to be loved again. That's wonderful!"

"I am ready, Ginger. The reunion may tell the tale. Brian's got me wrapped up every minute I have from Friday until Sunday when I come back. I'm so excited. He's really matured into a very handsome and thoughtful man."

The waiter was back asking about their meal.

Ginger, saying she knew she shouldn't, ordered the Jambalaya Pasta.

Kayla, saying that she was hungry too, ordered the Seafood Diablo Pasta.

They agreed that they'd pay for it later but right then, they didn't care.

SNR

Thursday morning, she was up before light cranking up Mr. Coffee before showering and dressing.

A cup of coffee and a bowl of cereal later, she noted that she'd missed a message from Lynn wanting to know if she was still in Greenville or back in Duplin Country?

I guess he's trying to keep tabs on me now since he knows that there's another man in my life.

Mr. Stocks, you should have corralled me when you had the chance instead of flying off to Paris without me. Now you're there and I'm here.

Greenville, going down for the weekend tomorrow - K

SNR

Thursday turned into Friday afternoon and she'd just arrived back home in Duplin County.

Her parents met her at the door. They both looked in perfect health. Perhaps she'd underestimated her mama.

Hugging them, she said,

"Daddy, you look healthy as a horse. Mama must be feeding you right."

"She is, Kayla, we're doing real good on the diet. I'm bout used to it now. Your mama's trying real hard. When Sam and Harriett came by yesterday. She brought her a ham biscuit. I told her to go ahead and eat it in front of me. I've done made up my mind. I'm going to be here a long time.

"Brian stopped by yesterday checking on us too. He's a fine man and he still thinks something of you."

It's good seeing him again, Daddy. We're going out to eat tonight."

Her mama, wanting to put her two-cents in, said.

"I told you, Kayla, he still thinks as much of you now as he always did."

"Come on in and sit a spell. What time's he is coming by?"

"About seven, Mama. I don't know where we're going but it doesn't make any difference."

"Daddy are you walking much? You know that you need to."

Her daddy, cracking a big smile, replied.

"I walked all the way out to the edge of the woods yesterday. It tired me a little but when I went back the second time, if didn't bother me at all. I'm getting stronger but it going to take some time."

There was a knock at the door.

"I'll get it. It's probably Brian."

It was. He came in and spoke saying he was taking Kayla to a restaurant in Wilmington.

"It will probably be late when we get back."

Wilmington, she hoped she was dressed for the occasion.

"Brian, do I need to change?"

He was wearing a sports coat and tie.

"You're fine. You always are. Would you like steak or seafood?"

His compliments were more than welcome. It had been too long and she craved each one.

"Steak?"

"Steak it is, we're going to the Port City Chop House. It's on Eastwood Drive just before you get to Wrightsville Beach."

"Good night, Mr. and Mrs. Herring. I'll take very good care of her."

SNR

The drive was only a little over an hour. He made reservations before pulling out of the driveway.

The drive down was nice. They talked mostly about the reunion and how much they were looking forward to it.

Arriving, they were seated at a table for two in a quiet corner. He'd been there before. The hostess recognized and addressed him as, Mr. Howard."

"Suzanne will take care of you tonight. Enjoy your meal."

"What beverages may I start you off with?"

"Start us off with a bottle of "Two-Vines," please."

While they were waiting, Brian suggested they choose starters.

"May I suggest the Bruschetta or the baked Brie. If you prefer seafood, the crab dip is excellent and the Calamari is too."

Suzanne was back opening the bottle of wine. She poured a small amount in one of the tapers for Brian to taste.

"Yes, that's fine."

Now she poured wine for both.

"Mr. Howard, will you be having starters tonight?"

He looked across at Kayla.

"What have you chosen?"

"The Bruschetta, please."

"And I'll have the crab dip, thank you."

"I'll have them for you in a few minutes, sir."

Kayla, looking around the room and then at him, remarked,

"This is very nice. Do you come here often?"

"Yes, I do. I have a cottage on the beach and sometimes spend the weekend here. I bounce back and forth between here and the Bridge Tender for dinner."

"Maybe sometime in the future, I'll be able to show it to you. If you'd like, I'll take you on a tour when you're down for the reunion"

That would be the perfect place for them to come together, to be one. She could feel the flames of desire intensifying.

Kayla, you can't do this. You shouldn't do this. You owe Lynn a chance!

She fought to regain her composure. She didn't want to but she had to.

Thankfully, their starters arrived

"This is very good, Brian. Thank you for suggesting it."

"Here, taste this. It's very good too."

They leaned forward and he placed a portion of spooned crap dip in her mouth.

"It's delicious too. Here, try my Bruschetta."

She knew that he didn't really taste it. He was looking too intently into her eyes. She was looking deeply into his too.

Their waitress, thankfully, broke the trance.

"Would Mr. Howard like to order now?"

"Are we ready?"

Kayla glanced once more at the dinner entrees', replying,

"I'll have the 6-ounce filet, medium-rare with the sautéed spinach and onion rings."

Brian ordered the steak Au Poivre, medium-rare, with Cajun rice pilaf and the creamed spinach.
"Also, bring a bottle of Anthology."

"Very good, Sir. I'll get your order in."

"Anthology?"

He replied,

"It's a Cabernet Sauvignon from Conn Creek. I think you'll enjoy its fruity taste."

If he liked it, she was sure she would too.

"How often do you come to Wilmington?"

"Once or twice a week. There are so many restaurants to experience and I really enjoy my time at the cottage. I'd like to bring you back down here for brunch tomorrow."

"That sounds very nice, I'd like that. What time are we leaving?"

"How does nine sound? Too early?"

"No, that's perfect. It will give me some time with mama and daddy. I'm already looking forward to it, thank you."

Their entrees arrived along with the wine that she found delightful. He certainly knew his wines.

"Brian, my steak is delicious. Yours looks so good. I've never had Steak Au Poivre."

"Here, taste this."

He cut a small portion, picking it up with his fork. Reaching across, he placed the morsel up to her lips. Tasting it, she exclaimed,

"Brian, that is so good. I'll have to try it, sometime."

"It's on Bobby's menu. We'll order it next time we're there."

All his next times seemed so wonderfully enticing to her. She was more than ready for them.

For dessert, they shared a Banana's Foster enjoying the tableside presentation.

An hour later, arriving back at her mama and daddy's, he walked her to the door and she turned into his arms. Their parting kiss was long and tender.

He released her, saying,

"I had a wonderful time tonight. I'll see you at nine in the morning."

"Brian, I really enjoyed our evening too. I'm looking forward to tomorrow too. Good night."

She practically floated into the house finding it quiet but her mama was still up.

"Mama, why aren't you in bed? Ya'll usually go to bed with the chickens."

"I know, Honey, but I wanted talk to you for a few minutes. I know now how wrong I was about the diet. I should have got right on it like your daddy did. I'm on it now, and we'll both stick to it.

"Please don't feel hard towards your mama. I'm old and set in my ways."

"Mama, I don't feel hard towards you. I'm sure what you've been through has been hard but what matters is now you're on the right track. I love you, Mama. Always know that I do."

They hugged and she walked down to hall to her room with tears in her eyes.

SNR

Saturday morning arrived with sounds coming from the kitchen. Putting on a robe, she walked down the hall finding her daddy reading the paper and enjoying his coffee.

"Daddy, you still get up with the chickens. Did you rest good last night?"

"Honey, I'm sleeping better now than I ever did. I guess that diet food ain't as hard to digest and what I'd been eating.

"Did ya'll have good time last night?"

"Yes, we did, Daddy. We had dinner at the Chop House in Wilmington. The food was delicious and I enjoyed being with Brian. We're going back to Wilmington for brunch this morning."

"Honey, I've always liked him. I don't know nothing about your other fellow but I hope you and Brian can hook up again."

"We'll see, Daddy; it's so nice being with him again. He's changed so much and all in the right ways but thankfully, he's still Brian, deep down inside."

SNR

Their brunch at the Basics in the Cotton Exchange was fun. Kayla ordered the Southern Grits and Brian chose the Southern Benedict.

Afterwards, they visited some of the many shops and boutiques in the exchange before driving over to the waterfront. The October air was a bit chilly causing their walk to be shortened, but it was fun.

Being with Brian anywhere was fun. She realized that more and more each time they were together.

Back in Kenansville, he asked if she had time to see his home?

She would make the time. She very much wanted to see it.

"Yes, I'd like that."

His home, beside the Graham House, was of the same time period and had been professionally decorated to mirror the eighteen-hundreds.

Totally rewired, plumbed, with an up-to-date HVAC system, it was beautiful but comfortable.

From the parlor, they walked through the dining room with its table for twenty-four. The place settings were exquisite. It appeared to have just been set for a party. Only the guests and food were absent.

The kitchen, while maintaining the period look, was fully functional and included a Viking gas range-top, double ovens, broiler, and grill. The refrigeration was Viking also. The cooking fireplace was left intact with the cooking rack still in place with several different sized cast iron pots hanging on hooks. Two Dutch Ovens dominated the space between the andirons.

Back in the hall that stretched from the front entrance to the rear leading to a veranda, he pointed out the library saying he used it as his home office.

Leading her up the winding staircase to the landing, he explained that originally, the upper level contained four bedrooms with no closets or bathrooms.

"On the back, I converted two rooms into the master suite including a master bath, walk-in closets, and dressing area. May I show it to you?"

"Yes, please. I know it's going to be beautiful."

It was, almost taking her breath. Entering, there was a seating group between her and the huge four-poster rice bed, complete with a canopy. The bed was accompanied by night stands on either side. The lamps were converted decorative kerosene lamps with beautiful globes from the period.

A lone chest-of-drawers was on one side of the fireplace and a dresser on the other. Two Lazy-Boy reclining rockers faced the fireplace. Across the spacious room on the rear wall were double French doors leading out on an upper-level balcony.

Standing on the balcony, the view of the formal gardens was breath-taking.

"If we have time, I'll walk you around the gardens."

Back inside, he led her to a dressing area with built-in drawers on the left and a huge walk-in closet on the right but nothing she'd seen prepared her for the master bath.

Entering, on the left, there was a huge walk-in shower, totally tiled with showerheads at various levels. Stemmed glasses populated the shelves above a glass-door wine refrigerator filled with bottles of wine.

Walking up one step, a huge Jacuzzi filled the bay window area. The view was of the gardens below. He explained that the windows were one-way. On the right, a double vanity occupied about six-feet of space and then there were private stalls for the bidet and water closet. Beside them, a linen closet filled the space to the entrance.

She was spell-bound, almost without words.

"Brian, I don't know what to say; it's too beautiful to describe. I know that you must be very proud of what you've done. Living in something like this is very hard for me to imagine. I know that you enjoy every minute you're here."

"I would enjoy it so much more if you were here with me."

She started to reply but instead, looked into his eyes and smiled knowing that if he touched her, they would not leave without becoming one. She'd weakened almost to the point of no return. Their high school reunion was only weeks away. It would happen then. She was sure of it and she was more than ready. She'd denied herself far too long, no more.

After showing her, the front two bedrooms separated by a full bath, he led her back to the landing and down the winding stairs. A tour of the gardens would come later. They knew there would be a later.

Arriving back at her parent's home, he walked her to the door, saying.

"Thank you for sharing your day with me. You'll never know how much I look forward to being with you. I've waiting and hoped for far too many years and now I'm with you. Kayla, it's so much more that I even dreamed it would or could be. You know that I love you. I always have and always will. Please know that."

"I've occupied so much of your time here. As much as I want us to be together, I'm going to allow you time to spend with your parents. I'll be in Greenville for a meeting Wednesday. Will you have dinner with me?"

"Brian, I enjoy every minute we've together. For so many years I didn't allow you, or anyone, into my life. Now, I look forward to each moment we're together.

I'd love to have dinner with you on Wednesday. Message, or text, me and let me know where we're dining and what time."

They were in each other's arms now, his lips on hers. He was kissing her and she was kissing him. Neither wanted the moment to end but it must. Wednesday couldn't come soon enough.

Inside, she found her parents asleep in their recliners. It was a good opportunity to check her messages. There were several from Lynn. From their content, he seemed more than aware that she was slipping away from him.

From her perspective, he's brought it on himself. He'd done almost nothing to hold on to her. She knew that he could have come home, at least once, but he didn't. Instead, he entertained himself with all that Paris had to offer leaving her to pine and wait for him.

He'd probably waiting too long. It was all his fault. Yes, she would have probably still been lonely and waiting if the series of events surrounding her father' heart attack hadn't brought Brian back into her life.

Now, Lynn was on the back burner where he'd placed himself. She still cared deeply for him but he was there and she, and Brian, were here.

Hi, Lynn. I'm visiting my parents. I came down yesterday and had dinner with Brian last night in Wilmington. Today, we had brunch and he took me on a tour of his home. It's beautiful. I'll probably spend the afternoon and evening with mama and daddy. I'd like to take them out somewhere for supper but I don't think they're ready for that. They're doing well with the bland diets and I don't want to tempt them.

Daddy has a doctor's appointment Tuesday. I think the neighbor's will take him. The doctor doesn't want him to drive for six-weeks.

That's about it from here. When are you leaving for the Rivera? I know you are looking forward to that. I guess I would. I've never been out of the country. I don't even have a passport but I've never needed one either.

Kayla

Before hitting the send button, she hesitated, knowing that by Monday, Mary would be all over her. She appreciated all that Mary had done for her over the years but now it was time to finally live again. If Mary jumped on her case, she'd jump back.

SEND!

It was done, now all she had to do was wait for the barrage that she was sure would come. Being in Brian's arms fortified her. She was ready.

SNR

That evening, she watched her mama preparing supper. It was about as bland as a diet could get. The baked chicken breasts would be okay but rice without any salt, butter, or gravy would be horrible. The frozen garden peas had been boiled with absolutely no seasonings. She was determined to act as if eating that way was normal but, every day, no way.

When they were seated at the table, her daddy returned thanks like he always, short and to the point.

They began eating as if the food was good. Maybe as the days slipped by, their tastes were really changing. She hoped so, one of her biggest fears was her daddy slipping off the diet and returning to his old ways.

SNR

Sunday morning, after a breakfast of poached eggs and grits, she said goodbye and returned to Greenville arriving just in time for lunch.

When she walked into the Three Steers, she saw Ginger seated alone and joined her.

"Hey, what did you order?"

Ginger greeting her, replying,

The hamburger steak, rice, gravy, and broccoli with cheese."

The waitress arrived taking a duplicate order and coffee.

"How was your visit? Did you see Brian?"

"It was nice, very nice, Brian took me out to eat Friday night in Wilmington and we had brunch Saturday at the Cotton Exchange in Wilmington before walking on the waterfront."

"When we returned, Ginger, he took me on a tour of his home. It was unbelievable. The house is 1800's colonial but has been updated with wiring, plumbing, bathrooms, a master suite that includes a dressing area with a huge walk-in closet. The master bath... Ginger, I couldn't believe it. I could spend the rest of the day just describing it.

"There are formal gardens out back that can be viewed from the master suite balcony, jacuzzi, or the veranda below. It's decorated with some of the plushest furniture I've ever seen.

"The kitchen still has the huge cooking fireplace but all the appliances are Viking. He's really turned his home into a showplace. He uses the library for his home office.

"When I go down for the reunion, he wants to show me his cottage at Wrightsville Beach and I'm so ready to see it."

Ginger was smiling now, she replied,

"You've seen Brian, that's for certain. When you mention his name, your eyes sparkle. If I were a betting woman but, I haven't met Lynn."

"Lynn's still in the picture but with each passing day, his image gets dimmer and dimmer."

"Brian will be in Greenville Wednesday. He's taking me out to dinner. There's no question that he still loves me and I'm beginning to wonder if he's is the only man I ever truly loved."

SNR

Wednesday arrived and with it, messages from Brian and Lynn. There were three from Lynn. One on Monday, One on Tuesday, and another late last night. She'd ignored the Monday one, and answered the Tuesday one saying again,

You're there, I'm here. I'm moving on with my life. I've been hold long enough. Enjoy your time with your son and the Rivera. I'm going to enjoy mine here.

The last one simply asked?

Are you telling me to move on?

Her reply was just as simple and to the point.

As I posted before, You're there and I'm here.

Opening Brian's, he wished her a good morning saying they would dine at Eli's Charcoal Steak House on the Waterfront in Washington.

"I'll pick you up at six-thirty. Our reservations are for seven-thirty. I miss you, Brian.

She's heard of Eli's but had been told that it was very expensive so she'd never been. She was looking forward to it and being with Brian too.

I'm looking forward to it, I'll C U at six-thirty.

SNR

She had lunch with Mary but chose not to mention her date with Brian knowing that it was church night for her and there wouldn't be any exercising.

Their whole lunch hour was about Lynn and how sorry he was for not coming home at least once.

"He said that it was a huge mistake and he felt that you were slipping through his fingers. He really wants to make amends when he comes back here Christmas."

Kayla wasn't going to address her remark directly but wanted Mary to understand where she was.

"Christmas is over two-months away. He's been gone over two-years keeping me on hold while he's been enjoying Paris and doing whatever he pleases. Now he's off to the Rivera with his son.

"What he's doing, Mary, says tons about where I fit into his life. He's only going to visit Christmas and then he'll be gone again."

"I think it's time for me to have a reality check, Mary. Don't you agree?"

Mary, the ball's back in your court. What' your response, now?

She knew that she'd backed her into a corner. It was time for her to come out of Lynn's corner and sit in hers for a change.

"Kayla, I have to admit that what Lynn done was wrong. I hope you'll give him a chance to make amends. I've known you for a long time and I'm sure you're ready to move on. If Lynn blew it, so be it.

"You have to do what you think is best for you. Please know that all I want for you is the best life has to offer."

SNR

It was almost six-thirty and she was so ready to see Brian. There it was, the doorbell, precisely at six-thirty.

"Brian, please come in."

He kissed her tenderly on the lips saying they should get started. His GPS would have to guide them.

"I haven't been to Eli's but it comes highly recommended from one of my major vendors. I'll soon know if he's as reliable with his recommendations of restaurants as he is with his choices of farm equipment."

"How has your week been?"

"It's been okay, I've been looking forward to tonight. The restaurant doesn't matter. I'm just looking forward to being with you."

"Me too, Kayla, each time we part, I'm already looking forward to the next time we'll be together"

Arriving in Washington, he turned south on business 17 crossing the bridge.

"It's on the left at the foot of the bridge. Mr. Latham said that years ago, there was an oyster bar there."

Seeing the restaurant, Kayla knew that it was going to be nice. It looked very expensive.

Inside, when asked about reservations, Brian replied,

"Howard, party of two."

"Very good, right this way please."

They were seated by a window with a panoramic view of the river and the waterfront. Someone had chosen a perfect location. Others must have thought so too. It was extremely busy.

"Hi, I'm Patsy, I'll be taking care of you tonight. What may I bring you for beverages?"

Brian looked across asking,

"Wine, Cocktail?"

"Wine, you choose."

"Please bring us a bottle of the Innocent Bystander, please."

"Very good sir, I'll only be a moment."

Kayla, looked across at Brian with her cute little smile,

"Innocent Bystander?"

Brian chuckled, replying,

"It's a Pinot Noir from Australia. I think you'll like it."

After tasting and approving, their waitress poured two-tapers while asking about starters?

He looked across at her, asking?

"Appetizer, soup, or both?"

"May I begin with the New England Clam Chowder, please?"

"Bring my lady the clam chowder and I'll have the wedge."

He reached over touching her hand.

"It's a little over a week before our reunion. I am looking forward to spending most of the weekend with you. Kayla, I haven't been this excited in years. I haven't been this excited since you left."

She could feel chills running up and down her spine knowing she hadn't been either. There'd been excitement with Jeff and there had been excitement with Lynn but it was different. She was sure that she loved Jeff and was very close to loving Lynn but somehow, this was totally different.

"Yes, we'll together most of the time and I am looking forward to it. I guess that we'll really turn some heads at the reunion."
"If we walk into Woody's, I'm sure that we'll turn heads there too."

Before their soup and salad arrived, Brian pointed to the Steak Au Poivre on the menu saying,

"You said you wanted to try this. Would you like to have it tonight?"

She'd seen it but it was expensive and had decided on something else but if he wanted her to try it, she would.

When their waitress returned with her soup and his salad, he placed their order saying,

"We're in no hurry so don't rush our steaks, please."

"Very good, Sir, I'll keep checking on you."

When their steaks arrived, Kayla knew from the presentation that they could only be delicious, they were.

"Crushed peppercorns and what else?"

"Kayla, the flavor comes from the bourbon. I watched Bobby cook them once. The steaks are crusted in crushed pepper corns and placed in a very hot cast iron pan. The bourbon is added as each side is seared. This is excellent. They must have a great chef."

"Dessert?"

"Could we split one?"

"Waitress, we'll split the double chocolate cake with cherries and ice cream. I'm sure the port wine really adds to the flavor too."

"Yes, Sir, it's our most popular dessert."

When she returned and they sampled it, it was easy to see why it was so popular.

"Coffee?"

"Please."

"Two coffees, please, black.

It pleased her to no end that he remembered everything. He was phenomenal in every aspect she could think of. Next weekend was going to be marvelous, it just had to be.

After spending a few moments walking along the waterfront, they returned to Greenville sharing a cup of coffee at Darla's before saying goodnight.
Standing at the door, he lingered, she wanted him to.

"Till next Friday?"

"Next Friday."

The Reunion, It Was Finally Here

The weekend and week breezed by without too much excitement. Lynn was all over her by text, message, and phone but he was still four-thousand miles away

Mary had subtly tried to advocate for Lynn but she was wearing thin with excuses and reasons to wait a little longer.

Ginger, on the other hand, was positive telling Kayla to go, enjoy, it was finally her time.

It was her time and she was going to make the best of it.

Leaving at lunch on Friday, she grabbed a quick bite at McDonalds on her way home. Her bags were packed. She'd change clothes when she arrived in Duplin Country.

Brian texted asking what time would she arrive?

She texted back indicating that it would be around three.

Would U like 2 see the beach cottage this afternoon? - B

Love 2 – K
C U 3:30 – B

The beach cottage, she was ready. She'd take a small overnight bag just in case they decided to spend the night. She really hoped they would. Her excitement was almost off the scale.

Arriving at 2:30, she spent an hour with her parents knowing Brian would be there soon. She couldn't believe how good they looked. They really looked younger.

"That diet must be agreeing with you."

"Honey, it's doing wonders for both of us. We're walking almost an hour every morning now. Sometimes, we miss that hog lard but we get over it pretty fast now."

"Are you looking forward to the reunion?"

"Yes, Daddy, I'm excited. I didn't believe I'd ever go to one but here I am."

"Brian, stopped by three or four times checking on us. He's excited too. You know I want ya'll to get back together."

"Yes, Mama, we'll see. This weekend may tell the tale."

Brian was right one time. He came inside to speak to her parents.

"Mr. and Mrs. Howard, you're looking healthier every time I come by. The diet is working wonders for you."

"Kayla, are we ready?"

"Yes, let me get my bag."

SNR

A little over an hour later, they crossed the bridge arriving at Wrightsville Beach. His cottage was located on the beach on Lumina Avenue.

It was located on the ocean front with beautiful views of the ocean. Her tour began in the entertainment room, then the den that led into the open dining and bar area. A gourmet kitchen contained two dishwashers, wine cooler, gas stove, granite countertops and a separate built-in twin-door refrigerator and freezer. There was an office nook in the hall that contained a pantry and laundry room.

Someone had done an exceptional job decorating the entire main level. She was sure the other levels would mirror the main level, and they did.

The elevator stopped first on the second level containing three bedrooms, each with a private bath and access to the spacious wrap around decking. The upper level opened into the master suite complete with walk-in closets, dressing area and bath complete with a jacuzzi with a panoramic view of the ocean and beach.

The master bedroom contained a seating area with a fireplace with gas logs, a huge king-sized bed and accompanying accessories all done in beachy décor. Double doors opened onto a large, partially covered balcony and hot tub.

All during the tour, thoughts were rapid-fire throughout her whole being. She knew that would be a perfect place for her to return to the land of the living. She'd been dead for far too long and she was ready to move on with a man she was sure she loved.

Back down on the main level, Brian opened a bottle of Carolina Red pouring two tapers.

"Let's walk out on the deck. It looks like a beautiful evening."

They remained for a few minutes but the October chill and ocean breeze sent them scurrying back inside.

"What time would you like to eat?"

It was almost six and the dark of night was relentlessly pushing the light of day further and further away.

"Now, if you're ready."

"Let's do. Are we coming back here?"

She was more than ready,

"Yes, if you'd like."

Before leaving, she called her parents,

"Mama, Kayla, we're not coming back until tomorrow. It will probably be after lunch... No, we're staying at his cottage... Yes, it's beautiful... Okay, I love you too, I'll see you and daddy tomorrow, bye."

Arriving at the Bridge Tender Restaurant, they were seated by a window with a view of the bridge.

Their waiter asked about beverages?

Wine?"

"That would be nice."

"A bottle of the Douro White, please."

"Very good, Sir, I'll only be a moment."

"You are exceptionally radiant tonight. May I ask why?"

She knew he didn't have to ask. She was sure he already knew."

"Being with you makes me glow. Remember?"

"I remember so very well. I cannot tell you how happy being with you, makes me, thank you."

The waiter interrupted showing first the bottle and then opening it, pouring just a little for Brian to taste.

"Yes, that's fine."

"Would you be interested in starters, Sir?"

"Give us a few moments."

"Very good, Sir."

"Would you care for an appetizer?"

"Yes, the coconut shrimp, please."

"Excellent choice, I think I'd like that too."

"A salad?"

"The Iceberg wedge looks good, may I?"

"An excellent choice again. That's my choice too."

Their waiter was back.

"Waiter, we'll both have the coconut shrimp with the wedge to follow."

"Thank you, Sir. I'll put your order in."

"Now, maybe we'll have a few minutes before he'll want to know about our main entrees.

"I'm excited about tomorrow night. Are you?"

She was probably more excited about tonight but that would have to wait until after dinner. Replying, she said,

"Yes, Brian, I am. I can't believe that when I received the invitation, I almost threw it away and would have if circumstances hadn't brought us back together.

"It's going to be interesting, and surprising to some, but I know it will be fun; especially since I'll be with you."

He replied,

"Yes, it will be a shocking surprise but not for me. I never stopped believing that we belong together. I love you. You know that I do and I want nothing more than to spend the rest of my life with you."

He'd placed the ball squarely in her court. It was up to her and she was almost sure what her decision would be. Tonight, would almost seal their fate.

Their starters and then their salads arrived and the waiter wanted to know about their main entrees?

"Have you decided?"

She'd looked at the choices,

"I'd like the crab-stuffed flounder please."

"And you, Sir?"

"The grilled salmon, please."

The seriousness of the moment had been broken but the probable highlight of the evening was still in front of them. It was for her and she was sure it would be for him too.

Their main entrees behind them, he asked about dessert. They looked at the offerings and chose to split a Fudge Brownie Napoleon.

"Are you ready?"

Yes, she was more than ready.

"Yes, if you are."

They had barely gotten in the door when he turned to her. She threw her arms around him a moments later, they were in the master suite with clothes falling carelessly here and there.

Now they were locked in a lover's embrace and as his lips kissed and sought her love. His hands were on her breasts then her hips.

She was whispering,

"Come to me, come to me."

They were finally one, climbing their mountain of love. Reaching the peak, they descended and climbed, more slowly this time, to the summit; holding the moment, savoring each moment they'd hoped and dreamed of for so many long years.

Finally falling asleep, still in a lover's embrace, their dreams wrapped around them delivering them into a new day.

SNR

Next morning, she awakened to the sounds of sea gulls quarreling outside. She smiled remembering last night and the events leading up to their becoming one.

That's when she realized that she was alone. Brian was gone. Where was he?

She showered and dressed before taking the elevator down to the main level.

When the door opened, she saw him sitting at the island counter, dressed only in shorts, drinking a cup of coffee and reading a paper.

"Good morning."

He looked around and smiling replied,

Yes, it is, good morning. I was going to wait another hour before awakening you. Did you sleep well?"

Did I sleep well, he knows I did?

"Yes, very well, and you?"

"You were beside me and in my arms, yes, I slept like lamb."
"Coffee?"

"Yes, please. When are we going to eat? I'm starving."

"He laughed, replying,

"You should be, it was all I could do to hold on."

"Brian Howard, I can't believe you said that. I begged for seatbelts half way up the mountain the first time."

He was grinning now.

"You didn't need seatbelts once you locked your legs around me."

"Feed me and we'll see who's holding on to who."

"Give me a minute."

He disappeared into the elevator and minutes later reappeared dressed in slacks and a collared polo.

"Waffles, pancakes, or omelet?"

"Omelet."

"Country ham, sausage, or bacon?"

"Bacon."

"Let's go."

Minutes later, they arrived at the Sweet N Savory at Pavilion Place finding it busy but they were easily seated.

They ordered coffee first and then bacon and cheese omelets.

"This is delicious, they could make a fortune in Greenville."

"They probably could anywhere but they're content right here."

"A second cup of coffee?"

"No, I have something better waiting for me."

SNR

Back at the cottage,

"Now, where were we?"

Minutes later, they were climbing their mountain again. The urgency was gone. Now, it was just them becoming one over and over again.

She marveled at the euphoric feelings surging throughout her whole being. All the years of emptiness had been erased. It was as if they'd never existed. There was only now and there was Brian. She felt fulfilled again.

"We've got to get a move on; our reunion is waiting."

She glanced at the clock on the nightstand. It was after eleven. Where had the morning gone?

They stopped at Paul's Place for hot dogs on their way back. It had been a couple of years for Kayla but they were a good as she remembered.

"The night I saw you in Wallace, Ginger and stopped by here on our way to tour of the battleship, Calabash, and Southport. She'd never had them but promised that she would again before she died.

"They are delicious. I've never tasted anything like them anywhere I've been."

"I know what you mean. It's hard to pass by without stopping; even if you're on I-40 and have to exit to get here."

Just before two, they arrived back at her parents.

I'll be by at six to pick you up. This is going to be fun now that we're back together."

With a kiss, he was gone. She walked into the house still floating on a cloud. Her parents were waiting for her.

Her mama spoke first.

"Honey, did ya'll have a good time?"

"Yes, Mama, we had a wonderful time. I'm the happiest I've been in a long, long, time. It's so good to be back with Brian. I may finally find happiness again."

Her smartphone interrupted her. It was Lynn.

She turned to walk down the hall saying,

"I should take this, Lynn, hello… You're where?… When did you get there?… No, I'm going to my reunion tonight with Brian. You know that… Not before early afternoon… Lynn, yes, I'm happy that you finally decided to come for a visit but why now? You've known about my reunion for months… No, I'm going to the reunion… No, I'm going with Brian. I told you a dozen times that I was… Yes, I'll call tomorrow when I get home, bye."

She couldn't believe he was doing this. How could he expect her to change her plans? No, she wasn't going to. She was going with Brian and that was that.

"Honey, who was that? You seem upset."

"Daddy, I am. That was Lynn. He's in Farmville and expects me to drop everything and go meet him. He knew the reunion was tonight. He's trying to wedge himself between Brian and me. It's not going to happen. I'm going to the reunion with Brian. I'll see Lynn tomorrow afternoon when I get back to Greenville.

"I can't believe he has the nerve to do what he's doing. Daddy, he's been in Paris for two long years leaving me here hanging and now he's back for two or three days expecting to pick up where he left me... I think a lot of him but now, Brian's back in my life.

"It can't get much more complicated but I'll work my way through it. I've been lonely and alone for far too long, no more. The emptiness in my heart stops here."

"Honey, you'll work it out, you seemed so happy when you walked in. That ought to tell you something. Listen to your heart, Honey. It will tell you who you love.

"Ain't that right, Hon?"

"Sure, nuff is, it's never failed me and yere mama."

Lynn was on the back burner now. It was time to dress for the reunion. She looked gorgeous in her orange side-ruffled dress. The emerald accessories were perfect. She was ready and just in time.

Someone was knocking at the door, it must be him. She heard a mama letting him.

"I'm ready."

"Kayla, you are absolutely stunning. I'm so ready for our classmates to see you."

First on Hwy 11 and then the Tram Road, they arrived at Britt's Seafood locating the banquet entrance on the right side.

Carolyn Kay Smith welcomed them.

"You don't have to tell me who you are. Neither of you have changed at all and you're still together."

She located their nametags while they signed in.

"Walk on in, there are quite a few already here."

They moved around the room recognizing some of their classmate but other's only after looking at their senior pics on their nametags. Many appeared old while a few, including them, appeared to have aged little.

At seven, someone on the PA instructed everyone to be seated.

"We'll eat first and then let everyone be introduced and tell us a little about the past 30 years."
"We'll begin with a prayer by Reverend Frank Sutton, remember him?"

After the opening prayer, the wait staff took beverage orders while others placed the food, family style, on the tables.
The entrees included: fried chicken, BBQ, fried shrimp, French fries, string beans, boiled potatoes, squash casserole, slaw, baked beans, and potato salad.

Sandi and Max Waters, set across from them. It was no surprise to see them together. They were married right out of high school. Max went to work for DuPont and Sandi first worked for a lawyer in Kinston until their third daughter arrived. At that point, she became a stay-at-home-mom.

Beside of them, Carol Mercer Hart and her husband, Douglas, joined in their conversation.

"Brian, you sat ahead of me in English. You were so wrapped up with Kayla, you barely knew any of the rest of us existed.
"Do you remember the time, Mr. Wells, made you come to the front of the class and recite Elizabeth Barrett Browning's poem because you were paying all your attention to Kaya?"

Laughing now, Brian responded,

"Like it was yesterday…

He took Kayla's hand and recited the poem.

How do I love thee? Let me count the ways.
I love thee to the depth and breadth and height
My soul can reach, when feeling out of sight
For the ends of Being and ideal Grace.
I love thee to the level of everyday's
Most quiet need, by sun and candle-light.
I love thee freely, as men strive for Right;
I love thee purely, as they turn from Praise.
I love thee with a passion put to use
In my old griefs, and with my childhood's faith.
I love thee with a love I seemed to lose
With my lost saints, --- I love thee with the breath,
Smiles, tears, of all my life! --- and, if God choose,
I shall but love thee better after death.

Neither realized that Mr. Edgar Wells was only a few feet away talking to one of their classmates and heard the recitation

"I loved her then and still do with all my heart."

"That's so sweet, you two must have had a wonderful life together."

"No, not really, we parted two years after graduation and have just gotten reacquainted a month ago."

It was Kayla's turn.

"I moved to Greenville to study at ECU and Brian stayed here. I married and had two children before my husband's wondering eye turned him into my ex. That was twenty-two years ago.

"Daddy had a heart attack six or seven weeks ago and they flew him to Greenville.

"Brian came by to check on him and as they say, 'the rest is history' and we're together again."

She hadn't told him about Lynn. She'd tried to a couple of times but his excitement wouldn't allow her to.

He'd probably want to take her to his home after the reunion. Yes, she'd go. She'd tell him then.

When it was apparent that most had finished eating, the MC, Travis Sutton, announced that it was time for introductions.

"There are a hundred thirty-seven stories, please keep it brief but tell us what's happening in your life."

There were three rows. The introductions began on the speaker's right. They were on his left about half way down on the outside. As each class member stood, it became very apparent that it probably wouldn't take very long. Most only introduced themselves and their other half, if there was one. Beyond that, a few mentioned college and children but little else.

Roger Hussey was one of the exceptions. He was a brigadier general in the Air Force and was the commanding officer at Shaw AFB in South Carolina. His wife, Kazumi, was from Tokyo, Japan. They had two sons. Both were married and officers in the Air Force. There were three grandchildren.

The introductions moved steadily on until it reached Mary Frances Stroud Foucaulti. She'd moved to Hollywood, California the year she graduated and attended Berkley where she met Michael Foucaulti. He was a professor in the geology department.

285

"We've spent most of the last thirty years at geology sites in the Mediterranean, mostly around Cypress and the Greek Islands.

"Michael made a significant fine on the Cyclades Island of Folegandros nine years ago and we return each year to further his study. He now heads the geology department. We have 2 children

"Dolan is twenty-six and is a professor at Duke. Bethesda, Beth, is twenty-two. She was born in a private hospital on the island of Crete. She has a Ph.D. in geology and is on staff in the Earth department at Cornell. She's married and has one child.

"We've had an exciting life and are eagerly looking forward to our next thirty years."

They were in the middle row moving right along past a sheriff, police chief, fire chief, chef, five school teachers, another minister, until they reached Damon Proctor. He stood, first introducing his wife. Cassandra, 'Cass,"

"We make our home on Kant Key. For the past eleven years, we've been hunting for sunken Spanish Galleons. Cass is from Nassau. I met her twenty years ago. I'm sure most of you don't remember when my parents were killed in an avalanche in Colorado. I sold the farm and equipment to Turner Farms and flew to Nassau with Shank Miller. He was a grade ahead of us.

"One the second day, we were having lunch when Cass, along with three of her friends came in and sat at the table beside us. We took one look at each other and we've been tied together ever since.

"She grew up in Nassau but went to school in Puerto Rico. She speaks, English, French, and Spanish fluently. Me, just southern although now I can read Spanish treasure maps.

"We started treasure hunting for fun until we ran across a small unexplored wreck between Cat Island and San Salvador. We didn't find a huge treasure but the doubloon and six pieces of eight along with some other relics whetted our appetites and we got serious about it.

"It's more research than anything else but cutting my story short, three years later we hit a big one. Big for us anyway. Because of a document we signed, we can't divulge the name of the wreck or how much treasure we found. It was substantial though.

"Now, we own an island and pretty much do as we please. Ours is a good life. That I can attest to."

Everyone knew that would be a hard act to follow but one by one, the line moved on.

Finally, on their line of tables it worked its way down the inner isle, Sandi and Max shared their stories and a little further down, Mac Batchelor stood introducing his wife saying he'd had a couple others but he guessed he'd probably stick with this one. and finally, to them.

Brian stood yielding to Kayla, saying,

"I'll let Kayla go first but to satisfy your minds, no, we haven't been together for the past thirty years but I hope we will be for the next thirty, Kayla."

No until now, we haven't been together for twenty-eight years. After getting my two-year degree at James Sprunt, I moved to Greenville to study a at ECU.

"I met my ex-husband there. We have two beautiful children. Kevin and his wife, Kylie, live in Concord. They have one son, Ray, he's three.

"My daughter, Amy is a junior at UNC-Chapel Hill.

"My ex-husband's wondering eye caused our divorce in 1987. Currently, he lives in Opelika, Alabama.

"Brian came back into my life almost two-months ago when my father had a heart attack. We've been together frequently since then. If it's meant to be, we'll be together again, this time for the rest of our lives.

"Brian, your turn."

He stood, kissing her before she could sit back down.

"Okay, she left Duplin County and I stayed. No, I didn't go to college. I worked on the farm until my parents were killed in a wreck on Sarecta Road.
"I sold the farm and bought my first tractor equipment dealership in Kenansville.

"Since then, I've purchased three others and am in negotiations for three, maybe four, more. I also invest in lucrative properties and businesses."

"I live beside the Graham House in Kenansville after doing extensive renovations. I have a beach cottage at Wrightsville Beach and another one in the Florida Keys on Long Key. I have investment property in Key West but have no interest in living there."

When Kayla came back into my life, I turned my attention to her. If she agrees, we will never part again."

He'd done everything but get down on his knee and propose. His classmates were holding their breath thinking at any moment he would but he stopped short knowing she wouldn't say yes. Not yet.

Finishing the introductions, the MC introduced several of their teachers. Mr. Edgar Wells, Jr. was one of them. When he stood, he singled Brian out.

"Brian Howard, I'm impressed, your recitation of Elizabeth Barrett Browning's poem as actually better than when you recited it thirty years ago. Kayla Herring, you realize, of course, that he had an advantage this time. He was looking directly at you."

"Each of you is my life and I try very hard to keep in touch with as many as possible. Thank you for inviting me to be part of your reunion."

The applause was long and thunderous. Many had tears in their eyes as memories of school days flooded through their minds.

The MC was asking who traveled the furthest? Malcolm Grady won the honors. He'd traveled from Manarola, Italy. His wife's family owned a villa on the coast.

It was time to close the official part though many would linger.

"Everyone, please stand as we sing our school song."

"Mr. Wells will play it through once and then we'll sing it.

Here's to you, Duplin General, True to you we'll always be.
Standing for our school together, One united family.
Wave the red, white, blue and gold, Show with pride your loyalty.
Though we part from one another, Duplin General we'll always will be. It's Rah,
rah for Duplin General. Duplin General we'll always be. Go with us now our
separate way but in our hearts, we'll always stay.

Tears were flowing everywhere. It was time to say goodbye until another day and maybe another reunion. It was time to tell Brian about Lynn.

SNR

Arriving at Brian's home, he took her bag and led her up the stairs to the master suite. After spending an hour in the jacuzzi, he led her to the bed. Still nude, they caressed and kissed. Climbing their mountain began slowly but then faster and faster until they reached the summit. Step by step, they came back down, rested, and climbed to the summit again.

Exhausted, they showered together before walking out on the balcony. It was too chilly to remain so they descended the stairs and walked into the den.

"Sit here while I make coffee. Would you like a cinnamon bun? They're frozen but it will only take a minute to thaw them."

"No, coffee's fine. May I help you?"

"I'll do it, it will only take a minute with the Keurig. Flavored or unflavored?"

"Unflavored, please."

He disappeared through the door. She had to tell him. She'd waited longer than she should have. How would he respond. Twenty-eight years ago, she knew. Now, she wasn't sure. It didn't make any difference. He had to be told.

He returned with the coffee sitting beside her. She tasted the coffee first before beginning. Clearing her throat, she began,

"Brian, Lynn is in Farmville. I'll have to see him when I get back tomorrow."

He looked at her, replying,

"Of course, you should. You have something special with him. I can only hope that what we have is stronger. I love you, Kayla. Maybe after seeing him, you'll know if your love is only for me."

She couldn't believe what she was hearing. When they parted so many years ago, he would have been ranting and raving but now, calmly, he was saying that she should see Lynn.

A choice had to be made. A choice only she could make.

She reached for him, kissing him tenderly at first, then, with more passion.

"Brian, you've changed so much. I'm so proud of what you've become. Hold me, please.

The coffee was untouched. Back in the master's suite, they were back in each other's arms, locked in a lover's embrace. They would climb their mountain again and again before the light of day slipped quietly into the room.

There's been little sleep, but neither missed it. They were together, together as one.

S.NR

As the colors of dawn filled the room with a pallet of orange and gold. He slipped from her arms, showered, and wearing only shorts, and stole quietly down stairs to the kitchen.

He returned a few minutes later with a steaming cup of hot coffee. She stirred as he entered the bedroom.

"Sleeping Beauty, has joined the living. Good morning."

Still nude, sitting up, she pulled the sheet around her. Why? She didn't know. Modesty probably demanded it.

"Coffee, good morning. You've already showered. It's still, early isn't it?"

"Not if we're going to church. You are still going with me, aren't you?"

She vaguely remembered saying she would.

"I'll have to go to mama and daddy's to change. How much time do we have?"

"Plenty of time, we could climb our mountain if you'd like."

The coffee got cold again.

"What happened to my coffee? It's cold!"

"Us, we're what happened. Get dressed and come to the kitchen. I'll make you another cup."

Finally enjoying her cup of coffee, and a cinnamon bun, they talked little about Lynn. Rather, they remembered the reunion and how much fun they had.

Squeezing her hand, he admitted that he would have gone without her but it would have been an empty experience.

"I only hope that we're together when they hold another one.

"We'll see, you know I have to see Lynn."

"Yes, Kayla, I want you too. May the best man, Me, win."

She wouldn't commit although she wondered if Lynn could bring the spark back that existed when he was pulled away. Two long years had passed and he'd done little to solidify his position.

Yes, he'd called, texted, and messaged, but that took little effort and he'd made no effort to come back for a visit.

She'd know soon.

"It's almost nine-thirty, take my car, or I'll take you, and go get dressed. I'd like to leave here at twenty of eleven for church."

"Go with me, I know Mama and Daddy would enjoy seeing you."

"Okay, I'll grab slacks and a tee. I'll dress for church when we get back."

When they drove past Woody's, Kayla mentioned that she hadn't had an opportunity to stop in.

"We can have lunch there if you'd like. I'd planned on the Squire but we'll do Woody's if you'd rather."

He was so accommodating, she couldn't believe the change but he was.

"The Squire is fine, I'll see Woody on my next time down."

At that point in time, she was sure it would be soon. After all, Lynn was only there for a few days.

Mama, Daddy, good morning. I'm going to change clothes so we can go to church."

Her mama's curiosity had to be satisfied first.

"Did Ya'll have a good time at the reunion?"

"Yes, Mama, we did. I'll let Brian tell you all about it while I change."

She walked to her room leaving Brian to answer a barrage of questions from her parents.

Her mama was still asking questions when she returned to the den.

"I'm ready."

"Okay, we need to leave. I have to dress now."

SNR

They walked into Grove Presbyterian Church knowing every eye in the congregation would be on them.

Reverend Bron, had greeted them outside alerting them that the congregation was all abuzz about the reunion saying in a small town, news traveled fast.

They took seats in the third pew from the front on the left. It was apparent that all eyes were on them, especially the ladies.

After Reverend Bron's message, they were inundated with greetings and well wishes. Half the congregation knew, or remembered, who Kayla was and everyone knew Brian and the part he was playing in their community.

It took thirty-minutes to break away. After a short drive down Hwy 24, they arrived at the Squire finding a lengthy line but their reservations had them seated quickly at Brian's favorite table in the pantry.

After ordering Pomegranate Orange Mimosa's, they chose the Grilled Chicken Caesar with shrimp. At Brian's suggestion, they added sides of home fried potatoes.

"What time do you need to leave?"

"I told him that I'd get back about two. That's not going to happen. I want to spend a little time with you before I leave if that's okay with you."

"Please spend as much time as you can. You know that I don't want to let you go."

Leaving was getting harder and harder but she knew she had to.

"I need to leave mama and daddy's by five."

SNR

Moments after arriving back at Brian's, they were climbing their mountain, not once but twice, savoring each moment together.

The time had melted away, she had to leave.

"Brian, I really hate to leave, you know I do but I have to. I'll reminisce for years over the time we've spent together this weekend.

"Being with you, at the reunion I wasn't going to attend turned into a dream. The time we spent together at the beach and in your home, will always be with me. Please know that."

"Kayla, I've waiting a long, long, time to hold you in my arms. If it's meant to be, you'll come back. If it isn't, I'll have these memories to comfort me for the rest of my life. I love you with all my heart and I always will."

If she didn't leave now, she wouldn't.

Arriving at her mama and daddy's, he walked her to the door and with tears in his eyes, he kissed her tenderly whispering one final time.

"I love you."

He turned and was gone.

Lynn's Proposal

She texted Lynn before leaving.

Late start, it will be 7, I'll call – K

She arrived in her driveway about quarter of seven. She unpacked first, and changed clothes before calling.

"Lynn, I'm back... No, it was hard breaking away from my parents but I'm here now... Okay, I'll be waiting."

She was almost panicky. Did she really want to see him? Brian had her in a state of confusion. Her heart was in a state of shock. She had to do this, she just had to.

There was the doorbell, he was already there. She struggled to regain her composure before opening the door.

He looked just as handsome as he did the last time she saw him.

He reached for her kissing her tenderly on the lips.

"I came back to make amends for leaving you hanging. I can't believe that I did but I know that I did."

"May I come in?"

"Of course, Lynn."

She closed the door behind him and they walked into the den.

"Kayla, I'm only here for a few days and I must return. I want you to go with me."

"With you? What do you mean?"

He dropped to one knee.

"Will you marry me?"

Shockwaves shot through her whole being. That was the last thing she expected.

"Lynn, that's so sudden. I'll...

Her smartphone alerted her to a call from Kevin.

My Grandson's Been in an Accident!

"Kevin, is there anything wrong? You don't usually call…No, is he alright?… I'll leave as quickly as I can… I love you too."

My grandson, Ray, was struck by a car in front if their home. They've taken him to Duke. It must be bad. I'm sorry, Lynn, I must go. He'd my only grandchild."

"I'm sorry about your grandchild but what about my proposal?"

"Your proposal will have to wait. I have to go. Are you coming with me?"

"I can't, Kayla. I'm flying out Tuesday morning. Just give me an answer. I'll fly you to the Rivera when this crisis is over."

"Lynn, I've waited two years for you and now, suddenly, you're in a big rush. I can't deal with your proposal right now. My grandson is hurting and I'm going to be with him."

"It's your time to wait, Lynn. If you can't wait for an answer, find someone else.

"I have to go, Lynn, goodbye."

He appeared not to believe what he was hearing but he turned and walked out the door.

Her nerves were in shambles. She had calls to make while she packed.

"Daddy, Ray was in an accident. The First Responders took him to Duke… I don't know, Daddy. I'm packing now. You let the family know. I'll contact everyone when I know something… I love ya'll too, Daddy, bye."

Her final text was to Ginger saying she would call when she knew something.

She would text Brian when she arrived.

She arrived at Duke Children's Hospital finding a spot in one of the parking decks.

The immensity of the complex was overwhelming but luckily, she'd parked close to the emergency entrance.

Make note of where you are parked. Remember what happened last time.

She made a notation in one of her apps and took four pics.

Arriving at the reception center, she asked to see Kevin Ray Harris.

"I'm his grandmother."

The receptionist checked and replied,

"He's been transferred to the East Wing - MICU-6 East."

She handed her a map saying,

"You're here, he was transferred here."

Following the map and getting lost twice, she finally located the reception desk.

"They're in the waiting room over there."

Kevin was rushing towards her with his arms outstretched.

"Mama, I saw you getting off the elevator. Kylie's in there. I'm so glad you're here."

"Kevin, you knew I'd come. What are they telling you?"

"Mama, not a whole lot. They ran a whole bunch of tests including a CT-Scan and a MRI. They're doing something with dye now. They'll come talk to us when they're ready. That's all I know. Mama, we're scared. We don't want to lose him."

Tears were streaming down his face. She huddled on a sofa with Kevin on one side and Kylie on the other.

Minutes trickled slowly by and then an hour. She was right at her breaking point when a surgeon is scrubs came in the waiting room.

"Is the family of Kevin Harris here?"

All three jumped up rushing up to him.

"Please come with me."

Dr. Bhatti shared that Ray had damage to his skull.

"It's causing fluid to exert pressure on the left frontal lobe. To exacerbate that, the frontal lobe is swelling. I've installed a stent to allow the fluid to drain. We have him in a coma to reduce the trauma. There are broken bones in both his right and left arm and left leg. We'll address those after the pressure is relieved on his brain. That will take some time to accomplish.

"I'll update you in the morning. Do you have any questions?"

Kylie was first.

"May we see him, please?"

"Yes, but only for a moment. He will not be aware of your presences. Please do not attempt to arouse him."

There were many other questions but they could wait.

Seeing Ray with a myriad of tubes and probes was almost unbearable but the worst part was seeing his head totally bandaged with two tubes apparently extending from his nose or mouth.

Back in the waiting room, Kylie was crying almost uncontrollably. Kevin was trying to calm her but finding it impossible. After a few minutes, she calmed to a whimper. It was going to be a long night.

Kylie finally dropped off to sleep in Kevin's arms and Kayla slipped out into the corridor to call the family.

She'd talked to her parents and Donna when she realized that someone was standing behind her. She turned seeing Brian. Immediately, the tears began to softly flow down her cheeks as his arms enveloped her.

"You're here, how did you find out?"

"Your mother called right after you talked to your father. On the way up here, I kept calling until I located your grandson.

"I went to the children's hospital first and because I was not family, they refused to tell me anything until I told them I was your fiancé.

"At that point, they told me about the transfer and of course, when I got here, I got the run-around too.

"It didn't matter, one way or the other, I was going to find you. I'm here now for you and your family."

She reached up pulling his lips to hers.

"I'm so glad you're here. I feel safe now. Kevin and Kylie are asleep. Could we go down to the cafe and get a cup of coffee?"

"Of course, you want to tell your son where you're going?"

"No, let him rest. If he awakens and sees me gone. He'll call."

They took the elevator down to the main level and followed the signs to the café. Seeing the packaged sandwiches, she realized that she hadn't eat anything since lunch.

"I'll get a cup of coffee and one of these."

"I'll get them. Find a place you would like to sit."

Again, she couldn't believe how accommodating he'd become or maybe she was being totally unfair. Maybe he'd been so many years ago and she was unfairly judging him.

She chose a table by the windows facing the terrace.

Setting her sandwich, two coffees, and two chocolate coated donuts on the table, he took a chair facing her.

"What have you found out?"

"Not a lot, Ray has skull damage and it's causing fluid to press against the front of his brain causing it to swell. The surgeon put a drain tube in it to relieve the pressure. He also induced a coma to help immobilize Ray. There are broken bones in both arms and one leg.

"Dr. Bhatti won't do anything about them until he gets the pressure off his brain.

"He's had a CT-Scan and MRI. They're doing a test with dye but I don't know what that is.

"He allowed us to see him. Brian, I almost wish I hadn't. He's got tubes and probes all over him and his head is completely covered in bandages with tubes extending out of his nose or mouth. I can't tell which."

"Dr. Bhatti says he'll update us in the morning."

Her phone alerted her. It was Kevin.

"Kevin, it's all right. I'm in the café... Really, I'm fine. Brian's with me... We'll go back up in a few minutes. I'll introduce you then... Kevin, you met him in Greenville when daddy was in the hospital... He was my boyfriend in high school, I'll explain it to you in a few minutes. Would you and Kylie like some coffee?... Okay, one with cream and sugar and one with two-sugars... See you in a few."

Brian was laughing.

"What?"

"This should be interesting. I'm sure he's never heard our story and here you are; lost in a huge hospital complex with some strange man."

Now, she was laughing,

"Brian, be nice. I'm not lost. I'm with you."

"Do I introduce you as my friend or fiancé?"

"Your fiancé, please."

"We'll see."

"Okay, I'll get the coffee and we'll go back up."

Kevin was standing when they walked in. She handed to coffee to Kevin and Kylie before making the introductions.

"Brian, this is my son, Kevin, and his wife, Kylie. Kevin and Kylie, this is Brian Howard. You met him in Greenville. We went to school together and were girlfriend-boyfriend until I moved to Greenville.

Over the years, we hadn't seen each other until about a month ago. Since then, we've dated several times and attended our thirtieth-class reunion Saturday night.

"I went to church with him yesterday before returning to Greenville."

Kevin extended his hand and Brian took it.

Kevin and Kylie were thoroughly confused. This wasn't the Lynn they'd heard so much about over the past year or two.

"Mother, help us out. We thought you were seeing someone that is in France or somewhere overseas?"

Kayla, holding tightly to Brian's hand tried to unravel the confusion.

"That was Lynn Stocks. He's been in Paris for the past two years. He surprised me Saturday calling from Farmville. He was supposed to come home for a visit during the Christmas holidays but he showed up early.

"He knew about my class reunion and about me attending with Brian. He also knew about our past relationship.

"I'm sure that's what triggered his surprise visit. It was his intent to fracture whatever was happening between us.

"When I got back to Greenville, he came over and had only been there half an hour when I got your call."

She was squeezing Brian's hand harder now. Her nerves were in shambles.

"In those few minutes, he totally surprised me with a marriage proposal."

Brian's hand was squeezing hers now.

In shock, Kevin and Kylie looked at each other and then at her.

"Marriage proposal? Really, are you that serious about him?"

This was going to prove interesting. How do you go about explaining what was and is now happening? She had no choice but to try.

"I'll try to explain. First…

Amy came rushing into the waiting room.

"Kevin, is Ray all right?"

She was hugging Kayla and Kylie while listening intently to what Kevin said.

With all he knew explained, Amy turned her attention to the handsome man standing beside her mother.

Looking at Brian, she began,

"Brian, this is my daughter, Amy."

"Amy, this is my friend, Brian Howard. You met him when daddy was in the hospital. I should have told you about us then, but it was so hectic."

"I was trying to explain Brian and Lynn to Kevin and Kylie when you walked in. I'll try again."

"Lynn first, I met him two years ago at a friend's home in Farmville. We became very close until his son, studying culinary arts in Paris, was involved in a serious accident.

"Lynn, immediately, flew to Paris and it was apparent that he'd be there for some time.

"He was a liaison for our congressman and he pulled some strings getting Lynn a position in the embassy in Paris. His son recovered but the embassy wasn't willing to release Lynn or so he told me.

"During the two years he's been gone, we've maintained contact via phone, messages, and texts.

"I waited, hoping he'd at least he'd come home for a visit but he didn't. Rather, he enjoyed Paris and the surrounding countryside.

"When his son was given the opportunity to study under a world-renowned chef on the Rivera, miraculously, he received a release from the embassy so he could join his son.

"That was about the same time daddy had the heart attack and was flown to ECHI.

"This is where Brian reentered the picture."

"But Mother, how…

"Give me a chance and I'll explain.

"Brian and I were sweethearts in high school and the two years I attended James Sprunt in Kenansville.

"When I moved to Greenville, we broke up and not under the best of circumstances. He wanted me to stay in Duplin County and marry him. I wanted no part of that. I wanted to see what was beyond the Duplin County line.

"I was very rude to Brian. I know that now but twenty-eight years ago, I paid little attention to how much I'd hurt him.

"Of course, you know about my marriage and divorce. You also know that I became an introvert and refused to date anyone for twenty-two years. I know now that it was a mistake.

"Brian never married but became a very successful business man. He dated many times but never seriously.

"Over the years, he visited mama and daddy. He was mama's favorite then and still is. That's how he knew about daddy's heart attack."

"He called asking if he could come up to see us. I invited him. That night, he took me out to eat. That's the first of several times we've been out.

"We attended the prom together Saturday night and I went to church with him Sunday. He's here now to support me and Lynn's flying back to Paris, the Rivera, or wherever."

"You know about my shelving Lynn's proposal and you see Brian here supporting me now. Are there any questions?"

She knew there were several but would they ask them.

"Mother, are you staying? You can bunk with me in the dorm."

Brian interrupted, saying,

"We have reservations at the Carolina Inn. I made them on my drive up. There are two bedrooms in each suite. There's adequate space anyone that would like to use the extra bedrooms."

"Brian, you didn't have to do that but thank you."

It was almost midnight.

"Kevin, why don't you take Kylie and get some rest. We'll do the first watch."

"Mother, are you sure?"

"Yes, Brian and Amy are here."

SNR

Next morning, about five, Kayla awakened in Brian's arms with Amy snuggled up against her. Brian was awake and Amy stirred.

"Mother, I'm going back to the dorm. I have classes at eight. I'll check back in at lunchtime."

"That's fine, Honey, thank you for staying. I love you."

With a hug, Amy was gone.

"Coffee?"

"Yes, that would be nice."

"Let's go to the café, we need to stretch."

The hot coffee was a perfect way to begin the day but a shower, first, would have been better.

"Brian, it seems that I'm tying you up again. I'm sorry, I don't mean to be such a bother but thank you. I really mean that."

You're not bothering me. Being with you is where I want to be."

Her smart phone alerted her to a call from Kevin.

"Kevin, good morning… No, not a word… She left a few minutes ago and we're having our first cup of coffee… In a few minutes… I love you too."

Finishing their coffee, they took the elevator to the sixth floor finding Kevin and Kylie refreshed but still very worried.

Just as Kayla was about to say something, Dr. Bhatti, walked in saying,

"The swelling on the frontal lobe has grown. We're prepping him for surgery now. The swelling isn't unusual but the pressure buildup must be relived. The X-rays and CT-Scan pinpoint the exact location of the pressure. I'll remove a small portion of the skull and replace it when the swelling subsides. It will take some time for that to occur."

Kevin and Kylie pressed him.

"How long Doctor?"

"Five to ten days. We'll keep him in coma during that period. It relieves the activity in the brain and he'll be much more comfortable that way."

"Please excuse me, they're waiting. The procedure could take four or five hours."

Kevin looked at Kayla, saying,

"Mother, you and Brian should get some rest. There's nothing left to do here but wait."

"Are you sure, Kevin. We can wait with you."

"No, Mother, we'll call if there's news."

Arriving, Kayla found the suites connecting. They were very spacious and well appointed.

"Brian, will you hold me? I need your strength and comfort."

"You know I will. Do you want to take shower and have breakfast first?"

She was hungry and a shower would help to awaken her.

"Yes, give me twenty-minutes."

"I'll freshen up and be here waiting for you."

SNR

Refreshed, they walked down the corridor to the Crossroads Restaurant. Seated, they ordered coffee and chose the Tar Heel omelets. She wanted grits with hers and he chose the hash browns.

"Brian, I'm worried, what the surgeon is saying, sounds very scary to me. Tell me that I'm wrong. Please tell me that I am."

He reached for her hand, replying,

"Kayla, your grandson must have been in a horrific accident. I know there are broken bones, bruises, and contusions but the major injury was to his skull. I'm not a doctor but know when something swells, there must be a way to relieve the pressure and removing a portion of the skull in the affected area will do just that.

"Look at it this way, the surgeon is only removing a small portion of the skull. He's not operating on Ray's brain. If he were, I'd be very concerned.

"Once the pressure is relieved, the brain will heal itself but it's going to take time. It may take a long time but Ray will recover.

"At three, he'll easily recover. At our age, well, you know."

She had found a smile.

"Brian Howard, are you telling me that I'm old?"

"Did I say that, me? No way, I couldn't have. No, Kayla, you're just right."

"All right, Sir. I'm not sure you admitted anything but I'll let it go this time but if there's a next... I won't let you off so easily."

He'd broken the tension. She felt relieved. After their breakfast, they went back to the suite.

It was seven-thirty, she had to call her boss. She punched in his private number.

"Cal, this is Kayla, I'm in Chapel Hill. My grandson was in a terrible accident yesterday and the surgeons at Duke are operating on him now...

No, I came up last night. Ray's father, my son, Kevin and his wife, Kylie, are here. My daughter, Amy, is here also, she's a junior at UNC here... Yes, Sir, he has a lot of broken bones but the head injury is the major concern... I will, Cal. Thank you very much sir. Please sign me out for sick leave until I get back. I'll be in touch, goodbye."

She texted Ginger saying she would try calling that evening.

She started to text Mary but was more than sure that Lynn had given her his version of incident. It would be interesting to hear his version but it could come later, much later, after her grandson recovered.

Back in her suite, she changed into pajamas and walked through the connecting doorway to his suite finding him waiting.

They pulled the covers back on the bed and she was asleep the moment he cuddled her in his arms.

Her phone awakened her a little before ten a.m. The distinct ringtone told her it was Lynn. She let it go to voicemail.

At eleven-thirty, she was aroused again. This time it was Kevin.

"Kevin, any word from the surgeon yet?... He's in recovery; thank the Lord. Did the Surgeon say anything else...? That's encouraging... We'll be over in about an hour... I love you, too."

Brian was holding her again,

"How long?"

"Kevin said at least two-hours. The surgeon said that the procedure was successful."

That's wonderful news, thank you, Lord. Do you want to eat before we go back over?"

"Yes, please, that would be nice."

She felt so secure in his arms, climbing their mountain would be helpful too. She proved her point, it was.

Dressing, they walked back to the restaurant enjoying chicken salad sandwiches and coffee.

"Brian, this is a very expensive place. Don't tell me you're involved in it too?"

Chuckling, Brian replied,

"No, I wish I were. Once a year, I bring my managers up for a weekend of UNC football. I prefer staying here. It's unique and offers every amenity a group could possibly need. Besides, it's a corporate write-off too."

Chiding him, she asked,

"Am I a write-off too?"

"The corporation is footing the bill but you'll never be a write-off, Kayla, never."

SNR

Returning to the medical complex, they found Kevin and Kylie, along with Donna, in the waiting room.

Introductions again, she hoped she wouldn't have to go through the whole thing again. She didn't. Apparently, Kevin had filled her in.

"Donna, this is Brian. Do you remember meeting him when daddy was in the hospital?"

"Yes, Mother, I do. Brian, thank you for coming to support Mother."

"Seeing you, Donna, is my pleasure. Different circumstances would be much preferred."

Kayla turned to Kevin, asking,

"Any further updates?"

"No, Mother, we're hoping to see doctor any minute now. I guess we should all sit down. Waiting is nerve-racking for me but I don't guess I have any choice."

Dr. Bhutti walked in asking the family to follow him into the corridor.

"The patient is still in recovery. As I've already reiterated, that's not unusual. His vital signs are all nominal. I'll keep him in CICU until tomorrow morning and move him to the children's hospital then. He'll remain in a coma until the swelling begins to subside. That will probably take another four or five days.

"At that point, I'll schedule surgery to replace the portion of skull I removed.

"During surgery this morning, I set ulna and radius in his right arm. That's the lower bones. I also set the humerus in his left arm. That's the upper bone. The tibia in his left leg was shattered and requires a more complicated procedure. I'll address that when I replace the skull portion. He's only three, and will bounce back rapidly.

"Please remember that he's in an induced coma and will not respond to you until I awaken him."

Kylie had to know, asking,

"Dr. when can I see him?"

"I'll send a nurse out but please limit you visit to a minute or two at the most."

With that, he disappeared behind the double-doors in the corridor.

Kylie was trembling.

"I know he won't know me but I have to see. Kevin, you will go with me, won't you?"

Kevin was holding her now.

"He's our son, of course I will."

A nurse approached and led them through the double-doors.

"Kayla, this has to be very hard on them. Nothing like this ever happened to Sandy or Jerry. I guess I've been blessed."

"You have been, Donna. I'm so glad that nothing like this ever happened to Kevin or Amy either."
"I don't remember any of us breaking a bone, growing up."

Brian inserted a comment,

"Ander did, remember, he was playing baseball the it stuck him on the end of his right index finger."

"That's right, it did and we picked on him unmercifully about the splint. That was a long time ago."

"Kayla, remembered, yes it was. I think I was nine."

"Brian, I remember when in was in high school, you used to come over to the house a lot to see, Kayla."

"That's right, we were sweet on each other from the fourth grade."

"That's right, remember the time you and Kayla got lost in the woods hunting for huckleberries?"

Kayla was blushing.

You didn't have to bring that up. We were in the sixth grade. Mama was going to make a pie if we picked enough.

Brian laughed before replying,

"Your mama and daddy had half of Duplin County out looking for us. It was way down late in the afternoon when we came out in Jesse Lee's new ground and almost dark when we came up on his back porch.
"I've wondered many times why neither of us got a whipping but we didn't."

Kevin and Kylie were back. She had tears streaming down her face and Kevin was trying to console her.

Holding Brian's hand, Kayla, suggested that they go back to the room and take a break.

"We'll be here. Go eat some lunch too. Did you have any breakfast?"

"No, Mother, Kylie said she didn't want anything."

"Go, get something to eat and get some rest."

Reluctantly, they walked to the elevator and were gone.

"Kayla, how long are you going to be here?"

"I don't know, Donna, it depends on how Ray does. I guess as long as I have to."

"Brian, will you be here too?"

"Yes, Donna. I'm here to support Kayla."

"I guess I'll get back to Greensboro, then. Call if you need me. I'm not that far away."

She hugged Kayla and turned to Brian, saying,

"Thank you for being here. She started to offer her hand but instead, put her arm around his neck and hugged him.

Now alone, they set holding hands, reminiscing about their reunion and weekend together.

The hours slipped by unnoticed as they continued to reminisce.

About eight, Kevin called apologizing, saying,

"Mother, I'm sorry, we grabbed a burger and when our heads hit the pillow, we were out.
"We're on our way over now."

She replied,

"We're fine, Kevin. At least you got some rest."

Her phone alerted her again. It was Lynn.

"It's Lynn, I guess I take. Answering it, she didn't move but stayed beside Brian.

"This is Kayla... No, we're still at the hospital... Brian, of course, he's with me... Lynn, Ray almost died. Did you not understand the gravity of the situation when I left...? Another week or ten days, there's a lot that still must be done... No, Lynn, you were concerned about missing your flight... Lynn, when you got the call about your son, what did you do...? Did you expect less of me? Ray's my only grandson, He'll always come first... Your proposal?

Lynn, I'll address that later, not now. How could you even ask…? Lynn, I'm tired, we'll talk later."

She was frustrated, Brian could easily see it on her face.

"He's still trying?"

She looked at Brian, saying,

"Please hold me. Yes, I don't understand. Does he not understand the seriousness of what's happening here?"

Brian had his arm around her when Kevin and Kylie walked in. She didn't attempt to remove it and neither did he.

"Mother, have they said anything else?"

"No, Kevin. No one's been out. It's going to be a long night but Ray will be better in the morning, you'll see."

She had to believe it or she'd go crazy.

"We're going to get something to eat and get a few hours rest. Call us if you need us."

You're saying, us, what's happening, you've made your choice, haven't you?

She hugged her son and daughter-in-law before taking Brian by the hand.

"Are you ready?"

Arriving back at the suite, they showered first and dressed.

"There are several great restaurants in the Raleigh-Cary-Durham-Chapel Hill area. Would you like to go out or dine here?"

"A change would be nice, surprise me."

"All right, I can do that. Buckle up, my lady."

From the intersection of Franklin and Columbia Streets, they traveled north on Columbia Street to Highway 86 following it past I-40 until he found the Farm House Restaurant Sign.

Turning left on Millhouse road, it was only about a tenth of a mile to the dirt road leading to the parking lot.

"We are here. They've been in business since the late 60s. Their streaks are grilled on an open-hearth charcoal broiler.

"My Lady, we don't have reservations. Let's see if they have room for us."

Inside, the setting reminded her of the Country Squire. The décor was rustic and the ambiance was cozy.

"Reservations?"

"No, we do not."

"We can fit you in, follow me please."

They were seated near the fireplace and there was a roaring fire. The lights were very low offering a very romantic setting.

Their waiter arrived asking about beverages.

"Wine?"

"Maybe later, a cup of coffee would be nice."

"Two coffees please, black."

"It's so quiet, it's perfect, Brian. It looks so much like the Country Squire."

He agreed saying he'd never been but one of his vendors highly recommended it.

Their coffee was back and the waiter was asking about appetizers?

They chose the chowder on the recommendation of their waiter.

It was an excellent choice and they really enjoyed it. For their main entrees, Kayla chose the 8-ounce ribeye,

"Medium-rare please and I'll have the baked sweet potato with butter."

Brian chose the 12-ounce ribeye,

"Medium-rare please and I'll have the baked potato with the works."

"Brian, you can never know how much I appreciate what you're doing. Seems like I've said the before but I really do appreciate it. You're making the trauma me and my family are facing so much easier. Thank you."

Brian, looked across the table at her. She knew that he loved her with all his heart and he'd be by her side until the end of time if she would let him.

"Kayla, as I've said before; I'm here because I love you and I want your family to be my family."

Their steaks arrived on a sizzling hot cast iron griddles with wood underliners being admonished by their waiter,

"Please be careful. The griddles are very hot. May I get you anything else?"

He looked across at her.

"Wine?"

"Yes, that would be nice."

"Yes, waiter, bring a bottle of the BV Coastal, please."

"Very good, Sir, I'll be a moment."

"Isn't this what the Country Squire serves on?"

"Yes, exactly, now, if these are a good as theirs, our steaks will be delicious. They were and the charcoal flavor was so scrumptious."

"I'm going to miss being with you when I go back to the real world. You're spoiling me. You know that of course."

"I'd like for this to continue, all you have to…

Her phone alerted her to a call from Kevin.

"No! We'll be right there."
"Ray's temperature spiked. We have to go!"

Brian summoned the waiter saying there was an emergency. Minutes later, they were rushing towards the hospital.

Buckling in, he raced back I-40 heading east to Durham exiting on 15/501 and then 15A that led to the hospital.

In moments, they stepped off the elevator finding Kevin and Kylie huddling together in the waiting room. When they saw Kayla and Brian, they rushed up to them clinging to both.

"What happened?"

Kevin, trying to regain his composure, tried to share what he knew.

"Dr. Bhutti, came out saying that Ray's temperature spiked to 103 F. Mother, he said that they were not sure why but doing several procedures to get his temperature back down while trying to discover why it spiked. He said the team would induce antipyretic agents and possibly use physical cooling methods.

"Mother, we don't know what any of that means. All we want is for Ray to get better. Please help us pray for him."

Kayla, holding on to them and Brian, began,

"Heavenly Father, our little Ray is hurting. We don't know everything that happened to him in the accident and the doctors are doing everything they can. Please God, heal Ray and make him well again."

Brian squeezed her hand,

"Precious God, our Loving Father. We come to you in our hour of need. Little Ray is in desperate need of your healing touch. Two-thousand years ago, Your Son, Jesus, healed many during his brief stay on the earth. He said that if we believe, anything is possible and we believe him.

"Please if it be your will, touch little Ray and make him whole again. We believe that through Your Son, Jesus, that all things are possible.

"Please, Heavenly Father, through your divine intervention, equip the doctors with the knowledge to make little Ray well so he will have an opportunity to live a full life serving you. In his holy name we pray, amen."

Tears were streaming down their faces. Kevin and Kylie seemed comforted and Kayla looked into Brian's eyes, whispering,

"Thank you."

A little after eleven, Dr. Bhutti summoned them into the corridor.

"We've managed to bring the temperature down to one-hundred F. The agents seem to be working. We'll monitor him through the evening. If the temperature continues to drop, we'll transfer him to the children's wing in the morning. Meanwhile, I suggest that you get some rest. There's nothing you can accomplish by waiting here. I have you cell numbers If there is any change; we will call you."

Kayla agreed,

"I'm sure he's right. Let's all go back to the suite and get some rest. Kevin, did you and Kylie have dinner?"

"No, Mother, we were going to get something in the café when we got the call."

"They still can, can't they Brian?"

"Yes, the packaged items and beverages are still available. We'll go with you and have coffee while you eat."

They took the elevator down to the main level and walked down the corridor to the café.

"Coffee still black?"

"Yes, thank you. I'll find a place to sit."

While they were having coffee and sandwiches, Kevin looked Brian, saying,

"Brian, you've been so supportive of Mother during Grandfather's heart attack on now. Thank you very much for all you've done."

Brian, acknowledged his compliment, saying,

"Kevin, as you know, your mother and I go back a long way. Yes, we're been apart for a long time but providence brought us back together again and I'm going to try very hard to not ever lose her again."

Finally, a smile, Kayla, looked at Brian, replying to his comment.

"It must have been providence, Brian. Whatever it was, the past month has been almost like living a fairy tale.

"Daddy's heart attack and now, my precious little Ray, have torn at my heart strings but you've given me the strength to overcome the downs and ride with me through the highs. I'm so glad that you're back in my life."

Thoroughly confused now, Kevin had to ask?

"Mother, you may or may not want to tell Kylie and me but what about the Lynn person. I thought the two of you were very close. I remember you saying that he went overseas a couple of years ago but I thought he'd come back and proposed?"

"Yes, we were, Kevin, until he went to Paris. Until a few days ago, he hadn't been back once until he got word of Brian. Then he tried to remotely orchestrate my life and my decisions. He did not want me to date Brian and certainly not go to the reunion with him.

"Seeing that he was losing the battle, he made one last desperate attempt trying to take Brian's place at the reunion. I told him emphatically, that I was going with Brian.

"When he came over Sunday; he had a ring. Just as he was proposing, I got your call.

"He wouldn't come with me but wanted an answer to his proposal. I told him it was on hold until Ray was out of the hospital.

"Kevin, he got on the plane flying back to the Rivera. He didn't have to go. He's not even employed. He put the Rivera in front of me and my family.

"Yes, he wanted me to drop my life and go with him. My life, Kevin, my everything. I can't, I won't do that."

"I'm sorry, Mother. You went through all of Amy and my childhood without dating once. Mother, we talked about it a lot of times wondering how you could go through your life with a man. I know that father hurt you. I'll never forgive him. I love him because he's my father but I don't like him one bit."

"So, Mother, you're saying that you won't marry Lynn. Where does that leave you and Brian?"

She looked at Kevin and then at Brian, reaching for his hand.

"All in due time, Kevin, all in due time. I think we all need to get some rest."

Brian's Proposal

Back in their suites, as soon as Kevin and Kylie were safely in their rooms, Kayla slipped into Brian's suite and into his protective arms. She felt so secure being with him and falling asleep came easily.

Brian awakened her at five.

"You probably should go to your room. If Kevin gets a call, he'll be looking for you."

She pulled him closer, replying,
"And you don't want to get caught with me? I'm just kidding, you're right but don't go anywhere without me. I'd be lost."

"Marry me and you'll never have to be alone again."

"Is that a proposal?"

"It is."

"I will."

"You will!"

"Yes, Mr. Howard, I will."

"Just a moment."

"Stand here."

He fetched the ring from his coat pocket.

"Kayla Herring, will you marry me?"

"Brian Howard, yes, I will. I love you with all my heart."

He slipped the three-carat solitary on her finger, saying,

"You've just made me the happiest man in the world. I've loved you all my life and I'll love you forever."

They held each other tightly and after a lingering kiss, she slipped back into her room only minutes before Kevin was calling her.

"Yes, Kevin… That's wonderful news… They have…? Yes, you're right, Kevin. God does answer prayers for all that have faith. I'll tell Brian and we'll go somewhere to have breakfast before going back over. I'm going to call Amy and see if she can join us… Yes, seven sounds good… I love you too, bye"

She raced back over to Brian's room finding him in the shower.

"I wish we were alone. I'd get in there with you. Good news, Ray's temperature is back to normal and they've moved him to the children's wing.

"I told Kevin that we would have breakfast before going back over. I'm going to call Amy and see if she can join us. We have something very important to tell my children."

He was standing in front of her with a towel wrapped around his waist.

"Yes, we do, my darling wife to be.   What time did you tell them?

"Seven."

"You'd better get a move on, it's six-thirty and you have to call Amy."

In her excitement, she'd forgotten the time.

"Oh, I'll never make it!"

Grinning, he asked,

"You are telling them our good news? Are you going to describe the circumstances? You in pajamas and me in jockey shorts, I'm looking forward to you telling them the rest of the story."

"Brian, absolutely not!"

"Why not? We could sell our story to the tabloids and get rich. Take a few selfies before you leave."

"Brian Howard, I don't know about you."

She did take a couple of selfies but there was no way she'd ever share them with anyone but, Brian."

"Amy, can you join us for breakfast. Ray is much better and they've moved him to the children's wing… Seven, meet us here in the lobby… I love you too, see you in a few minutes."

SNR

With everyone in the lobby, Brian turned to Amy, asking?

"Amy, do you have a preference where we should have breakfast? You're the expert here."

Amy, appreciating the compliment, responded,

This is the most sought-after place but it's also the most expensive."

"It's a corporate write-off. Let's eat here."

Walking down the corridor to Crossroads, no one except Kayla and Brian knew what was going to take place. Kayla had effectively hidden the ring from them. This would be the biggest surprise she would ever confront her children with. Hold her joy inside, was almost impossible.

Seated, Kayla shared her job about Ray. Apparently, he was on his way to a full recovery. "

Thank you, Lord, for giving the right tools to his doctor and his team."

Now, almost exploding with joy, she held her ring finger out for everyone to see.

Amy was first.

"Mother, is that what I think it is?"

With her eyes sparkling, Kayla replied,

Yes, Amy, we're getting married. I'm so happy!"

Kevin, shaking his head in disbelief, stammered,

"Mother, when did this happen? You were not wearing it last night."

What was she going to say? She couldn't tell them how it happened; they'd know that they slept together. She looked at Brian seeing a slight grin on his face.

"It was earlier this morning, we were in his suite having coffee. He looked at me saying that he was going to propose. Was I ready? I thought he was joking but he wasn't and I said, yes. Now, after twenty-eight years, we're finally going to get married."

 She could see Amy looking at Kevin and Kylie, almost sure there was more to the story but she left it alone.

Sitting across the round table from Brian, Amy got up and walked around to him. With a big hug, she said,

"Brian, welcome to our family. I'm so glad it's you. That other guy wasn't right for mother. I believe that you really love her and you'll make her happy."

Kevin was sitting beside Brian. He extended his hand offering congratulations.

"Brian, welcome to our family. Do I call you, Pop, or Brian?"

Laughing, Brian shook his hand saying,

"Brian, works for me."

SNR

They arrived at the hospital complex finding little Ray in a room. The bandages were still in place and now there were splints on both arms and his left leg.

A nurse was adjusting fluid inputs when they walked in.

Kylie asked if Ray was still in a coma.

The nurse replied that he was and was oblivious to his surroundings.

"How long will he remain that way?"

The nurse replied that she didn't know but Dr. Bhutti was making his rounds and would be in shortly.

He walked in about ten-minutes later.

Kylie was in his face, asking,

"Dr. when will you awaken my son?"

He replied that the swelling was going down.

"I'll replace the skull fragment on Friday and if all goes well, I'll awaken him on Monday. It's all contingent on his vital signs. When I awaken him, if he shows signs of being in a lot of pain, I'll put him back under.

"I'd rather him be under than taking excessive amounts of pain killer. That only exacerbates the length of the healing process and veils what's going on."

"His vitals look good this morning and I want to keep them that way."

In moments, he was gone. There was some relief in what he'd told them but it was awfully apparent that the healing process would be lengthy.

Kevin looked at his mother, saying,

"Mother, I think the Lord's got this. I'm sure you need to get back to work. We love you, and Brian for all you've done."

Brian, if we could just stay in the room one more night, it would be extremely helpful. I'll contact the Ronald McDonald House today. It looks like we'll be here for some time."

Kayla was hesitant about leaving.

"Brian, are you sure. You know I'll stay."

"Mother, the worst is over, the Lord's taken care of that. We'll be here until Ray leaves and besides, we have Amy. We'll be fine."

"If you're sure, Brian, please take me back to the hotel so I can pick up my car."

"I'm ready, Kevin, I'll tell the desk clerk that you'll be staying another night and if necessary, as long as you need to."

Supporting hugs and kisses were exchanged. They were already treating Brian like he was family.

SNR

Back at hotel, Kayla gathered her luggage and Brian walked her out to her car.

"When am I going to see the man I'm going to marry?"

"Tomorrow evening, we'll dine at Bobby's"

"Mr. Howard, that sounds nice and sir, you'll be staying with me."

On her way back, she texted Ginger.

B home 2night – engaged – K

The response was immediate.

Engaged – who? G

Brian – K

Congrats, how's gndson? G

Better – K

Great – G

3 steers 7? K

Yes – G

She arrived home a little before noon after stopping by Bill Ellis' for an early lunch. She knew she shouldn't but did the pig-picking anyway. Her exercise schedule would have to double for a few days but not tomorrow. There would be exercise but it would be climbing a mountain.

She waited until after one to call in saying she would be back to work tomorrow. Work had to be discussed, not only that, where would they live? She felt very sure they would call Kenansville home. Maybe she could get on at Vidant Duplin?

Kayla, maybe you and Brian should decide when you're getting married first?

She and Ginger arrived at the Three Steers almost simultaneously, walking in together.

As soon as they were seated, Ginger wanted to see her ring.

"Oh, that's beautiful, congratulations, Kayla, you're finally getting married and I think you made the right choice."

"I've got a hundred questions and I'm sure you don't have any answers yet so I'll wait."

"Please tell me about your grandson."

"Ginger, he's on the road to recovery. It was touch-and-go for one of the longest twenty-four-hours of my life but Brian was there every minute. Ray will be a long time in recovery but the keyword is recovery. The doctor says it will be complete, no after-effects.

"You cannot know how happy that makes me."

The waitress had been back twice asking for their orders.
Ginger said she was getting a salad. Smiling, Kayla responded,

"Me too, I stopped by Bill Ellis BBQ for lunch and did the pig-picking thing. I don't have a choice."

"You've been a bad, bad, girl. I wish I'd been with you."

Laughing, they made their way to the salad bar building their salads.

Back at the table, Ginger wanted to know?

"Didn't you say that Lynn was with you when you got the message about your grandson?"

"Yes, he was, he was proposing."

"What, he proposed before Brian did?"

"Yes, but he showed no concern about Ray and didn't offer to go with me. He's called a dozen times asking for my answer. Next time he calls, I'll give me one and we'll be finished. I can't believe how little concern he had for Ray or for that matter, me either."

"What's Mary saying about this?"

"I don't know, I haven't talked to her. I'm back now, I'll give her a call tomorrow. Maybe we can have lunch. I'll fill her in then."
"Brian's coming tomorrow evening, he's taking me to Bobby's, and yes, he'll be staying with me."

SNR

Next morning about six, her phone alerted her to a call from Lynn.

It was time for her to say, goodbye.

"This is Kayla... Thank you, I guess it's past noon there. No, I came back yesterday... He's better but recovery will take a long time... Your answer? Yes, Lynn, I'll give you an answer; it's, NO. I'm engaged to Brian now. We'll be married soon... No, Lynn, I'm not rushing, he asked me twenty-eight years ago. I don't think that's rushing at all... No, Lynn. You came into my life when I sorely needed someone but you were pulled away and made no effort until recently to come back... Lynn, you left me high and dry for two-long-years... Yes, I missed you but apparently you didn't miss me. Go your own way, Lynn. Have a happy life, I am. Goodbye."

I Do

"Brian, do you take, Kayla, to be your lawfully wedded wife, to have, love, and hold for the rest of your life?

"Yes, I do."

"Kayla, do you take Brian to be your lawfully wedded husband, to have, love, and hold for the rest of your life?

"Oh, Yes, I do."

Smiling, Reverend Bron, looked out into the packed sanctuary of Grove Presbyterian Church and then back at them, saying,

By the power invested in me by Almighty God and the state of North Carolina, I pronounce you, man and wife. Brian, you may kiss your wife."

On a sunny, afternoon, almost a year to the day that Brian proposed, they were married on November 2nd, 2010.

After a two-week honeymoon in Europe, yes, they stopped over in the French Rivera but made no attempt to contact Lynn. As far as Kayla was concerned, he was a part of her past but had no place in her future.

After their honeymoon, they came home and hosted the family for Thanksgiving. It was a gala affair being catered by "We Cater Too; one of Bobby Carraway's spinoffs that had been financed by Brian's investment group. It was based in one of the storefronts in Kinston and was doing a booming business.

Christmas was just around the corner and they insisted that the family gather there too. Raymond and Dolly Herring would be the official hosts.

Kayla didn't worry about them anymore. They were sticking to their diets and looked ten years younger.

Little Ray had completely recovered from his ordeal and no one would have ever known except a small part of the scar was still visible outside his hairline. The doctor said, in time, it would completely disappear.

It would probably be gone by the time his eagerly awaited sister, expected in February, would be old enough to notice.

A lot had taken place over past twelve months. Kayla had found a position at Vidant Duplin. She was a supervisor in data processing and although she missed Mr. Newbold and her friends in Greenville; she was the happiest she'd ever been.

She'd promised to retire when she got her thirty-years in and she had a little less the three years to go once she cashed in her sick leave and vacation time

Brian cut back on his travels preferring to stay at home with the woman he'd loved all his life.

Amy was a senior now and Brian was encouraging her to remain in school as a graduate student to work on becoming a doctor saying that her education was now his responsibility.

At first, Amy had declined but after he insisted, she gave in saying being a doctor was her dream.

Epilogue

Five years had rushed by since their wedding. Kayla retired in 2013 and Brian had retained a management group to oversee his umbrella corporation that had grown to six farm equipment dealerships.

They were spending most of their time either at Wrightsville Beach or their third home on Long Key often flying to the Atlantis Resort at Nassau in the Bahamas. They occasionally gambled a little but found the other amenities much more enjoyable.

Next week, they would return to Kenansville. Ginger was getting married in Greenville and wanted Kayla to be her bridesmaid. Of course, she would. They were looking forward to seeing many friends there and would take the opportunity to dine at Bobby's at least once, if not twice.

The following weekend, they planned to host the family. Amy had gotten engaged and wanted her family to meet the man in her life, Dr. Ira Thompson from Charlotte.

Few plans were in place but Amy wanted her mother to be involved in every decision. She'd confided that she wanted to be married in the formal gardens at Kayla and Brian's. She, of course, already had their permission.

After years of indescribable loneliness, love had returned to Kayla and Brian. Their time together, would more than make up for the lost years.

"Brian, I love you more than you can ever know."

"Kayla, I love you now and forever."

Just a note:

I hope you enjoyed reading She'd Never Return. It's my most thrilling novel yet. As with my previous novels, it's fictitious and all the characters in my story are figments of my imagination.

Some names and locations are from my past but are only there as background for my story.

If you enjoyed reading this book, may I ask a favor? Please go to amazon.com and write a favorable review. Like everything else today, it's all about the "clicks."

You may also enjoy one of my other novels listed below.

His Recurring Dream

His Dark-Haired Darling

Darlene

JD

Gina

She Walked Through His Heart Again Today

III (Three) Islands

I am Janie

You may also enjoy my cookbook.

Bob's Country Recipes and Other Interesting Stuff II

All my books are available online at createspace.com, amazon.com or other online bookstores. Some are available in Kindle and other eBook formats.

P.S. Look for my next book soon. "She'd Never Return"

All of my books may be reviewed at: bobLholt.net or amazon.com.

Best Wishes!

Bob Holt